Pack Shift

by

AJ Skelly

The Wolves of Rock Falls

This is a work of fiction. Names, characters, places, and incidents are either the product of the author's imagination or are used fictitiously, and any resemblance to actual persons living or dead, business establishments, events, or locales, is entirely coincidental.

Pack Shift

Cover Art by *Jennifer Greeff*

The Wild Rose Press, Inc.
PO Box 708
Adams Basin, NY 14410-0708
Visit us at www.thewildrosepress.com

Publishing History
First Edition, 2022
Trade Paperback ISBN 978-1-5092-4353-2
Digital ISBN 978-1-5092-4352-5

The Wolves of Rock Falls
Published in the United States of America

Two sets of red eyes gleamed at the edge of the forest bordering the football field. Dread cramped my middle as a breeze blew the tang of blood from the mangled corpse several yards away.

Praise for AJ Skelly

Chapter 1

Friday Night Dance at Rock Falls High
February

Sarah

"Oh, crap," Cade said.

I turned from where I was headed across the football field, the frigid grass stinging my bare feet.

Two sets of red eyes gleamed at the edge of the forest bordering the football field. Dread cramped my middle as a breeze blew the tang of blood from the mangled corpse several yards away.

The bound wolf at Cade's feet gurgled in unconsciousness. I'd knocked him out minutes before, and my foot still smarted. But that was nothing compared to what was going to happen when those mongrels broke the tree line.

Adrenaline surged beneath my skin. Terror clawed at my belly, and Wolf burst to the front, scenting, gathering information.

"Raven, go find Bowen, Sam, anyone you can. I don't know why they're not here yet. Sam knows what's going on. I linked him. Use your link to Bowen. We need back up," Cade ordered his sister. And he was right. We needed all the help we could get. Because once the werewolf on the ground regained consciousness, he could use his mind control against us, and there was nothing we could do to stop it.

A word that would have raised my dad's eyebrows shot out of my mouth. "I knew I wouldn't get to enjoy one night in a fancy dress." The words tumbled out after, bravado my constant cover so the rest of the world didn't see me shaking in my fur. I yanked the zipper of my frilly blue dress and let Wolf out.

White fur prickled along my arms. My snout pushed out along with white tufted ears at the sides of my head. Snapping crackled along my backbone as my tail disengaged. White paws pounded down on the turf, black claws gouging the top layer of the manicured football field. Many yards behind the building itself, a tall fence, the press box, and a sizeable stand of bleachers separated us from the school where the rest of the Rock Falls High student body was enjoying their homecoming dance. Blissfully unaware of the battle about to take place. I growled at their general ignorance.

Two mottled gray werewolves stalked from the trees. Moonlight glinted off wicked canines; strings of saliva hung between incisors. They were big and battle scarred. I clenched my teeth to keep my panic-laced tremors from showing. A lethal snarl echoed behind my bared teeth.

"Go, Rave. Use that speed. We'll hold them off as long as we can." With his last instructions given, Cade morphed into a black wolf, bigger than me, but still smaller than the two hulking brutes creeping toward us.

Raven blasted off on four paws, racing over the chilly grass to find someone—anyone—who could help. I focused on the encroaching enemy.

These were wolves with one purpose. Mania

emanated from their red eyes.

Cade moved beside me, standing at my shoulder. He nudged me once with his nose. It calmed some of my terror and, even in the middle of a coming confrontation, sent tingles dancing to my paws. Shoving away the unhelpful thoughts, I focused all my energy on the two approaching werewolves.

Wolf snapped her jaws while Cade growled, low and menacing.

As if on command, the two brindled wolves barreled over the ground separating us. With a clash of fur, fangs, and yelps, we met them. Cade took the one on the left while I battled the one on the right.

He was huge. Nearly twice my width and mottled gray with rough, scarred skin poking through his mangy fur. He reeked of the woods—a wolf too long in his fur without the humane influence of his other half. A wolf like the one that murdered my mom.

Growling, he lunged at my throat. I twisted out of his way, shooting out with my back leg and catching him in the flank. It wasn't enough to do any damage; he didn't even budge an inch. He was an immovable wall of granite. And as I dashed away from his incisors once more, I realized that mountain of granite would crush me given half a chance. The wolf charged at me again, head down, trying to ram me. I leaped, my paws brushing his ruff. Using him like a springboard, I vaulted off his broad back and landed several paces away, whirling to face the onslaught.

Chancing a glance at Cade, I saw he was locked jaw to jaw with the other wolf, both on their hind legs, pawing at each other. Fear iced through my veins, but I couldn't stop to think, couldn't help, because the beast was after me again. This time I stood my ground, sidestepping only at the last moment in a move my father had drilled into me so long that it was second nature to do it. As the gray fur passed me, I bit down hard at his neck. I caught a lot of fur, but enough muscle underneath that blood flooded my mouth.

Wolf snarled and shook as the animal in my mouth howled, hurt and enraged.

Before I could do anything else, pain lanced through my side as a third wolf sank his teeth into my ribs.

Yelping and thrashing in panic and agony, I let go of the wolf in my jaws, and he immediately bounded away, only to turn and face me. Scrabbling at the wolf who had me in his mouth, I tried to rally my thoughts against the panic and the pain, and focus—to think through the haze fogging my brain.

Blood dripped down the chest of the big wolf slowly advancing on me. A fourth materialized from the woods and ran to join the fight. This was not good. Oh, this was *so* bad.

Suddenly, a roar cut through the air, and the wolf let go of my side. Wild-eyed, I craned my neck enough to see him sail through the air and land in a heap near the disemboweled body in the middle of the football field. He was still.

Cade stood over me protectively, sides heaving and smelling of fresh blood. Smothering a burning whine, I shakily got to my feet, turning so we were flank to flank, facing our enemies.

The remaining three wolves surrounded us, pacing in an ever-tightening circle.

A harsh bark echoed across the field, and relief

momentarily made me weak in the knees.

Sam Wolfe, Beta of Cade's pack, rushed over the green, a snarl following his bark and lifting the hairs on my neck. The wolves surrounding us broke formation, one branching off to take on Sam.

Then the other two sprang at us.

Yips, tearing, and more blood filled the night as we battled for our lives.

"Stop now." The world quivered to an abrupt halt, and I stood panting, tired, a little light-headed, and momentarily confused.

The four attacking wolves stood stock still. Hate and fear radiated off their matted fur. Gasping for air, I leaned against Cade. He met my weight with his own, and we sagged against each other. We'd done it. We'd held them off long enough. Sam stepped between us and the enemy wolves.

Searching, I found Raven dressed in Cade's dirty dress shirt, standing next to Bowen and another boy I'd seen on an opposing basketball team. Power singed my nostrils. My eyes widened as I realized *Bowen* was controlling the other wolves.

Suspicion and a hint of fear coiled in my belly. Bowen had kept his powers hidden from me—from my pack. The omission sat heavily in my gut. As Beta of the Thornehill pack and a close ally, I should have been privy to something this gigantic.

"Sit," Bowen commanded. The wolves sat as their fear choked the air.

Drew, the wolf I'd bound and knocked out earlier, whimpered, having shifted back to his skin. Narrowing my eyes, I wondered if Drew or Bowen had the stronger will and who could control who. Bowen wasn't even breaking a sweat. The boy next to him was Kyle. That was his name, I remembered. He was deathly pale; the stench of his fear was the strongest.

"We're here!" Megan called. Sam's attention instantly lasered in on his mate before going back to the wolves under Bowen's sway.

Footfalls thumped on the ground as Dominic Wolfe, Dad, and several other adults swarmed the football field. Another wave of relief nearly had me collapsing on the frigid grass.

Gordon Rockwell, a wolf from Dominic's pack and also on the local police force, took charge. "You all need to get out of here. Right now. Let the adults do this. The police will have enough questions they can't answer without finding all of you here."

"Is it safe to let go of their wills?" Bowen asked Gordon.

"Probably?" he replied.

Cade wheezed next to me and nudged me with his nose. My legs felt like rubber bands, all bendy, stretchy, and limp. Dominic grunted where he and Dad had taken charge of the other wolves on the field. Dad looked down at Drew, the ropes I'd used to hog-tie him still tight even though he'd shifted from his fur back to skin. Resha, a woman from my pack, hauled Drew none too gently to his feet.

"Sarah, you do that? Those are some tidy knots." Dad looked up at me, grinning as pride shone from his eyes. It kindled that spot in my chest that made some of my rubberiness disappear. I nodded, tongue lolling, and stood a little straighter under my father's praise. Drew snarled, the rope having slipped from his mouth once he'd shifted from fur to skin.

Cade nudged me again. I made my way over to the heap of shiny blue material as he went to find his pants. My poor dress. The one night I'd gotten to be a normal high schooler and go to a fancy dance. Not that I'd expected a completely trouble-free event, but it would have been nice to just be a girl for an evening without having to be a Beta and second in command of a pack of werewolves.

But at least the world was safer now. Drew and the rest of his pack were done. Gordon Rockwell had the boy next to Bowen in cuffs. Resha was lugging Drew up to the others to be taken into custody. A loud snarl ripped through the night.

Morphing in mid-air, faster than I'd ever seen a shift, Drew latched his wolf's incisors around Kyle's throat. Blood spewed from Kyle's neck, a wet gurgle all that marked his final words. My stomach quivered as a fresh wave of adrenaline blasted through my limbs.

Growling, Rockwell yanked his giant human hands around Drew's neck, and Wolf recoiled as a cracking snap echoed around the field. Drew's head lolled, Kyle's blood slicking the front of his chest.

Stunned, I only barely registered when Raven retched. I wanted to. Swallowing back bile, adrenaline, and a shudder, I turned my face away and ran to the shadow of the field house, shifted, and struggled back into my dress.

Chapter 2

Cade

So much blood. It was the second major battle I'd fought, and it left me with a confusing mix of disgust and elation. Catching Sam's eye, I nodded to him. I knew my best friend would interpret the motion correctly. I was okay, and I'd make sure Sarah was, too. Snatching my pants off the ground, I ducked into the shadows and shifted back to my skin.

I jammed my legs into the dress pants I'd abandoned on the edge of the field before running to my sister's rescue. Glancing back to Raven as I buttoned the dark material, I exhaled in relief. Bowen, her mate and Beta of the Kypson pack, scooped her up, and they were heading toward the parking lot. She was safe.

I needed to find Sarah. Wolf pawed inside me, suddenly frantic to have eyes on the girl we were falling for.

Scenting, I picked out her wild honey and citrus smell from the other grisly smells surrounding the area. I found her against the wall of the field house, adjusting her skirt. Blood streaked her arm.

"Hey, you all right?" I asked softly. Concern knit my brows together, but I didn't fawn. Sarah didn't like to be seen as anything less than strong and capable, so I tried not to crowd.

She gave her head a quick shake, her light-blonde hair twisted and tangled, a few stray sparkly pins sticking out of it. She'd been so beautiful, all dressed up for the dance.

"Yeah. Let's just go."

"Come on." I reached my hand out, offering her support. I wasn't sure if she'd take it or not. She slid her trembling fingers against my palm. Shivering as a cold February breeze blasted over the field and chilled my naked torso, I knew we needed to go—not only to get away from the murder scene, but because Sarah's dress was strapless and hit just above her knee. She'd be freezing, too.

"Are you okay to drive?" she asked as her teeth chattered. We jogged to the parking lot and my new truck. Well, new to me. I'd traded my car in last week.

"I'm fine. Mostly just cold. The shock of everything will probably set in later," I confessed. She nodded.

I opened the door of the truck for her, and she hopped in. Jumping in on my side, I gunned the motor and rubbed my aching fingers together.

"Wow, Cade. You're covered in…gore."

I looked down and realized my chest and stomach were swathed in blood and a few errant pieces of fur. Blades of grass stuck to my side. A few nicks on my chest were already healing.

"That's disgusting," I blurted, revolted at my own body covered in the aftermath of the battle. I glanced at Sarah.

"Ooh, and you're oozing." Fresh concern ratcheted up my backbone.

"I am?"

"How deep were those punctures in your side?" My belly tied itself in knots, looking at the blood seeping through her dress.

Sarah grimaced in a silent snarl. "I'm so keyed up right now I can't even feel them."

"Let's get you to your house and take a look." That seemed to be the safest option right now.

"Sorry. I'll try not to bleed on your seats. I could have driven myself if I'd known there was going to be an all-out attack like this. You're probably ready to be at your own home."

"No. I'd still rather have come with you." I reached for a gym towel I knew was in the back seat and passed it to her. I gave her a cheeky wink as my heart tried to stutter into a more normal rhythm.

She snorted.

"You know, I hear the middle seat is warmer than the one way over there by the door," I quipped as I pulled onto the main road that would take us to the subdivision where the Wolfe pack lived and where several of the Thornehill pack were living temporarily, having banded together to fight Victor Atwood—a common enemy. I shivered. Drew had been Victor's lackey. Fortunately, both threats were now done.

"Funny, Cade," she said, but not with any venom. She dabbed at the blood dripping down from her punctures. A tired smile hid at the corner of her mouth, even though she stayed on her side. We'd been dancing around this attraction between us for weeks. I bit back a sigh and guided the truck around a turn at Walnut Street.

She made a surprised noise in her throat. "Hang on," she said when I glanced at her. "Dad's using the link."

As Alpha of the Thornehills, Sarah's dad, Austin, had taken a big risk when he and half his pack moved down here. But it had paid off. Our packs were close. Solidified allies. And Sarah was here.

"You're not going to believe this," Sarah said after a few minutes of silence.

"What?"

"Dad just filled me in—it wasn't Drew that could use the mind control at all. It was Kyle Mason—the kid from the Eagles basketball team! He was another one of Victor Atwood's kids!"

"Seriously?" Though I supposed I shouldn't have been so surprised that Victor had yet another illegitimate offspring, the news rocked me. After Victor's death, I thought we'd seen the last of his evil. So much hate and so much bad from one werewolf. Although, on the other hand, two of his sons had turned out well. One of them—Bowen—was now my brother-in-law. And Kyp was shaping up to be a fine Alpha for their pack.

"Is the madness really over now?" Sarah groaned as she yanked sparkly bobby pins from her hair.

"It's done." Wolf whined inside me. But if all the threats were dealt with, if danger no longer lurked around every corner, then the Thornehills would move back to New York. Sarah would go. A cold lump lodged in my throat.

"Hey, you just went all ashy under the gunk," Sarah said, her tone forcibly light, though I heard her concern.

I shook my head. "It's fine." It was not fine. But I wasn't sure baring my soul to Sarah right now would win me any points. I swallowed hard as her fingers ghosted over my arm.

It didn't take long for us to reach the subdivision and to park in the drive of Sarah's borrowed house.

"So…I'll see you…Monday?" Sarah ventured as she sat in my truck, not getting out.

"No. I'll stay with you until your dad gets home." I gave her what I hoped was a disarming smile.

"I don't need a babysitter, you know." She raised an eyebrow.

"Maybe I do," I retorted. I cracked my door open and reached behind the driver's seat for the duffle of spare clothes I always kept in my vehicle.

Sarah snorted. "Can't argue with that," she said with just a touch of her normal sass back in her voice. We made our way up the short path, and Sarah unlocked the door and flipped the lights, flooding the room in a soft amber glow.

She took a deep breath and leaned against the door as she shut it.

"Sarah?" She shut her eyes, and her chest rose and fell once in the silence.

"The adrenaline is fading. I feel the teeth now."

"Want me to look?" I said it with the express purpose of making sure she was okay. Wolf chuffed. I wouldn't object to seeing her skin either. Well, the unbruised bits.

Sarah rolled her eyes, a half grin playing at the corner of her mouth. "I'll go wash them out and assess the damage after that." She pointed down the hall, wincing at the movement. "You can use the shower off the guest room. Towels are under the sink. Do you need anything?" Her celery-green eyes softened as she glanced at my face. "Are you hurt anywhere?" Her voice gentled, and for just a second, I could see inside the crack in her armor.

Resisting the urge to let my fingers trail down her cheek, I glanced down at myself. "Nothing I don't think will heal up by tomorrow or Sunday."

She nodded, then turned to the stairs.

Twenty minutes later, I'd showered off the nasty, texted my parents, and was plopped on the Thornehills' couch with two glasses of water and a bowl of snacks I'd raided from their pantry. Sarah came into the den and gingerly perched on the other end of the couch.

I handed her a glass. "Thanks," she said tightly.

Letting my gaze deliberately slide to her ribs and back to her face, I carefully said nothing, waiting for her to offer information if she wanted to.

She huffed a sigh and raised the back of her shirt up, showing me an angry red, blue, and purple bruise surrounding a few punctures on the back side of her ribs. "I can't reach these very well."

Quelling my inner urge to freak out over her injury, I whistled through my teeth. "I can do that." I held out my palm, and she thrust a tube of ointment and a large gauze pad at me.

Swallowing hard, I dabbed as gently as I could at the cuts. I winced more than Sarah did. She was seriously the toughest girl I'd ever met. And most of the time, it was so hot. But right now, I wish she'd let me in.

Smoothing the gauze pad over the bite and sticking down the edges, I couldn't resist letting my thumb stroke once down the curve of her spine near the edge of the gauze.

The faintest hint of gooseflesh broke out over her skin, igniting mine and sending Wolf pacing. Was that the faintest hint of a shiver? Was it truly possible she felt a fraction of what I felt for her?

Chapter 3

Sarah

He ran his finger down my back, and Wolf nearly went euphoric. My mouth dried, and I knew I had to put some distance between the two of us, or I'd be all over him. And that was a line I shouldn't cross.

Never mind that he was gorgeous with his thatch of black hair and ice-blue eyes. Never mind that he understood me in a way no one else ever had. Never mind that he was staring at me in a way that curled my toes. Never mind that his teasing knotted my belly up in the most delicious way. Never mind that we were intellectual equals. Never mind that I wanted him. I was Beta of the Thornehill pack. It was my job to marry another Alpha or Beta and to someday take over my dad's place as Alpha. Cade didn't fit those parameters. So he had to stay just a nice guy who happened to be one of my best friends.

Carefully, I moved away from his fingers and let my shirt fall back down.

"You want to watch a movie?" he asked hoarsely.

I nodded, not trusting myself to speak. Cade snagged the remote off the coffee table and held his arm out. A welcome invitation to snuggle up against him on the couch. His springy scent of watercress and mint teased my nostrils, and I wanted so badly to have him wrap his arms around me. But I gave him a playful smile and leaned gingerly against the arm of the couch, careful not to overextend my abused flesh. I did let my toes poke him in the ribs. I didn't want him to think I didn't want the closeness—because I desperately did—but I didn't know a good way around the obstacles set before us.

Cade smiled, a twinkling flash in his blue eyes as he grabbed both my feet and put them on his lap, his hand draping lazily over my ankles as he stopped flipping at some sci-fi movie. It was just as well that I hadn't snuggled up next to him, because after the day's trauma, we both fell asleep not long after.

That's how my dad found us in the middle of the night when he got home.

"Sarah? Cade?" My dad's deep rumble of a voice nudged me out of a heavy sleep. I ached. My ribs were healing, but they hurt like all get out.

"Dad?" I mumbled.

"I'm home. Come on. Everything is taken care of. It's all over. Go on up to bed. Cade, you all right to drive, or do you want to stay on the couch?"

"I'm good, sir. Sorry. I didn't want Sarah to have to wait here by herself until you got home. Everything get cleaned up?" Cade's voice gradually lost its edge of sleep.

"What didn't get cleaned up, Rockwell is taking care of with the police. Rest easy. You kids did well tonight. We're all very proud of the way you handled yourselves." Dad smiled, the corners of his eyes crinkling even as pale shadows cupped his eyes.

Wolf warmed at Dad's praise. Cade gently squeezed my foot, and I snatched it back, a flush creeping up my cheeks as I realized half my legs were still draped across his lap. Not that there was anything improper in it, but the way I felt toward Cade made it *feel* improper.

"I'll walk you out," I said as I rose stiffly from the couch.

"Sarah, that a bandage under your shirt?" Dad's brow creased in concern.

"Yeah. It'll be fine in a few days. Got a couple teeth to the side."

Dad grunted. "Well, keep an eye on it. Cade, see you around." Dad bobbed his head and went toward the stairs and his room. Glancing at the clock, I stifled a yawn. It was almost four in the morning.

"Cade, do you want to just crash on the couch? It's almost dawn as it is."

"Nah. I'm awake now anyway." He turned at the door and gave me a sleepy smile, belying his words.

Wolf nudged me inside. Biting my lip, I let my fingers graze his hand. His eyes widened in surprise, his fingers quickly folding around mine.

"Thanks. For...tonight," I finished lamely. I could have died of mortification. Was that really the most eloquent thing I could come up with?

"Yeah. Anytime. Although maybe without the excessive gore next time. But I'm always up for a good tussle." He wagged his eyebrows suggestively, and I couldn't help the smirk that formed on my lips as I disengaged my fingers.

"Good night, Cade." A grin hovered at the corner of my mouth.

"Night." For just an instant, his gaze darted to my lips, and my belly clenched. But then the moment was gone, and he was out the door, climbing into his truck.

****

I slept late Saturday morning. By the time I peeled myself from my bed, the sun was fully up. My side was sore, but when I checked it in the mirror, most of the cuts were healed up, pale scars ringed in ugly bluish-green and yellow bruises. My lip curled back. I wasn't crazy about the scars. I had no desire for a permanent reminder of last night.

Dad had coffee going in the kitchen and a box on the kitchen table.

"Morning, Sarah. Well, afternoon, really." Grayish circles still ringed under Dad's eyes.

"Morning. What's with the box?" I asked while helping myself to a mug of coffee but eying the tin of my favorite tangerine tea on the counter beside the coffee maker. I blinked, then took a sip of the coffee. I needed the caffeine today.

"Well, the immediate threats are over. I figured we'd be heading back to New York this week." He wrapped a glass in a piece of newspaper and put it in the box.

Ice lodged in my middle as fear clutched at my heart. I set the mug back on the counter. Wolf squirmed inside. I cleared my throat. "What if I told you I want to finish my senior year here? At Rock Falls." I was proud that my voice held none of my inner tremor.

Dad paused. "Anything you need to tell me?" he hedged.

"No, no, nothing like that," I answered quickly. Possibly too quickly. What could I tell him? That I liked a boy I could never have? Even though Cade was a big reason I wanted to stay in Rock Falls, he wasn't the only reason. I took a breath. "This is the first time

18

I've ever had friends my own age who weren't my subordinates. I've never known what it's like to have friends who are on equal footing with me. There are Betas here my own age—and their mates are girls I genuinely like and get along with. Besides. We *need* strong alliances. Someday I'll have to keep these alliances intact. Deep friendships would only help that."

A grin played over Dad's lips. "You've made your case. All you needed to do was ask." His grin broke into an outright smile. "But you do have several very good points. And I'm glad to see you happy with friends your own age. I wish your life had been easier." He stepped closer and gently squeezed my shoulder. A lump formed in my throat the way it always did when I knew Dad was remembering Mom. I wished I could remember her.

"I've always had you," I said softly.

"And you always will," Dad answered before wrapping me in a comforting hug.

I winced slightly as my ribs pulled.

"Is your side worse than you let on last night?" Dad asked as he moved back.

"The wounds are closed, just some bad bruising." I turned and flipped the back of my shirt up so he could see.

"Ew, Sarah. That's a *bad* bruise. You need anything for that?"

I shook my head, setting my jaw. "It's fine."

"All right. Don't let your stubbornness keep you in unnecessary pain. I guess I'll unpack, then. I'll call back to the home pack and let them know our plans. Most of us are down here anyway. I imagine some will be eager to get back to New York, though."

I nodded, relief shooting through me. My phone dinged up in my bedroom. I took my coffee and a packet of breakfast pastries and went back upstairs.

Tingles and guilt ran to my toes as I glanced at the screen.

Chapter 4

Cade

I woke up thinking about Sarah. I woke up thinking about Sarah most mornings because most nights I dreamed about her. My muscles were tight and achy after last night's fight. Immediately, my thoughts tracked to Sarah's side and back. I fumbled for my phone on the nightstand.

It was just after noon. Pursing my lips, I debated whether I should text her. I didn't want to seem desperate—I mean, I was close to desperate, but not there entirely yet. On the other hand, I did genuinely want to know how she was.

I fired off a quick text to Sam first.

—How'd things turn out?—

He might not be up yet. I decided to text Sarah. Wolf perked up.

—How're you feeling this morning?—

That was subtle enough, wasn't it? When she didn't immediately answer either, I began to wonder if I was the only wolf awake. The house was quiet. Too quiet. Ever since Raven had moved in with Bowen, everything was too still, too noiseless. Too lonely. Wolf whined.

I stared at my ceiling, letting my thoughts drift.

My phone vibrated, and I nearly jumped out of my skin.

—Sore and bruised but okay. You?—

My heart beat quicker just seeing her words on my screen.

—Sore. Cramped from your couch. I give great back massages.—

She sent me a winky face.

—What are you doing today?— I sent back.

—Helping Dad unpack!—

—Unpack? Were you packing to leave already?—

Fear pounded in my chest. Was she going to leave without even telling me? I knew she was a private person, but I thought we were pretty close. But wait…unpack?

—I got up this morning, and he was packing to go back to New York. But I convinced him to let me finish school here in Rock Falls.—

—YES!—

We texted off and on the rest of the day. Sam called me later that afternoon to fill me in on some more of last night's happenings.

"Rockwell got things squared away and has seen to the details. Dad and Austin helped him clean up things, so that only the evidence they wanted left was what the humans found when they got there," Sam said as I cracked open a bottle of juice. Mom brought a package of meat in from the deep freeze, put it on the counter, and smiled at me.

"Anyone else hurt? Anything else happen at the dance?" I asked as I gave Mom a quick hug around her shoulders before I took my glass of juice back up to my room.

"Just minor cuts and bruises from what we can tell. Resha got the worst of things aside from you and Sarah.

22

And then there's the backlash that's slowly building and rumbling about Bowen's mind control."

Dread slithered into my gut. "What's going on with Bowen on that end?" Wolf whined, and I suddenly felt torn between my own pack and my sister's mate. Bowen was my brother-in-law—the one who took care of my sister, but the Wolfe pack was my home. Who owned more of my allegiance? I suppressed a shiver as Sam continued.

"Right now, nothing. He's Kypson pack. I can tell you I was equally shocked and grateful when he used it last night. Did you know?"

"Of course, I didn't. You know I'd tell you something like that." I was mildly offended my best friend thought I'd hold out on him that way.

"Yeah, I know. Just…sorry. I'm tired and processing. I don't doubt you, Cade. You know you're my second." And just like that, we were back on the solid footing we'd always had.

"Don't you forget it," I said teasingly. "For what it's worth, I trust Bowen. I don't like that he didn't tell us about his mind control freakiness, but given what he had to go through living with Victor for four years, and how we would have perceived his mind control, I get it. I don't like it, but I get it."

"Your trust in him does make me feel better. You know him better than I do. And he did save us all last night. I trust him, too." He was quiet a second. "I think we need to reaffirm our friendships. Not me and you, but with the others. We've still got three packs represented in the immediate territory. We need to remember we're all allies. Our allies are more important than ever now. Who knows what else may pop up?"

"I'm all for hanging out. What did you have in mind?"

"I hadn't gotten that far yet."

"Let's crash at Raven and Bowen's house. I like his hot tub." And Sarah would come. In her swimsuit.

Sam laughed. "Hey, Bowen, as penance for keeping secrets, we're all coming to schmooze in your pool."

"Just tell me the time, and I'll be there."

Chapter 5

Sarah

"Hey, Sarah," Rachel's voice chirped on the other end of the phone.

"Hi, Rachel. What's up?"

"There's a few of us going to hang out at Raven and Bowen's tonight. Wanna come?"

"Oh. Sure. What time?" Time with friends would be welcome.

"Around six thirty-ish. Bring some snacks if you want. I just baked a batch of basil bread. Trying out a new recipe. I'll have that. I think Meg is bringing brownies."

"Mm. Chocolate."

"Right? Anyway, that sound good?" Rachel's voice carried her typical happy enthusiasm.

"Yep. I'll see you there."

We chatted a few more minutes before hanging up. A smile played on my lips as I moved to my drawer to rifle for my swimming suit.

My swimming suit.

Momentarily abandoning my rummaging, I crossed the room to the mirror on the back of my door. Lifting my shirt in the back, I craned my neck and grimaced.

"Ugh." I groaned softly. My back was looking better, but it was still ugly shades of green and yellow with shiny little crescent marks where the brute's teeth had cut into me. My swimsuit was a tankini—but the top didn't quite meet the bottoms. It had a V-shaped fringe on the front that gave my athletic frame more curves, which I loved, but it would leave part of that nasty bruise exposed in the back.

I sighed. Maybe I could just make sure I faced toward people all night so no one saw the bruise. Although Cade had seen it at its worst last night. My cheeks heated. If I were totally honest, he was probably the only one who would be looking. Or that I wanted to look.

****

Six thirty rolled around just as I pulled into the drive of Bowen's two-story brick house. He and Kyp had both inherited houses once Victor had died. Both were impressive. Snagging the meat and cheese tray I'd picked up at the corner deli on the way out of town, I shivered against the wind and rang the doorbell.

"Hey, Sarah! Come in. Here, I'll take this. Thanks for bringing it—ooh, these little pepperonis are some of my favorites." Raven's eyes twinkled. She had the blush of someone in love—and the pheromones to prove it.

"Thanks for having me." I came in and shut the door. Shrugging out of my jacket, I draped it over the arm of the chair with a few others.

"Sure! Come on back through. Sam and Meg are in the kitchen."

We went through, and I immediately noticed the stiff set of Bowen's shoulders. He gave me a tight nod. Wolf bristled, still annoyed, and still slightly fearful, that he hadn't shared his mind control abilities.

"We didn't know either," Sam said before Bowen

26

or I could say anything. My gaze flicked to Sam. His blue eyes were steady, calculating. Wolf snorted before tipping her head to him. I'd bet money that Sam had organized this outing to make sure everyone was still on friendly terms. It was smart. We all needed our alliances intact. The circumstances of my mom's death and Victor's treachery against his own race had shown us that.

"And now that we do?" I asked, encompassing both Bowen and Sam in my stare.

"It will go back to being as dormant as it was before last night," Bowen said without pause.

I lifted an eyebrow. Not exactly skeptical, but more curious than anything at his cryptic remark. The doorbell rang, and the door opened before we could continue the conversation.

"Hey!" a familiar voice shouted.

My heartbeat picked up, and I really hoped the flush stayed off my cheeks. Cade, with Kyp and Rachel behind him, tumbled into the room, bread, cookies, and a few liters of soda between them.

Cade's gaze immediately swung to me. He gave me a quick wink, then put the drinks on the counter.

"You guys want to fill plates and eat in the hot tub?" Bowen asked, his shoulders having lost some of their tenseness with Kyp's arrival.

General agreement circled the room, and we broke off into groups. Those with their suits already on started opening food and getting plates out while the rest of us went to change.

Since I'd stopped at the store on the way over, I hadn't put my suit on under my clothes. I changed quickly in the bathroom off the downstairs hallway, glad that the lengthening shadows might be enough to cover my bruises. They made me feel exposed. Less—like I couldn't take care of myself. Like they somehow reflected badly on my ability to one day lead my pack. I shook my head. I knew it was silly, but they still fed that insecure part of me that had been forced to grapple for every shred of respect I'd ever received. Being a female Beta in a world of Alpha males was tough in more ways than one.

Wrapping my towel around my waist, I went back to the kitchen. Kyp and Rachel were the only ones still in the house. We quickly finished filling plates and went out to the back patio. Shadows hugged the outer edges, and trees seemed to stretch impossibly long and black, snaking over the ground as the sun began its descent.

With a pang, I realized that the only open spot left in the tub was beside Cade. Not that I didn't want to sit next to him, but because everyone else was already paired off. Cade and I were the only ones not officially together. Wolf whined inside as loneliness surfaced.

Gritting my teeth and putting on a pleasant expression, I put my towel next to the others and made my way toward Cade on the far side of the hot tub—careful to keep my back turned away from everyone as much as possible.

Cade caught my eye and gave me a flirty suggestive quirk of his eyebrow. Butterflies rushed in my stomach. Wolf preened.

Chapter 6

Cade

The door shut behind Kyp as he, Rachel, and Sarah came outside. Finally. I ignored the way my sister was sitting close enough to share Bowen's breath. She smelled different. I tried not to gag thinking about why she now carried a subtle hint of Bowen's scent. They were married, mates. They were supposed to…do things with each other. But she was still my little sister. And the thought of any guy touching her made Wolf see red—or in this case, see through a haze of green. *Ew.*

But Sarah was the perfect distraction. No one was paying any attention to me as I watched Sarah take off her towel, careful to keep her back turned. I wondered if her bruises were still bad. They'd be visible in that delicious strip of skin where her top and bottoms didn't quite meet.

She scanned the pool, and I could tell the second she realized the only open spot was strategically next to me. I lifted an eyebrow, letting her know I was watching. With the tiniest twitch of her lips, she held her plate to the side and strutted—she didn't walk— there was no other way to describe that little extra wiggle, the way her slender hips swayed, the way her tight abs flexed slightly as she took each step.

She knew exactly what she was doing, and it was

working. Wolf was practically frothing. My mouth was dry by the time she gingerly set her plate down and slid into the water. Not quite touching, but close enough I could feel her even under the water.

"Since we're all here now," Bowen started and then cleared his throat. I ruefully turned my gaze from Sarah on my left to Bowen on my right. Raven angled subtly, her shoulder touching her mate's. "I wanted to tell you I'm sorry for hiding my…*abilities* from you all. It wasn't something I was eager to share after everything that happened with Victor." A pained expression flitted over his face. "It's not something I'm proud of or ever plan to use again unless I have no alternative. I hope this won't damage relations between our pack and yours." Bowen met each of our eyes. A collective weight seemed to rise from the group. Kyp watched his brother, acceptance and maybe pride shining in his dark eyes.

"I've spoken with my dad. Our alliance with you has not changed," Sam confirmed, his eyes serious.

"I have not spoken with mine, but he has said nothing to indicate a break in our alliance," Sarah said. "I want to keep it."

A knot of tension I hadn't noticed released at her words. We were all still allies. We were all still friends.

"Thank you," Bowen said quietly. He met Kyp's gaze across the tub. They nodded solemnly at each other.

"Speaking of Victor, Sam, tell them what Rev found," Megan said as she slid a chip laden with cheese dip into her mouth.

Sam swallowed his bite of bread and nodded. "Rev may have found the crux of Victor's enmity with us—

why he targeted the Wolfe pack and not some other pack." He took a sip of his drink.

"He said once that you all—the Wolfes—were always stealing what didn't belong to you," Kyp said.

"That's all I ever got out of him for an explanation, too, though I never outright asked," Bowen added.

Sam nodded. "Rev has been doing research like a madman. But he found what he thinks was the spark to the eventual powder keg. Way back in my family line, one of my ancestors, Anderson Wolfe, came for *Lacessere* right here in this area."

"Hang on, I'm still new to this world. What's *Lacessere?*" Rachel asked.

"It's an ancient ritual where wolves come to fight over a claim to a she-wolf and the title or lands she inherits upon her Alpha father's death or his relinquishment," Sarah said woodenly.

Wolf pricked his ears forward at Sarah's tone. I knew she was intended to marry another Alpha or Beta. That's the only reason I'd met her—Dominic and Austin had brought Sarah and Sam together in hopes that they'd strike an attraction, or better yet, a mate bond. But Sam already had a mate bond with Megan. Surely, Sarah had more choice in her future than Sam's ancestor from hundreds of years ago? Wolf whined. I shoved a cracker and cheese in my mouth, pulverizing them under the tenseness of my jaw.

Sam continued. "Rev thinks Victor's ancestor—a wolf named Richard Woods—was here for the *Lacessere*, too. By the end of the trials, Anderson had been declared the victor, but there was some murkiness to how he won one of the points in his favor. Richard thought he'd been cheated, and it started a blood feud.

Over time, things settled, but the animosity between the two packs never went away, only spread out into different territories over time.

"Victor called Wolfe lands his rightful ancestral lands. I think he saw this as his rightful inheritance. Wolfe territory won in the *Lacessere*."

"So wait. Anderson won the *Lacessere*. Then what?" Rachel's nose wrinkled.

"He won, got the girl, and got the land. When her father passed, his Alpha title went to Anderson," Meg summarized.

"Why not to his own daughter?" Rachel asked.

"Because it's only been in the past half century or so that it's become acceptable for female Betas to inherit their father's packs," Sarah said softly. There was the barest edge of pain in her voice. So slight I doubted anyone else picked up on it. Carefully, I put my hand on her knee underneath the bubbles that distorted the surface of the water and kept my actions private.

She nudged her thigh against mine, igniting fire in my veins. Wolf shivered inside.

"But you inherit your father's pack, right?" Raven asked, her eyebrows drawn together.

"I do." Sarah's voice rang with quiet finality.

We were all quiet for a minute.

"I'm going to go grab a refill. Anyone want anything while I'm in?" Sarah said as she rose, effectively ending our contact and sloshing water on my shoulder.

"I'd actually love some more water. You sure you don't mind?" Rachel handed up her cup as Sarah skirted around the hot tub.

"Nope. Be back in a sec," Sarah said with a smile that didn't quite reach her green eyes. She quickly wrapped her towel around her waist and went into the house.

"Cade, do you still have that playlist you showed me the other day?" Bowen asked casually.

"Yeah. It's on my phone. Why?"

Bowen gave me a sly look from the corner of his eye, and Wolf came alert. "If you want to grab it, you can plug it into the dock on the kitchen counter, and it'll play through the speakers out here."

"Yeah, okay." I resisted the urge to grin like an idiot. Maybe my new brother-in-law wasn't so bad.

I slid from the burbling water and traipsed to my towel then inside, shutting the door behind me. Sarah stood at the kitchen sink, staring out the window, her expression unreadable.

Chapter 7

Sarah

Cade entered the room. Wolf shook her coat out while the human part of me stood still, staring into the blackness falling across Bowen's backyard. He made next to no noise as he padded across the floor and hovered behind me.

His fingers ghosted up my arm, raising gooseflesh. My eyes slid shut. I relished his touch, memorizing the way he made me feel inside before swallowing hard against the attraction threatening to suck me under.

"Hey, Alpha Girl," he said softly.

"Hey, Wolf Dude," I whispered back.

His fingers traced up both my arms, resting against my shoulders before he started gently kneading my taut muscles with his thumbs.

A groan escaped without my permission as my muscles surrendered under his light pressure.

"Girl, your muscles are tighter than a—"

My snort cut him off. "What are you doing, Cade?"

"Trying to save you from a miserable existence with knots the size of tennis balls in your shoulders. I might be hitting on you, too."

A smile ghosted over my lips. His palms pressed against my shoulder blades, his thumbs rubbing near my spine.

"How're things down lower?" He could make the

most innocent question sound naughty. I fought the stupid girlish impulse to giggle.

"Still bruised. It looks pretty gross."

"I'll take a look for you and confirm or deny if you'd like."

"I'm sure you would," I quipped. His fingers stilled and slid back to my upper arms, turning me to face him.

His blue eyes twinkled but then settled. "Seriously. You came in here kinda quick. I'm guessing not only for a refill." His hands cupped my elbows, but he didn't push any farther.

Wolf nudged me, and I couldn't help the longing that filled me as I stared at his face. My gaze dipped to his lips. His quick inhale startled me out of my trance, and my gaze flew back to his. He was lasered in on me, his hands tightening around the back of my arms, pulling me farther into his space.

I had to stop this.

My hand landed on his bare chest, and I winced inside as skin on skin didn't exactly diminish the sparks flying between us.

"I'm fine," I whispered thickly past the boulder of emotion ready to combust in my throat. I pushed his chest lightly. He stepped back. I grabbed the refilled cups and fled back to the patio.

Chapter 8

Cade

My jaw clenched as my eyes slid shut along with the door. She ran from me. Again. I knew she liked me. I could still smell her interest lingering in the air. My chest tingled where she'd pressed her hand flat against it. She'd wanted to kiss me. Maybe I should have just made the move and kissed her first.

Why? Why did she run from me like a scalded cat every time I got close? It left me frustrated and achy. I hurt every time she jerked away. But every time, something always pulled me back. Back to her. I was a glutton for punishment.

Sighing, I retrieved my phone from my coat pocket and put it in the dock. Flipping it to the playlist Bowen had suggested, I hit play and adjusted the volume so it would be just background noise outside. Sensitive wolf hearing didn't need loud music.

The laughter that hovered both eased my tension and rankled my nerves as I rejoined the group. I needed to get a grip. The tumultuous emotions between Sarah and me didn't need to affect all parts of my life. The water was warm against my skin, but my skin burned even hotter when Sarah nudged my knee with hers. Like she was contrite for not kissing me in the kitchen.

I was so confused.

****

My mood didn't improve come Monday. I'd been too distracted with Sarah and forgot about a quiz in Calculus. I bombed it. I wasn't in danger of failing the class by any means, but it might have been enough to drop me from an A- to a B+. And that sucked. Because I needed my grades as high as I could get them if I wanted to be the full package colleges were going to want. I knew there were several college scouts that had come to games. I'd even talked to a few, but I hadn't had any formal offers yet.

I wanted to play college ball. I loved basketball. Loved the camaraderie, the physical exertion, the high that came from a game well played. I didn't want that to end after high school. Plus, I knew I was good enough to go to college on a basketball scholarship if I played my cards right.

The day went from bad to worse. Someone's soda exploded all over me at lunch. I put on my practice shirt, but I couldn't get all the sticky out of my hair. Fizz was permanently lodged in my nose.

The guys noticed my foul temper before practice even started. Jamie even sidestepped around me so as not to cross my path.

Bowen nudged me in the locker room. "Long day?"

"Yeah." I bit the word out tersely.

"We're all on the same team here," Bowen said quietly enough only I heard him.

Scrubbing a hand over my face, I blew out a harsh breath. "Yeah," I said with less venom this time.

****

Coach called me over after practice. "Cade, you were a little off tonight. Make sure you get your head on before games this week. Big ones. You know state championship is a distinct possibility if we keep doing as well as we have."

"I will, Coach," I promised, resisting the urge to groan at the pressure his words added. It wasn't the game. It was Sarah. My infatuation with her was distracting me from the rest of my life. I swallowed hard against the ache that formed in the back of my throat as I untied my tennis shoes and stuck them in my bag back in the locker room.

I wanted her. Badly. But for whatever her reasons, she didn't want me—I didn't have enough to offer her pack. I wasn't a Beta. I wasn't an Alpha. I was just a nice middle-of-the-pack guy who happened to be crazy about her. Resisting the urge to growl, I thrust my hoodie over my head and shoved my arms through the sleeves with more force than was necessary. Wolf rumbled low in my chest.

We were not in agreement. The rational part of me knew that a relationship with Sarah was impractical and improbable. But that didn't stop the rest of me from wanting it. Acutely.

I was the last one out of the locker room, and nearly the last one in the parking lot. As I was heading out the doors, the last of the guys were pulling out.

"Cade."

The word stopped me in my tracks, and I froze like a bucket of ice water had been dumped over my head. Wolf surged inside me, and despite my internal war in the locker room, my nerve endings started firing. I wheeled around, and there she was, standing against the corner of the building.

"Sarah? What are you doing here?" Wolf whined

and pawed inside me. She had no reason to be here this late after school.

She bit her lip. "I stayed after to do some work in the library. How was practice?"

My eyes slit. Her voice came out higher than usual.

"A little rough. How was the library?" I stalked closer to her. The sun was just starting to set, and the orange rays lit up her face.

"It was all right."

I was in her space now, less than a foot between us. Her eyes widened, and her lips parted. My insides tied themselves in knots.

"What do you want, Sarah?" I whispered, the words jagged and edged in double meaning.

For a fleeting minute, vulnerability flashed across her features. Her hand closed over mine as her mouth opened. Then she shut it, snatched her hand back, and her features fell into the haughty mask that I knew hid the things she was really thinking.

After the day I'd had, it was the last straw. I couldn't keep doing this to myself. Basketball, and potentially my future college and career plans, were on their way to derailment because of my preoccupation with this girl. And the thing was, I'd happily change all the tentative plans I'd made for myself after high school if it meant I could make new plans with Sarah. If she'd let me in.

I ran angry hands through my hair, tugging the black ends. Wolf gnashed, frustrated and hurt.

"Sarah, I don't know what you want from me. I can't do this"—I waved a hand between us—"anymore. I need to either go all in or make a clean break of things." My insides withered, waiting for her response.

She leaned against the wall, the mason blocks washing out her pale skin and light hair. She was gorgeously ethereal. My heart twisted painfully. I meant what I said. I couldn't keep doing this dance around us. I was falling for her. Hard. And I felt like she was teasing me, stringing me along. I knew she liked me. I saw it in her celery-green eyes when she thought I wasn't looking. Knew the way her wolf responded to mine.

I lit up when I was with her. She made me feel alive and ache in places I hadn't even realized I had.

Her eyes slid shut, her turmoil evident in the crumpling of her eyebrows and the way she braced her palms flat against the wall.

Wolf nudged me. Without meaning to, I stepped closer. All the way into her space.

"What's it going to be, Sarah? I can't do this without you. It only works if we're both in or we're both out." The words were soft, whispered on a breath charged with anguished anticipation.

She swallowed, her eyes still shut.

Finally, she looked at me. Searched my face. Vulnerability crawled across her features in a way I'd never seen. Then my beautiful, strong, independent girl crumbled before my eyes.

I opened my mouth to speak, but before I could, her hands shot out from her sides, fisted into my hoodie, and dragged me flush against her.

Her lips crushed against mine as a shocked whimper escaped my throat. She held me tighter against her, every one of her curves snugged up against me. Her lips were insistent, not waiting for me to get over my shock. Her tongue found its way into my mouth as my stunned body remembered how to react. Wolf pushed me from the inside, and I had no trouble obeying his wishes.

Careful of her bruises, my hands gripped her sides, my tongue tangling with hers, breathing each other's air, stealing each other's noises as they surfaced. One of her hands released my sweatshirt and snaked into the hair at the base of my head. Her other pressed flat against my chest, right over my thundering heart.

At some point we slowed down. I let my fingers explore over the soft cotton of her shirt underneath her jacket. Her sides, the small of her back, coasting along the waist of her jeans. Her hand cupped the corner of my jaw, slid down my neck, over my shoulder to my bicep. She rose on tiptoe to reach my mouth better and the brush of her chest against mine sent another wave of heat ricocheting through my middle.

Her tongue stroked against mine once more before she pulled back. For a minute, nothing but our heavy breathing broke the silence.

"Does that mean you're in?" I asked, aching for her to choose me despite all the reasons she shouldn't.

Sarah's hands rested on my chest. My heart picked up again under her touch. "Cade, I don't know how this is going to work. I don't think it can." She frowned, and my heart fell somewhere down around my ankles. Had that been a goodbye kiss? The first time we kissed was going to be the last? She continued, "But I don't think I can live with myself if I don't try to make it work. I lo—" She broke off, her cheeks flushing darker.

The corner of my mouth tipped up. "You love me and you know it."

"Shut up." She mock punched my shoulder. Her

embarrassed flush crawled down her neck.

"It's okay." My voice came out ragged and breathy. "I'm falling in love with you, too." I didn't give her a chance to respond, but nudged her back against the wall again, lips swooping in to cover any words she could have offered.

Chapter 9

Sarah

I'd never felt cherished the way I did as Cade's gaze drank me in right there outside the school, the wind whipping around the corner of the building and tangling my hair in my face. Heat wrapped around me from the inside out as Cade gently pushed a few strands back behind my ear.

"It's getting late. We should be getting home. My parents are going to wonder where I am," he said, his voice low and slow.

"Yeah." I didn't want to leave this bubble we'd created in time. I felt like once I left, I'd lose this magic that welled up inside me and flooded the space between us. Wolf rubbed her head against me.

"Do I need to speak with your dad? Um, ask him officially to date you or anything?"

A silly grin spread across my face. "Probably. Let me talk to him first. He's not unreasonable, but he does have specific ideas about the way he'd like things to go as far as my dating and potential mates goes." My face fell. Dad liked Cade. But I'd never told Dad how much *I* liked Cade. If Cade were a Beta, there'd be no questions asked. But he wasn't. And I was the sole carrier for the next generation of Thornehill wolves. I alone carried the Alpha gene. I *needed* to someday marry a wolf with dominant genes to ensure my pack survived. A shiver worked over my skin.

"Hey. Did I just lose you? Now that I finally got you?" He smiled, but his eyes were worried.

"No. You still have me." I wanted him to always have me. "Just trying to sort out how this is going to work. I don't want this to be a secret, but you know there are complicating factors here."

"I'm not a Beta." His mouth tugged down slightly at the corners.

I shook my head.

"Can we use Sam and Megan as an example? She wasn't a Beta when he fell for her."

"No, but they're true mates. That's different." I sighed.

"We'll figure it out. Together." He brushed his knuckle under my chin.

"Together." One word had never inspired such hope and such dread at the same time.

"Want me to drive you home? I'll pick you up in the morning. I kind of don't want to say goodbye yet." He gave me a shy smile that pricked at my insides. Cade was always self-assured and confident to the point of cockiness. It was part of his charm. Underneath all his bravado was one of the most genuine people I'd ever met. But I couldn't remember ever seeing him shy like this.

"I suppose we could make that happen." I didn't want to say goodbye either.

He laced our fingers together and tugged me toward his truck.

"You gonna sit in the middle this time?" he asked with a teasing smirk as he opened my door.

I lifted an eyebrow, held his gaze, and deliberately

scooted over to the middle of the bench seat.

"That's my girl." Light seemed to emanate from inside him, and it gave me a contented sort of joy deep in my belly.

He hopped in and brought the truck to life, put it in drive, then promptly squeezed my knee, leaving his hand there.

"This is what middle seats are for," Cade quipped as he pulled out.

"I could like the middle seat." A grin hovered on my lips as giddy little sparkles floated in my belly.

We were quiet on the drive home, just happy to be together with all the walls down. Cade pulled into the driveway of my borrowed house too soon, and it was time to get out. He put the truck in park and turned to face me, a sly smile tugging his lips.

"Can I kiss you good night?"

"Honestly, I'm surprised you asked."

"I'll remember that next time," he said as he leaned in. I met him halfway. His lips were firm and warm and knew exactly what they were doing. He was an exceptional kisser. With a quick sweep of his tongue over the seam of my lips, he pulled back, blue eyes half hooded.

"I could kiss you for hours," he rasped quietly.

Wolf shivered in pleasure. "Well, probably not tonight, but maybe sometime soon," I replied breathlessly.

Cade groaned. "Don't say things like that unless you mean them."

With a cheeky grin I scooted to the passenger side door. "Who says I didn't mean it?" Cade's mouth dropped open as his eyes practically shot sparks. "See you at seven tomorrow morning." A girlish giggle escaped my throat.

"Tomorrow morning, Alpha Girl!" Cade called after me.

I loped up the walkway and waltzed into the house.

Chapter 10

Cade

I was grinning like an idiot when I walked into my own house a few minutes later.

"Cade? You're home later than usual. I was just getting ready to call you," my dad said as he came in from the kitchen to the living room where I was kicking off my shoes. "And you're practically glowing." Dad smiled, his cobalt eyes crinkling. "Come tell me about it while you help me make the salad for dinner. Your mother should be home soon."

Letting my bag fall with a thud near the door, I followed Dad through to the kitchen. The scent of beef, roasted vegetables, and yeast rolls wafted through the room, and my belly growled.

"Basketball related?" Dad asked as I washed my hands.

"Nope." I grinned harder. We did this sometimes. Dad would guess what was going on, kind of checking up on how different areas of my life were going. It was our own sort of special banter together. "Actually, practice today kind of sucked."

"Oh?" Dad raised an eyebrow as he handed me a bunch of radishes and a knife.

"Later. Keep going."

"Grades? You ace a difficult test?"

"Nope. Tanked a calc quiz."

My father's face took on a sterner note. "Do you need help studying?"

"No. I just got too distracted by things and forgot I had a quiz today. I should be able to bring my grade back up with the next two or three assignments."

Dad nodded, knowing I knew the importance of keeping my grades up. "Hmm. Not basketball, not school. Friend related?"

"Not this time."

Dad's mustache twitched. "Then it must be the most important topic of all. It must be girl related."

My face about broke in two. "Sarah kissed me."

The lettuce in his hands dropped unceremoniously into the bowl as he let out a startled guffaw. "She kissed you? Austin's daughter?" Pride and surprise shone in Dad's eyes. Wolf sat up straighter as I hacked at another radish.

"Yeah." I tamped down the urge to giggle. Men did not giggle.

"I'm guessing you kissed her back?"

I cleared my throat. "Um, yeah." I hoped my cheeks weren't burning.

"I see."

We were silent a minute.

"Are you guys officially dating now? Are you thinking of pursuing her? Seriously? You know as next in line for Alpha, she doesn't have the luxury of dating around unless she plans to be serious."

"I know. She wants to talk to Austin tonight." Wolf nudged me, and I let loose a sigh as I finished the radishes. Dad handed me a tomato. "I've never been serious about a girl like I am about Sarah." I was pretty convinced that she was The One for me. I just needed to convince her. And her father. And then figure out how to be what she needed as she planned to take over as Alpha someday. Wolf shivered. Until now, I hadn't paused to think about those implications for me. I didn't care that she'd be Alpha someday. I just wanted her. How did I become what she'd need? Anxiety slithered into my belly. That was a tall order.

"Be careful, son. If this is the path you're choosing, you've got some tricky bits ahead. For what it's worth, I think Sarah is a fine young woman. She'd be fortunate to have you, and you'd be fortunate to have her." Dad looped an arm around my shoulders and gave me a quick squeeze. "You know your mom and I are always here." His eyes twinkled as he smiled at me, and some of my trepidation lifted.

Chapter 11

Sarah

"Dad? I'm home."

"I'm in the den," Dad called back.

I dropped my stuff off at the table, then started rummaging around the fridge for sandwich stuff. I plopped cheese, lunch meat, and sandwich spread on the counter. I needed to go grocery shopping.

"How was school today?" Dad asked as he came into the kitchen. "Sorry. I've had a lot of phone calls to make today. I didn't get anything started for dinner."

"That's okay. How is work going?" Dad owned his own business and could do everything remotely. He'd made the switch once Mom was killed so he could be around for me.

"Went well. I've got a new client filling out forms. How was school?" he asked again.

I couldn't stop the blush that infused my cheeks. "It was really good," I stammered, suddenly lost for words now that Dad was here. This wasn't familiar territory for us.

"Sarah?" Dad's eyebrow was raised as an amused smile hovered near the corner of his mouth.

I put bread on two plates and wordlessly handed one to Dad. He waited silently while I collected my thoughts now that they'd scattered.

"You know how it's always been expected that I'd

marry another Alpha or Beta?"

"Yes," my father said slowly as he layered meat on his sandwich. He paused and gave me his full attention, worry crowding the corners of his eyes. My belly clenched, and Wolf whined. I swallowed.

"What if I really, really liked a guy who…wasn't…an Alpha or a Beta?"

"Liked him how?" Did Dad's voice sound slightly strangled?

"Like enough that I think we could easily forge a mate bond," I whispered.

Dad blew a breath through his mouth and stared unseeing at his plate. He blinked twice before pulling his gaze back to my face.

"Who, Sarah?" he asked quietly, not angry, but…resigned. This wasn't going as well as I'd hoped.

"Cade Rivers."

Dad's head tipped back, and he pinched the bridge of his nose as his eyes squeezed shut. Dread spiraled down my backbone.

"Why didn't you say something the other day? When I asked you if there was anything I should know?" His eyes were sorrowful, and I felt like I'd been kicked in the gut.

"Because I've been trying to convince myself for weeks that he's off-limits. I know I shouldn't like him like this. But I do. So much."

Sweeping his hands down his face, Dad groaned. "I wish you would have told me this before today."

"Why?" I whispered. Dread and anxiety slithered like snakes in my gut, twisting up painfully tight.

Dad turned his anguished eyes to my face. "Because just today, I accepted the interest of three other packs who want to see if you are a potential match for any of their Betas. Since things obviously didn't work out with Sam, and you hadn't mentioned anyone else, I went ahead and made arrangements."

Trepidation and despair sat heavily on my shoulders as my belly cramped, and Wolf thrashed as I sank defeated into a chair at the table. "Is that it, then? There's no way possible for me to be with Cade?"

Dad pursed his lips. "No. I'm not saying that."

Hope flared hot and vibrant in my chest. I jerked my head up, staring at Dad. "What does that mean?"

"Sarah, I'd never do anything to intentionally make you unhappy. You know that. You also knew that this was the expected outcome—that you'd have to entertain the advances of other Betas and Alphas as possible mates. I like Cade. He's been good for you as a friend. I'd far prefer him be a Beta, as that's going to be most compatible with ensuring a strong leader for our pack someday, but if you have a shot at real love, I don't want you to squander that, either."

Hope burned against my ribs. But I could feel a weighty addendum coming.

"You *have* to entertain the offers of the other packs. There's no way around that. I've accepted. We're stuck between a rock and a hard place right now. Their overtures have been made and recognized. Rejecting them now would be an insult heavy enough to spark bloodletting between the packs. I've been making arrangements with all concerned packs this afternoon. Dominic Wolfe has graciously allowed us to continue here on his pack lands while you finish school. Representatives from the other packs will rendezvous here as well so you can get to know them and see what you think."

Air whooshed from my lungs. "And Cade?"

"I think you'd better call him and see if we can all three sit down and have a discussion about this."

****

An hour later, Cade knocked at my front door. Wolf wiggled in excitement as I pulled back on the handle. My breath caught as Cade stood there, black hair shiny and blue eyes flashing in the porchlight.

"Hey," he said softly with a cocky grin that made my toes curl.

"Hey," I replied, unable to stop myself from touching his arm as he walked past. His fingers brushed the inside of my forearm as he moved and entered the kitchen. I shut the door while Cade shrugged out of his jacket.

"So what are we talking to your dad about?" he asked quietly. "You were kinda cryptic on the phone. Are we talking about this?" He motioned his hand between us and let his fingers grasp mine on their way down.

My lip found its way between my teeth. "There's good news and bad news." Cade's eyebrows lifted as his jaw muscles clenched, likely in anxious anticipation. "The good news is that Dad's not opposed to *this*. The bad news is that there are even more complications than there were two hours ago."

Cade frowned. I squeezed his hand before letting it go.

"Come on. Dad is in the living room."

Cade followed me through the house to the back where we'd fallen asleep watching the movie the night of the fight. Dad sat in the armchair. When we came in, he put his newspaper aside and rose gracefully.

"Cade, thanks for coming down."

"Sure, Mr. Thornehill."

"Why don't you both take a seat? I think we need to have a very frank discussion." Dad's words weren't unkind, but they did have a ring of finality to them. He sank back into the armchair.

Cade brushed his fingers against the small of my back, and Wolf shivered. Sitting on the couch at one end, I was gratified when Cade took the middle seat of the couch next to me instead of sitting on the opposite end. I leaned into him, letting my shoulder rest against his.

Dad cleared his throat and bent forward, steepling his hands in front of him. My belly clenched. "I'd like to start by saying that I didn't realize how interested the two of you were in each other. I probably should have, but I didn't."

Cade stiffened beside me. Guilt wormed in my belly. I regretted not telling Dad about Cade when I'd had the chance.

Dad continued, "Cade, I assume you know that Sarah has always been intended to marry another Alpha or Beta."

"I do. I also know it's not wolf law that she does so," Cade answered. There was an easy respectful confidence in his voice that warmed my frozen insides.

"And you're not a Beta or an Alpha," Dad said to clarify the point.

Cade's jaw set as he considered his next words. "I understand how important Sarah's position is in your pack. I'm not trying to jeopardize that in any way." Cade knew who I was. I realized in that moment that my inheritance didn't matter to him. Wolf shook out her coat. My position—the power I held now and what I'd have someday as a female Alpha was highly sought after. Not that I was a bartering chip, but in some ways, it made me an exceedingly desirable commodity. I'd bring a pack and power to whoever I married. It would be mine by rights, but as an extension of me, my mate would have a share in that. With the realization that Cade wanted me just because I was me, my attraction to Cade—already considerable—grew inestimably. With a rosy glow filling me despite the less-than-perfect circumstances, I pulled my thoughts back to the conversation.

Dad was nodding. "It is not my desire or my intention to keep the two of you apart, but events have been put into place that make any relationship between the two of you an issue right now. Three other packs have made overtures of interest, and they've been accepted. The only way to back out of them now would be if Sarah found her true mate."

Cade's shoulder and arm tensed against mine.

"Sarah?" Cade turned to me.

"I didn't know," I said softly, aching as I realized Cade felt that I'd betrayed him. I had never wanted to have a true mate more than I did in that second. And I wanted it to be Cade.

"Sarah didn't know about the overtures. Not these specifically. It was always the plan to entertain them when they came, but I didn't tell her until this afternoon when she got home that now is that time."

Cade sighed, and his bicep lost some of its rigidity. "What does that mean for Sarah and me exactly?" Cade asked carefully.

"I've been thinking on this, looking at this from all the angles I can imagine. The best solution I've come up with is for you all to call things off between the two of you for the time being. Wait it out. If your attraction is deep enough, it can withstand a few more weeks. I'm not going to give you an ultimatum, but know this: pack alliances are tenuous things. Sarah, if it looks like you're showing favoritism to Cade, who is not among your potential paramours, it's going to be interpreted as a slight against the other packs. Wars have been fought over lesser infractions. Given the state of things, we don't know if there are other werewolves out there like Victor. We *need* to continue the alliances we have and forge ahead with these new ones. Insulting these new potential allies could have consequences we can't yet imagine. A slight like this could be enough to turn them from ally to enemy. We can't afford that right now. Especially not while we're still recovering and regrouping from Victor's assaults."

The weight of Dad's words and the implications if Cade and I continued our fledgling relationship crashed down on me, suffocating me with their responsibility.

Dad sighed. "I'm sorry for the unwitting part I've played in this. I'm going to go upstairs to the office. I'll turn some music on so I can't overhear anything. Why don't the two of you have a conversation and talk things over." Dad hauled himself from the chair to his feet.

Cade stood abruptly, and I blinked.

"Mr. Thornehill, thank you. For not dismissing me outright. I know my position in my pack doesn't make me an ideal candidate for Sarah, but my intentions and my feelings do."

Dad smiled tiredly. "You're a good man, Cade.

And if you ever cease to be one, my daughter will probably disembowel you." Dad winked as I blushed, and a grin tugged at the corner of Cade's mouth.

"I believe it," Cade quipped. Dad laughed—a laugh from his belly that erased some of the tension lurking at the corners of his eyes.

"Sarah, let me know before you head to bed. Cade." Dad nodded his head and then trudged up the stairs. The office door snicked shut moments later.

Anxiety wormed its way into my middle. What could I possibly say to make things better and less awkward right now? I'd made an amazing mess of things today.

Chapter 12

Cade

I ran a hand through my hair and glanced back down at Sarah, still seated on the couch with one leg tucked underneath her and her cheek caved in like she was chewing the inside of it.

"That kind of puts a lot of pressure on the whole wanting to kiss for a few hours," I said trying to break the sudden tension between us. I lowered myself back to my seat, careful not to touch her, unsure where we were now. Wolf whined. I wanted to be with her so badly. Had wanted to be in a relationship with her for weeks. But if putting things off for a while longer let me have her for keeps later, surely we could do that?

"I'm so sorry, Cade." To my horror, the barest film of tears lined her eyes. "This is all my fault. I...I shouldn't have pushed things this afternoon."

Ice lodged in my chest. Was she trying to back out completely? "Hey. I was the one who gave the ultimatum." And now it felt like we were back at that same crossroads. "Do you regret this afternoon?" Wolf whined at the question, but I needed to know.

She angrily swiped at her eye. "No. I don't." Her light-green gaze met mine. "I don't want to be with anyone besides you," she whispered.

Relief was like a hot spring gushing up inside me. "Good." Before I could stop myself, I tucked a piece of hair behind her ear. My eyes widened when she turned her face and kissed my palm. My mouth dried, and Wolf stirred.

"Cade, I'm going to have to spend time, get to know these other wolves at least well enough so they're satisfied that I made an effort when I reject them. Can you...will you wait for me?"

The breath left me in a whoosh. "For you? *Yes.* I'll wait."

A small smile played at the corners of her lips. "Could...could we still *be* even though it looks like we aren't?"

A grin curled the side of my mouth up. "You want me to be your secret boyfriend? Didn't we outgrow this sort of thing in, like, fifth grade?" I teased, elated that she still wanted to feel connected to me.

"Shut up!" She snorted and smacked my shoulder. She glared at me, but I could see the amusement deep in her eyes.

"Only on one condition," I said, trying not to let my eyes twinkle.

She raised an eyebrow. "One condition?"

"Mm-hmm. You have to be my secret girlfriend, too."

"Shut up and kiss me, Cade. This is probably the last chance we'll have for a while."

Wolf rumbled low in my chest. I leaned in but pulled back, suddenly desperate to make sure she knew I wasn't going anywhere. "Sarah?" I whispered.

"Yeah?" she whispered back, mere inches from my face.

"I meant what I said earlier today." I leaned back enough to look her straight in the eye. "I'm falling in love with you."

"Don't tell the other wolves yet, but I think I'm falling in love with you, too." Her voice broke on the last words, and it was mutual when our lips met.

****

Tuesday, I caught Sam before lunch. I hadn't had a chance to talk to him in a few days. Sam and I had been best friends practically since birth, but since he'd married Megan, the time we spent together had slowly ebbed away. I didn't resent it. I had filled that time with Sarah. And I wanted to fill *more* of my time with Sarah.

"Hey, guys." I nodded to Sam and Megan outside the cafeteria. "Sam, a word?" I tipped my head to a secluded part of the hallway.

"Sure. Meg, grab me a tray? I'll be there in a sec."

"You want an extra sandwich?"

"Please." He smiled at her, and I smirked as a light blush stained Megan's cheeks. I didn't try to figure that one out but hoped I could someday have the same effect on Sarah.

"What's up, Cade?" Sam turned his full attention to me.

"I just wanted to tell you." I swallowed. "Sarah and I are kind of serious about each other. But we're putting things, well, the appearance of things, off while the new wolves are in town."

Sam chuckled. "Dad told me about the overtures. I'm sorry the timing is crappy. I wondered Sunday if you'd finally persuaded her. She kept staring at you out of the corner of her eye at Bowen's place."

"She did?"

Sam nodded, then studied me a minute.

"What?" I asked, rubbing the back of my neck.

"I've just never seen you this serious about a girl."

"Are you telling me I shouldn't be?" Wolf pawed inside me.

"No. Being serious about the right girl is the best thing that's ever happened to me." Sam winked.

"Well, it's probably easier when you're true mates," I quipped, wishing Sarah and I were.

"Yeah—but you know Megan made the choice to be my mate. You and Sarah could, too."

I smiled. "I think I've made mine."

Sam nudged me with his elbow. "I hope it's everything you want it to be. I'll run interference with the potentials if I can."

"Thanks, Sam."

****

The rest of the week sped by. Sarah and I tried to go back to just being friends—at least for appearances. Our text messages grew considerably more flirtatious. It was tough. She was finally letting me in, but I felt torn—I couldn't act on anything. It was harder than I expected to be near her and not try to act like her boyfriend. Wolf wasn't helping. The more we opened up to each other in our communication, the more protective Wolf got.

Friday night was a big basketball game. Not just big—huge. It was the first regional game. If the Rock Falls Wolves did well tonight, we could find our way to state playoffs. And that could attract college scouts.

The excitement in the locker room was tangible. Bowen nudged my shoulder.

"You ready for this?" Exhilaration shone in his brown eyes.

I bounced on my toes. Wolf was leaping around,

keyed up with pent-up energy. "I'm *so* ready."

"You're the Alpha here. This is your pack. We're all behind you. Take us to that championship," Bowen said low enough only I could hear him.

I nodded, appreciating his confidence more than I let on. Inhaling the strange smells of the borrowed locker room, I let undertones of sweat and gym equipment, as well as the familiar scents of my team, engulf my senses. I had to focus. I was the team captain. I was the point guard. It was a lot of responsibility, and my team deserved my best.

"Huddle up!" Coach called. We crowded into a circle and put our hands in. "Big game tonight, boys. You're up for the challenge," Coach said. He nodded to me.

"Just like in practice," I said. I met every pair of eyes on the team. "On three."

"One, two, three! *Wolves!*" And then we all howled. A note of Wolf's true voice crept into my own as I let the wash of power behind it creep into my muscles, bunched and taut with adrenaline.

We bounded out onto the court amidst thunderous cheering. We were playing at Tri-Falls Community College, and it looked like half of Rock Falls and half of the town of our opponents had all turned out.

As a team, we made a lap around our half of the gym and retrieved basketballs to take warm-up shots. I glanced around to see if Mom and Dad had made it in yet. An ear-piercing whistle ripped through the air, and Wolf grinned. I nodded to my parents, my mom taking her fingers from her lips. Ripples of longing shivered over me as I saw Sarah seated with a group of my friends—human and werewolf alike—sitting near my parents.

"I'm here," she said. She probably only mouthed the words, but I felt them to my core. Wolf surged within, and I sank a three pointer.

I was ready to play ball.

Chapter 13

Sarah

Cade swished the ball through the net, glanced up, caught my eye, and winked. Heat slid through me as Wolf practically batted her eyelashes at him. Something twinged in my middle as I watched his focus change. He led the basketball team. I'd been to plenty of his games. A lot of our werewolf circle went regularly. Sam and Megan sat a row below me while Raven, who had jammed her toe and was sitting out of cheerleading for tonight's game to keep up appearances, even though her werewolf healing had already kicked in, sat next to me. Rachel and Kyp were on my other side. Cade's parents were here. I think Dominic and Mary Wolfe were planning to come, too. My dad would have, but he had a late business call that couldn't wait. Gazing around me, I saw more wolves I knew from Kyp and Bowen's pack, from Sam and Cade's pack. But no others from my own. There weren't many younger wolves in my own pack. And those that we did have were all back in New York.

Wolf nudged me, and with reluctance, I acknowledged that I felt more at home with the two packs surrounding me than I did with my own. I'd forged friendships here that were deeper than any friendships I'd had back in New York. I felt understood here. And valued because of *who* I was, not just *what* I was in the pack hierarchy.

A sigh escaped without my meaning it to. Raven bumped her elbow against mine.

"You okay?" she whispered. I heard her easily over the din of the crowd.

I smiled. "I'm all right." And I was. Or at least I would be. Raven smiled back and turned her focus back to the teams huddled up before tip-off.

"Ugh. Ever since Kyle Mason, tip-off makes me nervous," Raven commented as Bowen loped to the middle of the floor. As one of the biggest and strongest on the team, Bowen's job was getting the ball to Cade right off. Kyle Mason—I shuddered remembering the way his throat had been ripped out in front of my eyes—had played for the Eagles and had bloodied Bowen on the court after a particularly ferocious tip-off earlier in the season.

"Look who he's up against. That poor kid doesn't stand a chance." The Tigers' player was tall and lean. A stiff breeze could probably bowl him over.

My gaze tracked to Cade, poised in a half-crouch, ready to receive the ball. The ref blew his whistle, and the ball soared upward.

Raven gasped beside me as Bowen launched himself into the air, easily capturing the ball and flicking it back to Cade. The breath caught in my throat as Cade snatched the ball and pounded it against the wooden floor, wheeling around an opponent and sprinting toward the basket as he dribbled. Out of nowhere, the other post, I think his name was Jamie, dashed in front of the red-haired kid chasing Cade down the floor.

"Now!" Jamie hollered. Cade pulled up at the

three-point line and sank a beautiful arc straight into the basket.

The bleachers erupted as Cade threw his fist in the air. The teams ran back down the court, and Cade slapped Jamie on the shoulder as he passed.

I lost myself to the thrall of the game, the way Cade moved, the way he encouraged his team, the way he led them. Like an Alpha. With a start, I realized that's exactly what Cade *was* for his basketball team. He was their Alpha. A longing ache set loose inside my chest as I watched him with closer scrutiny. I saw with new eyes. This side of Cade made him infinitely more suited to being the mate of a leader. Possibly *my* mate someday.

Certainty settled in my heart even as dread of tomorrow rode tense on my shoulders. Tomorrow the Betas were coming.

****

The Wolves won the game seventy-three to sixty-seven. It had been close, but they did it. They'd advance to the next round of regional games next week. Wolf snorted enviously as Raven ran limping to Bowen after the game and kissed his cheek. He swooped an arm around her waist, triumphant smile wide across his face.

My heart constricted as Cade's head popped up behind them as he left the locker room. While running and jumping into his arms the way Raven had run to Bowen wasn't exactly my style, I'd have given up chocolate for a month to be able to go up to Cade and kiss him possessively the way I wanted to. Wolf's hackles rose as a few other girls from school crowded around Bowen, Cade, and the other guys coming out of the locker room.

Cade met my gaze across the room, and he nodded. Blue fire seemed to flash from his eyes and wrap me in its heat. I nodded back, reminding myself that a few weeks and we could be together openly. I just had to survive tomorrow first.

****

I was jittery that night after I was home, showered, and lying in bed. My heart drummed, my brain obsessing about tomorrow. The three Betas from other packs would be coming into town. I'd have to meet them, give them a fair shot. I hated that a tiny part of myself was excited. That stupid rebel part of me that relished the power of my position reveled in the thought of the Beta males' interest in me. I quickly reminded myself that they weren't really coming for me. They wanted the connections—what my genes could offer. I equally hated that the power of my position took away my choices. Because all of me—even the rebel part—wanted Cade.

Grabbing my phone, I gave in to temptation and texted him.

—*Great game tonight!*—

—*Thanks! I'm glad you came. I play better when you watch.*—

—*Show off.*— I smirked as I sent it.

—*For you? Always.*—

I grinned, Wolf rubbing her head against me. He texted again before I could reply.

—*Are you thinking about tomorrow?*—

It was as if he could read my mind half the time. —*Yeah. You?*—

—*Obsessing about it.*—

—*Why?*— I was pretty sure I knew the answer to that question but asked anyway.

He didn't respond for a few minutes. My lip tucked between my teeth.

—*Because part of me is terrified that you're going to find your true mate and that'll be it.*—

The breath left me in a hard rush as an ache formed in the pit of my stomach. Part of me was terrified of that, too. I didn't know what to say.

—*I only want you.*—

—*I hope that's still true after tomorrow.*—

I slept fitfully.

Chapter 14

Cade

I was up with the dawn, even though it was Saturday, and my body was tired after the game and adrenaline surge last night. But Sarah's would-be mates were coming into town, and I was going to combust if I didn't burn some of this anxiety out of my system.

"I'm heading for a run," I called to Mom as she was starting coffee in the kitchen.

"Okay. Be safe!" she called back.

Dressed in one of the gray robes we all wore when leaving and entering the woods in skin, I moved to the tree line not far behind my house. The river made soft shushing sounds that helped calm some of my taut nerves.

Several paces into the thick underbrush of the forest, I let the robe fall and shivered as a chill wind swept over my naked skin. I let my head fall back and my eyes shut as I spread my arms wide out to the sides. It had been two days since I'd gone in fur, and even that short amount of time felt like an eternity.

Black fur rippled through the skin of my arms. My fingers retracted, shiny claws protruding from my footpads as my palms grew rough with dark gray skin. My muzzle pushed out from my face, elongating the shape. Whiskers poked through, slicing just a little as the sensitive wisps quivered with the motion of my shift. My ears, tufted with black fur, edged out from my scalp.

I fell to all fours. My backbone shattered, my tail protruded and my form grew, heaving, cording with muscles and sinews. With a last shake of my head, my ruff settled, fur still twitching in the breeze as scents blasted into my nostrils.

I inhaled, bringing all the forest scents in and holding them, letting their familiarity soothe the wild terror that flashed under my skin. Sarah would meet the other wolves. She would spend time with them. Then they would go home, and she'd choose me. Because none of them would be her true mate. Because that wasn't an option I would even entertain.

Churning up the dirt behind me, I ran hard. Ran until my sides hurt and my lungs burned. Flopping down beside a creek that eventually fed into the river behind my house, I lapped up some of the frigid water. A howl rose in the distance, and my ears pricked up.

Sitting on my haunches, I howled back and then started jogging toward the other wolf. Ten minutes later, Sam's gray-and-white wolf materialized from the underbrush. He snorted at me and tossed his head. Somehow my best friend had sensed my inner turmoil. He'd come. With a quick bark, he jumped so that he faced the open meadow. I yipped, and we were off.

We ran together, two wolves, two friends.

I hadn't realized how much I needed the extra support.

After another long run, we turned and headed back through the trees to where I'd left my robe behind my house. I wasn't surprised when I found a second robe beside mine.

"Feel better?" Sam asked once we were both back in skin. I sat on the pine needles blanketing the forest floor. My stomach growled.

"Yeah. Thanks for coming."

Sam nodded, an understanding smile on his face as he sat next to me. My belly rumbled again.

"I have to eat."

Sam laughed. "Megan is shopping with Rachel for her wedding today. Want to go into town and get something?"

I turned the idea over. It would be a good distraction. Sarah wasn't sure what time she was meeting the wolves today, so I wasn't expecting to hear from her until this evening when it would be safe to text without fear of too many questions.

"Breakfast would be great. Meet at your place as soon as I'm showered and dressed?"

"See you then."

****

An hour later I was practically faint with hunger as we walked into Scrummies, the local mom-and-pop diner that had the best omelets this side of the Mississippi. Snagging a booth near the back, we only just slid in before our waitress appeared.

"Cade Rivers, I heard all about your game last night. Congratulations!" Miss Nora crooned at me with a huge smile. She'd been waiting tables at *Scrummies* for years, and she was one of my favorite ladies around town. Her plump form was covered in a white frilly apron, and her dyed red hair was piled on top of her head. She'd been the one to train Mom when she worked at the diner for a while after she first moved to Rock Falls.

"Thanks, Miss Nora. It was tight a few times, but the team pulled it off," I replied with a grin.

Miss Nora gave me a motherly look that said she knew I was being modest and clicked her pen. "Well, what'll we be having for our celebratory breakfast? Sam, orange juice for you?"

"Just like always. Thanks, Miss Nora. I think I want French toast today. Extra side of bacon and scrambled eggs."

"Cheese over the eggs today?" she asked as she jotted down his order.

"Sure. That sounds good."

"And how about you, Cade?"

"Ham and cheese omelet. Actually, just give me a sampler platter with the omelet." I was pretty sure Wolf had turned into a ravening beast inside me and was going to start eating my backbone if I didn't feed him soon.

"Hungry today. Must have worked up quite an appetite winning that ballgame. What do you want to drink today?"

"Chocolate milk." Because Sarah loved chocolate milk, and I couldn't escape thinking about her if I tried.

"I'll bring it right up, boys." She smiled fondly at us and collected our unused menus.

"Well, what's up with you, Sam? Pretty sure you know all my business," I said with a rueful smile.

Sam chuffed through his nose. "Your life is more exciting than mine right now. Megan and I have settled and are finding our routine together." He shrugged, his face content. For a brief instant I envied his contentment but then tamped the irritating emotion back down. "Dad's partners at the law firm asked if he wanted to be the one to go to California to do some presentation at their annual conference."

"Dude. Don't they ask him to go every year?"

"Yep. And every year he makes an excuse to stay here." Sam smiled to himself. Dominic, though gruff and a little rough around the edges, cared deeply about his pack and our collective well-being.

"Here you are, dears," Miss Nora chimed and set our drinks down and a plate of toast. "I heard your belly growling when I was taking your order." She winked at me. I smiled appreciatively. "Sam, I remembered the honey, just for you." Miss Nora pulled out some packets from her apron pocket and put them by the plate of toast. Strawberry jelly, grape jelly, and butter were kept on the table. But Sam liked honey. Miss Nora always remembered.

A pang shot through me as it only served as a reminder of Sarah's wild honey and citrus scent. I could practically smell it if I concentrated hard enough.

I snagged a buttered toast wedge and popped it in my mouth, not even bothering with another spread.

"Heard anything else from colleges?" Sam asked as he took the time to spread honey on his slice.

"Nothing official. Dad and I have talked with a few colleges, and I've filled out forms for several places. Truthfully, I'm getting a little concerned that season is almost over, and those opportunities for showcasing are going to stop."

"Think you'll go to state?" Sam asked, following my train of thought from school to scholarships.

"I hope so. Bowen drastically improved our chances when he joined the team."

Miss Nora brought our food out soon after, and we

caught up with each other but were careful to steer clear of Sarah as a topic.

Just as we were finishing up, the bell above the door chimed, and a guy close to our age walked in. His scent of bergamot and musk permeated the room and stood every one of Wolf's hairs up on edge. This was one of the new Betas that had come for Sarah. Sam's eyes widened as he turned to face the door. The new wolf's head swiveled straight to us, immediately recognizing that we were his kind.

His chin came up, and with a confident swagger, he sauntered to our booth.

Nodding regally to us, he paused at the edge of our table. "You all in town for important matters?" he asked.

Wolf snarled inside, and I clenched my teeth to keep any sound from escaping.

"No." Sam shook his head. "I'm Sam Wolfe. This is Cade Rivers."

The stranger's thin brown eyebrows rose. "Ah. This is your land."

Sam nodded. "Where are you from?"

"Oh, sorry. I'm Max Fielding. From Michigan."

"Nice to meet you," Sam said. I nodded tightly, trying to make my face look neutral.

"Tell me, is Sarah as pretty as her pictures are? Man, from what I could tell, she's a *fine* piece of tail. And her pedigree! Impressive. I'm quite the catch, you know. She'd be lucky to have me and my associations."

I was going to go ballistic. He was *not* allowed to speak about Sarah that way. Wolf growled. Max's eyes shone as his eyebrows took a conspiratorial bent as he whispered. He leaned toward us like we were about to share some big secret. Wolf pulled his lips back and bristled. Who was this upstart pup?

"You know, true mates run in my family." His quiet words sent ice shooting through my heart. My parents were true mates. Raven and Bowen were true mates. They ran in my family, too, but had cruelly seemed to skip me. Wolf thrashed.

"Good thing about the true mates. Makes up for any other missing bits." The words leaped out of my mouth. What was I doing? I did not need to antagonize Sarah's potential beau. Regardless of what a jerkwad he was. What was wrong with me? Wolf seethed beneath my skin.

Max's eyes narrowed—possibly catching on that he might have been insulted.

Sam cleared his throat and broke in, kicking me under the table. I tried not to flinch. "Sarah is very beautiful. I'm sure there will be plenty of, uh, opportunity for you to share your associations with her and her father. Austin Thornehill has earned himself a lot of respect around here, as has his daughter."

Was that just a hint of an edge in Sam's voice? Wolf simmered down some, realizing that Sam was affronted on Sarah's behalf, too.

Max nodded his head like we were all pack brothers. "I'm on my way there just as soon as I grab some grub. Hey, move over, I'll join you, and you can give me all the inside details. Always helps to know your conquest," he said, dead serious, an arrogant tilt to his chin.

It was possible steam was coming out my ears.

"Sorry, but we just finished and have some stuff to get to. I'm sure we'll be seeing you around," Sam said peaceably with a tight smile.

I shoved to my feet after throwing bills on the table with enough for a generous tip for Miss Nora. I couldn't bring myself to speak as I darted around Max and sped toward the door.

Chapter 15

Sarah

"Sarah, you're going to wear a hole in the carpet," Dad said, concern wrinkling his brow.

"I can't seem to stop myself," I countered. Wolf was jittery. Even my fingers were twitching. "I'd better get it all out now before the Betas get here." I flicked my hands to the sides like I was slinging water off them.

"Come here. Let's sit down and go over who they are again. It'll help you focus, and you know you do better when you have information."

Dad was right. I did best when I had all the facts and could make a decision I felt good about. While I had no intention of choosing any of the Betas that would be coming today, I did need to keep up appearances. Because we did still need to make alliances with them, or at the very least, be on friendly terms with them. Wolf paced. Part of us was terrified one of these Betas would be our true mate.

"Fine. Give me the lineup again." I clenched my teeth hard enough the base of my skull started to ache.

"All right. Let's take a few breaths. Bring the air in. Calm your wolf." Dad's soothing voice spoke to me like I was a child again. Not patronizing, but grounding. I let my eyes slide shut and focused on being in tune with Wolf. We breathed in; we pushed the air out.

"Better?" Dad asked.

"Some. Hit me with the first one," I said. I stretched my arms slowly above my head, letting oxygen flow into my veins as I stretched and brought my hands back to my sides. Dad handed me the now cool cup of my favorite tangerine tea. I took a sip as Dad spoke.

"Donovan Hazelton."

"Son of Hal Hazelton. Beta. Graduated last year, will be nineteen this year. Taking classes toward a business degree."

"Good. Where's he from?" Dad nodded encouragingly.

I wracked my brain. Hazelton—where they grew hazelnuts. "Oregon."

"Good. Greyson Sage."

"Greyson Sage, Beta, though he has a twin brother." I paused, pinching the bridge of my nose. "I can't remember the brother's name."

"That's all right. He's not coming anyway." Dad stopped, cupping his hands on my shoulders. "Sarah," he said softly. I glanced at his face. His eyes swam with remorse. "I'm sorry. I should have seen how you felt about Cade."

Just hearing his name sent a stab of anxiety through my heart, even as Dad's words registered. I glanced away.

"I did a good job hiding it. I didn't try to fall for him." It was my fault—I should have been more honest about what I was feeling with Dad.

"I know. And so long as no one else finds out while the other wolves are here, things should be fine." His big hands squeezed gently as he wrapped me in a comforting hug. I pressed my cheek against my father's chest—the safest place in the world—and inhaled his spruce and lemongrass scent. "You want to do more review?"

Just then a knock sounded at the door. "Too late," I squeaked.

Dad squeezed me extra tight. "I'll get it. Wait here."

While Dad's footfalls echoed down the hall, I straightened my shirt and folded my hands in front of me. Wolf tossed her chin in the air, and my aloof façade settled into place. I had the luxury of my nerves no more. They had to be put away until later.

Male voices sounded from the kitchen. I tamped down the urge to fidget. Wolf sat perfectly still on her white haunches inside me.

Dad entered the room, a tall, athletic man beside him. Brown eyes set over a smattering of freckles met mine. I willed my heart to feel nothing as interest lit his features.

"May I present my daughter, Sarah Thornehill," Dad said as he swung his arm to indicate me standing awkwardly in the middle of the room.

"Sarah, this is Donovan Hazelton."

"I'm pleased to meet you." His rich, cultured voice wrapped around me, not uncomfortably.

"Thank you for coming," I managed steadily.

He crossed the room, confidence in his swagger, his shoulders straight. He stopped a foot in front of me and politely dipped his head to scent me. Relief that he didn't actually touch my skin as his nose followed the curve of my neck made leaning in to sniff his earthy clay and nut scent easier.

I locked my knees in place as relief swelled when I felt no pull—no attraction to him. He was not my true mate. Donovan pulled back, the faintest frown of disappointment flashing over his face before he schooled it.

"Can I get you anything to drink?" Dad offered just as another knock sounded at the door. Donovan's eyebrows rose.

"Guess I'll have competition right away," he said to me with a wink. His words held no arrogance, only confidence and a hint of flirtation. It reminded me of Cade. Wolf twitched her tail. I reminded myself that Cade was still waiting for me.

"Oh," I heard Dad say from the kitchen.

"Maybe we should head that way?" I said, moving before I'd finished speaking. Whatever had surprised Dad wasn't something we'd planned for.

"Sarah, it seems both Greyson *and* Tate Sage have come," Dad said, his voice giving nothing away. His jaw gave the slightest clench, and I knew Dad was annoyed that we'd planned for one Sage wolf, and two had shown up.

"Hello," I said, trying to keep the surprise out of my voice. I'd never seen twin werewolves before. Werewolf birth rates were generally low—and having a set of twins was extremely rare. Two identical boys my own age stood before me. Four gray eyes shaped like large almonds stared at me. One had a hint of a scar through his left eyebrow. If their hair hadn't been dark, I probably wouldn't have even noticed it.

"I'm Greyson," said the one without the scar.

"I'm Tate," the other said. In tandem, they came across the kitchen, and before anyone realized what they were doing, Greyson scented the left side of my neck while Tate scented the right.

Okay. That was weird. I stepped back before I'd scented either of them. Dad cleared his throat. I wasn't sure if it was directed at me or the odd behavior from the Sage boys.

"I'll scent one at a time." I gave them a smile that felt too tight. The boys shrugged. Donovan raised an eyebrow and glanced at the newcomers.

Gingerly, I leaned in and scented Greyson. Oddly enough, he smelled like sage and charcoal. Tipping my head to Tate, Wolf pulled back in confusion. Sage and charcoal. I'd never smelled two wolves with scents exactly the same. Family bloodlines carried similar undertones. Dad and I both had hints of a citrusy lemon flavor, but never had I smelled two wolves exactly the same. I blinked. Wolves identified each other by scent. I couldn't do that with Greyson and Tate.

Dad cleared his throat, and the boys stepped back.

Testosterone seemed to flood the space as awkward silence descended on the kitchen. I was already counting down the hours until this was over.

Chapter 16

Cade

"Cade, are you going to the gathering tonight?" Dad called up the stairs.

I yanked the earbuds out of my ears and glanced at the clock.

"Crap!" I muttered as I closed my computer and jogged to the top of the stairs. I'd been reviewing footage of the basketball games of our opponents that Coach had sent over. As captain, I considered it part of my job to be as informed as possible so I could help direct the guys. They all had access to the footage, too, but I wasn't sure anyone watched it as intently as I did. Bowen might.

"I'm going! I didn't realize it was so late!" I bounded down the stairs.

"You might just want to go in fur at this point," Dad commented as he glanced at his watch. "We'll be over later. I'm sure Sarah would feel better if you were there for all of it, though." Dad winked at me. I'd told him and Mom what was going on. They were supportive but cautionary, knowing how important it was to keep alliances intact. They also wanted to keep my heart intact. For that matter, so did I.

Wolf jerked. Basketball had been the only thing that could remotely distract me from going out of my mind thinking about Sarah and her potential true mates.

Wolf growled. I'd immersed myself. So much so that now I was going to be late and Sarah would probably worry. If she wasn't already kissing the face off some significantly more suitable werewolf with claims to the biggest pack in the United States.

"Calm down," Dad said with a smile as he squeezed my shoulder.

"I'm calm," I nearly snarled.

"Perfectly calm," Dad said and patted my shoulder before letting his hand drop. "Better get a move on it. Maybe running over there will help."

I hoped so. Grabbing a gray robe out of the coat closet, I dashed to the laundry room and stripped. Cracking the door open, I shifted, grabbed the robe in my mouth, and was a streak of black shadow against the setting sun.

Running did help. My muscles stretched, the earth reached up to boost my paws over fallen trees and around crackly bushes. It was easier to believe that Sarah was still waiting for me when the scents of the forest rushed over me and settled next to my fur.

It wasn't long before dusk had consumed me in its shadows, and the glare of the bonfire behind Sam's cabin grew in the distance. The rumble of voices, a few grunts and snuffles, let me know that I wasn't the only one in fur, and that helped relieve some additional tension. I dropped my robe next to a tree and slowed to enter as unobtrusively as possible.

Anxiety clutched my belly. If Sarah had found her One, then I could observe and then melt back into the trees and go curl up in a ball somewhere and let the agony overtake me. I shook my head to clear the negative thoughts. She'd have let me know if that were the case. Wouldn't she?

Sliding up to the tree line, I immediately homed in on Sarah. She stood in her skin, firelight playing on her light-blonde hair, down on her shoulders. Unable to help myself, I padded closer until I was in her direct line of sight. Her eyes widened slightly, but otherwise, she gave no indication she saw me. Her body lost some of its tension, and so did I. She was still mine.

Recognizing the back of Max from the diner, I sidled up to him and perched on my haunches, close enough he could have yanked my whiskers if he'd leaned over. Someone needed to keep an eye on him. Only then did I tune in to what he was saying. He was talking to—at—Sarah, much like he'd expressed his arrogance at the diner. I bit back a snort of disgust.

"Good reflexes run in my genes. I once detected a wild cat from nearly a mile away. I have the true werewolf's nose."

"Is that right?" Sarah said. I picked up on the trace of amusement in her voice, but I'm not sure anyone else around did. A few others—mostly young werewolves close to our age—had gathered around, since this bash was all for Sarah and her suitors. The Alphas and adults would join us later.

"It is," Max confirmed.

A tiny spark crackled upward and brushed my nose. I sneezed.

Max jerked around and let out the most undignified yelp I'd ever heard.

A few titters and a few outright laughs broke out from the group. Sarah kept her face impassive, but her lips twitched, and her eyes twinkled.

I resisted the urge to let the smugness I felt show

on my wolf's features. It hadn't been my intention to make him look a fool, but clearly, he'd been completely unaware of my presence right next to him as he was bragging about his nose. Moron. Color burst across Max's cheeks, then mottled as rage overtook his humiliation. His eyes slit as he focused on me. His fists clenched, and a growl simmered deep in his chest.

Lifting an eyebrow, I stared him down. I was more than capable of taking any challenge he wanted to issue, though it would be unwise for either of us to give or accept a challenge at a gathering meant to celebrate relationships.

He stared at me. I could almost feel him willing me to wither under his glare. I licked my lips. Max's nostrils flared.

"Megan, are those chocolate chunk cookies?" Sarah turned, drawing the attention of the crowd to the table where Megan and Rachel were setting trays of snacks out and effectively ending Max's audience with her. Anger radiated off him.

"You will regret this," he ground between clenched teeth before he stalked off, trying to salvage any shreds of pride he still thought he had.

Wolf chuffed through his nose. It wasn't my fault his talk was bigger than his actual abilities.

Chapter 17

Sarah

We went for a run. All of us. A giant pack of teenage wolves, moving seamlessly through the forest, sleek as shadows, fast as deer, lithe as mountain lions, and I was as annoyed as a wet hen.

One of my paramours was constantly underfoot.

When we started the run, the freedom of the wind in my face and the exultation of stretching my muscles had been wonderful. And then Donovan pounded up beside me. Of all of them, I minded him the least. He was older than the rest of us, and that extra year's worth of maturity showed. But he still tried to run ahead of me. And as the Beta who would succeed him as Alpha, whether we mated or not, he should have kept pace at the most, not gone charging ahead.

Taking an unexpected turn, I leaped over a dead tree, and Donovan lost his lead, but Greyson and Tate soon took his place. One on either side of me. Their footfalls beside me were in tandem with each other. They even breathed together. Their twin presence was suffocating.

Yipping, I splashed through the creek, leaving them scrambling to follow me. But then—I should have expected it—Max, the youngest at sixteen and with a chip the size of Delaware on his shoulder, came charging up next to me.

He barked, nudging my shoulder with his and nearly knocking me over. My mood was growing blacker by the second, and I snapped back at him before I could control it.

Max whined and tried to lick my cheek mid-run. Jerking my head away, I wasn't quite fast enough, and he caught the inside of my ear. Nasty!

I stopped and growled at him then. I did not appreciate his overt show of affection, and I was going to let him know it. No one touched me without my permission.

Instead of cowering like he should have, he wagged his tail, head cocked to the side, having no clue how repulsed and offended I was. I wanted to snarl in frustration. I was so over this already.

Sam gave a quick howl a few trees over in the forest. I barked back, grateful for his suggestion. Cade materialized beside Sam. I could just make out his eyes, the rest of him blending into the shadows. My heart rate picked up, and Wolf scratched her paw in agitation. Cade never crowded me. He let me lead. That's how this was supposed to work. I was going to be the Alpha.

Sam barked again, tipped his nose to Cade, then dashed off through the trees. Cade sent up a long howl, and the rest of us scattered. Werewolf tag in the dark was so much fun. But it was the one time my white fur worked against me. In winter, with snow on the ground, I was unbeatable.

We played for an hour or so, and things were tolerable once I had a little breathing room. Once I let my tail brush over Cade's flank in passing, but otherwise, we stayed apart. It was harder than I thought it'd be. After so many years trying to keep it hidden away from the world, I'd finally given my heart to a boy, and now I could do nothing about it but keep my distance.

It was maddening.

The adults joined us later for a pack run. We split off into smaller groups, as there were so many of us with the Wolfe pack, the Kypson pack, and the few of us remaining from my pack and my new paramours. Even so, I found myself surrounded by my would-be mates. They flocked to me like sharks to chum.

****

—Definitely no true mates.— I texted Cade late that night when I finally made it into bed.

—Good. We still secret boyfriend and girlfriend, then?—

I giggled into my empty bedroom. *—For sure.—*

—How was today?—

I sighed. How was today? Strenuous. It had taken a lot more mental energy than I'd been prepared to give. And I hadn't expected to miss Cade so much. He was still right there, but so out of reach. *—It was a long day. How was yours?—*

—Much better knowing you're still mine.—

My heart fluttered. I was tempted to text the word *always*. I bit my lip. I sent him a heart instead. I was beginning to realize that I did want Cade…for always. Just contrasting him to the other Betas today highlighted all the ways Cade was vastly better suited to me and what I needed. I sighed. Maybe someday he might feel the same about me?

—Miss you.— I texted.

—Miss you back.—

****

It was a relief to go to school on Monday. None of my would-be mates came with me to school. Until lunch.

I walked into the cafeteria, heading for my table over by Megan, Rachel, and several others. I caught Cade's eye over at the basketball table, and he winked before turning back to his conversation with Bowen. My insides warmed, sending little pings of excitement through me.

Then the cafeteria doors opened, and I caught a whiff of the very last thing I wanted.

Max strutted into the lunchroom like he was the king of the cafeteria, immediately finding me and striding purposefully toward me. I could practically feel Cade's hair standing on end and hear his growl. Pasting on a polite smile, I continued to my table and slid in next to Raven.

She sighed, and it was gratifying to know someone else found Max irritating, too. I got the vibe that he felt he had something to prove. Though his father was an Alpha, he was the younger brother of a Beta—Max himself would be Beta only until his brother's child reached majority and usurped him. Max was also the youngest suitor. There was a lot that didn't work in his favor. But he was doing his level best to try to ingratiate himself to me. Unfortunately for him, and also for me, he picked up on none of my subtle hints that he was coming on way too strong.

"Sarah, hi. I thought I'd drop by your school, and we could have lunch together," Max said, crossing his arms across his chest and attempting a confident pose.

"That was nice. I'm sorry, though, Rock Falls High has closed-campus lunches. I have to eat here."

"Oh, that's too bad. You know, back at my school, we leave all the time for lunch." He winked at me. Was he trying to imply or suggest something? To let me know he was big enough to take himself to lunch? Wolf rolled her eyes. I barely pulled back my grimace as he shoved his way onto the bench next to me.

"Not to butt in, but did you get a visitor's pass? I don't see you wearing one, and they're pretty strict about that sort of thing here," Sam said conversationally, but I didn't miss the underlying warning to Max in his words. If only Max could read a situation as well as Sam did.

Max blustered. "Oh, I mean, yeah, of course I did," he stammered as his gaze darted around the room.

"Max, I appreciate you coming all the way up here, but school isn't really a good place for this. Why don't we talk later?" I said to appease him.

His face brightened. "Yeah! Yeah, that's great. Hey, I'll pick you up for dinner tonight. It's a date," he said with a giant wink as he hopped up from the table and dashed out the doors as a teacher started rounding toward our table.

I groaned. Raven patted my back in sympathy.

"He's…persistent, isn't he?" Megan quipped as she munched a cherry tomato.

"Very. Here. Have my scone. You look like you need it more than I do," Rachel said kindly as she passed me a napkin-wrapped triangle. Normally, I'd have politely declined. But not today. A headache began crawling up the back of my skull.

"Thanks, Rachel," I said sincerely.

"You bet. It's vanilla bean with caramel melts. New recipe. Let me know what you think."

I nibbled a bite. The caramel and vanilla exploded on my tongue while the pastry crumbled.

"It's divine." I took another bite. Rachel beamed.

"I'm putting it on the list for possibilities." Megan nodded at her best friend.

"Sarah, I didn't get a chance to tell you yet, but Rachel and I officially opened our website for online ordering." Megan smiled. "Well, I should say Raven has opened up our website officially. She did most of the design work."

"And…" Raven gave a drumroll on the tabletop. "Guess what just came in the mail for me yesterday?"

"What?" I asked. All eyes at our table were on Raven.

"I got the graphic design internship!"

Rachel squealed as a round of excitement circled the table.

"I bet Bowen is super proud," Kyp said around a smile.

Raven blushed prettily. "He is. We already started making plans for what that's going to look like for us."

I glanced over at Bowen, sitting next to Cade, at the basketball table. The whole team sat together religiously during season. After, they'd disperse and melt back into the rest of the student body. Cade met my gaze. I held it a second, sighed, then dropped my gaze back to my group of friends. My heart ached at what I wanted, what I saw my friends enjoying, but what was still just outside my grasp in my current circumstances. A surprising shard of loneliness pierced my chest.

Wolf nudged me inside. Soon. It would be ours soon, too.

****

Max showed up at my door at four thirty p.m. on the dot.

"Hey. You ready to go?" he asked cheerfully as I opened the kitchen door and saw him standing there on the stoop, bright eyed and fresh faced. The back of my skull throbbed.

"Um, let me just go tell my dad."

I met Dad coming down the hallway and quickly ushered him back into the TV room, where I could whisper safely without being overheard.

"Max wants to take me to dinner. Is there anything I can do to get out of it?" I whispered fiercely, Wolf pacing inside me.

Dad grimaced. "You've got to give him a fair shake. Chin up." Dad winked at me and squeezed my shoulder. I sighed, resigning myself to a long evening. I had an English paper I needed to work on. I was totally using the homework card if things dragged out too long.

I didn't bother changing clothes. My jeans, fitted shirt, and cardigan were fine.

"Let's go," Max said and grabbed my hand as I came back into the kitchen. Wolf seethed.

I disengaged my fingers. "Maybe when we know each other better," I said evasively.

"Sure," he said, unperturbed. I shut the door behind us and stood on the concrete stoop. There was no third vehicle in the driveway.

"Did you drive here?"

"Oh, no. I walked. I figured you'd drive." He shrugged. He figured I'd drive. I blinked and resisted the urge to shake my head.

"Okay. I'll drive. Did you have someplace in

mind?" I asked as I slid into the driver's seat.

"I checked a few places online this afternoon. Do you know how to get to *The Angus Steakhouse*?"

"I've been by it a few times. You sure that's where you want to go?" I was pretty sure even their appetizers cost double digits. Their main plates were closer to fifty or sixty. And that was for chicken.

"That's the place." Max settled back against the seat, looking confident and content.

"All right." I cranked into gear and backed out of the drive. I wasn't going to argue with a nice dinner. I just wished it was with someone else.

"Tell me about your pack history. I can trace my roots back five generations to early settlers, but we're not sure where they originated. Probably Germany."

"That's cool. Both my parents are descendants of fairly long Alpha lines," I said. I was proud of that. I came from generations of leaders. Alpha ran thick in my blood.

"You know the Fielding pack is one of the largest in the United States? You'd be smart to choose me. I'd bring a lot to the table." He winked at me as he stretched his arms behind his head.

I smiled tightly. Max himself didn't bring much to the package, but he was right about one thing. The Fieldings were a big pack. They'd make solid allies. I swallowed. They'd make impressive enemies, too. I needed to watch myself and ignore Max's irritations. Reminding myself that he was young, and apparently had very little experience with girls, I steered us back to less touchy topics.

"Are you still in school?"

"Oh, yeah. I used to go to our main campus but do

all my courses online now."

He said nothing else. Wolf blew a raspberry with her lips. "So…what do you want to do after high school?" I ventured as I turned into town.

"I'll help lead our packs."

I blinked again. "You're so sure of yourself as all that, then?" I tried to keep the *are you serious* tone out of my voice.

He shrugged. "Aren't you?"

"Sure of myself, yes. I know my place and what is expected of me." I was acutely aware of what was expected of me.

"It's good to know your place in the world."

My eyes rolled of their own accord. Hopefully, he didn't notice.

****

The steakhouse wasn't overly crowded when we got there, and we were ushered to a booth pretty quickly.

"Hi, I'm Sean. I'll be your waiter this evening. Can I get you all anything to drink?"

"I'll take lemonade. She will, too," Max said.

"Actually, I just want water, thanks."

Sean flashed a confused look between the two of us before resuming his cheerful smile. "Sure. I'll be right back with those."

A slight frown appeared between Max's eyebrows as an awkward silence stretched between us.

"Peanuts?" I offered him the bucket at the end of the table.

"I'm good," he said a touch stiffly. "Why didn't you let me order for you?"

My eyebrows drew together. "You don't need to

order for me. Besides, you didn't even ask me what I wanted first. I wanted water."

"My dad always orders for my mom when we go places." Max pursed his lips, trying to figure me out. I wasn't sure what to make of that.

"Does your mom like for your dad to order for her?"

"Yes. She always ends up liking what he gets better, so she just has him order two of whatever looks good to him. She trusts his judgment."

"Oh. Well, that might work for them, but I'm not your mom," I said, unsure how to be any more polite about that. Max frowned a little more, either deep in thought or highly displeased with me. "What was it like growing up in your pack?" I said, biting back a sigh.

Max nodded like he was appeased and launched into several stories that ran into each other and had my eyes glazing.

"Sorry to interrupt, but are you ready to order?" Sean asked as he rounded to our table again.

I took a sip of water, grateful for the interruption. "I'd like the Caesar salad with grilled chicken," I told the waiter.

"You should get steak. We're at a steak house," Max protested.

"But I'd really prefer chicken." Also, it was the cheapest entrée on the menu. And anchovy breath might detract Max from trying to invade my space later. So help me, if he tried to kiss me good night, he'd have more than anchovy breath to be concerned about.

"Fine," he huffed. "I want the filet mignon. Medium rare. I'll take mashed potatoes, green bean casserole, and I want extra fried apples. You got all that? I don't want the wrong thing brought to the table."

"I've got it," Sean said, smile in his voice. "I'll take your menus."

We handed them to him, and then we were alone at the booth again.

"You know if you request a steak medium rare, they'll actually bring you a better cut of beef." Max nodded like he was telling me the secrets of the universe. My head pounded so hard my eyeballs jiggled in their sockets.

"That's nice. I'm sorry. I need to go find the restroom. I'll be right back." I grabbed my purse and dashed toward the sign showing me the ladies' room.

It was blessedly empty. I leaned against the cold tile wall and took a few deep breaths. The tension in my neck eased, and my heart rate slowed in the silence. I didn't need to use the restroom; I just needed a minute away from Max. Clearly, his pack norms and expectations were different from mine. Customs varied from pack to pack, but there were universals we all clung to. Ordering dinner for your date wasn't a universal. I stretched my neck, trying to relieve some of the tightness still ratcheting up my skull. I dug my phone out and checked my messages.

My heart galloped when I saw one from Cade. Ignoring all the rest, I opened his message.

—*Thinking about you.*—

That's all it said, and that's all it took for Wolf to rub her head against me. A wave of longing swooshed over me, and for one horrible second, tears pricked the backs of my eyes. I clicked his face.

Chapter 18

Cade

The phone rang at the edge of my desk. I paused
the basketball footage I was going over again and
snatched the phone up. Wolf danced in circles as *her*
name flashed over the screen.

"Sarah?" I hadn't expected to hear from her until
later that night.

"Hey," she rasped. Wolf pricked his ears forward
as adrenaline thrummed through me. I sat straight up in
my desk chair.

"What's wrong?"

"I'm on a date with Max."

Cursing under my breath, I took a deep inhale,
trying to calm the emotions now raging inside me. "On
purpose?" I bit out.

She snorted, and some of the tautness ebbed from
my shoulders. "There wasn't a graceful way to back out
of it. Besides, as he so politely reminded me, his pack is
one of the biggest in the States. It wouldn't be good to
offend them if I haven't already." She sighed, and I felt
it deep in my own chest where an ache was starting. "I
just needed to hear your voice," she whispered.

My head tipped back against my desk chair as my
eyes slid shut. For her to admit that told me how she
was feeling. "I love you." My voice didn't waver. I
didn't hesitate. The rest of her life was up in the air

right now. I wanted her to be sure of me.

"Say it again?" she whispered, the words barely audible. My heart squeezed, and my arms ached to hold her against me and whisper the words into her ear.

"I love you," I said again. Opening my eyes, even I could hear the emotion in my voice. I did. I loved Sarah. Having the other Betas in the area and their pursuit of Sarah had shown me just how much I couldn't be without her.

"I love you, too." The words seemed to slip from her lips through the phone. I wasn't sure she'd meant to say them out loud, but they warmed me right down to my core. She'd never said the words so directly to me before. Of all people, Sarah wouldn't say those words unless she meant them. Wolf savored the feel of them as I turned them over inside me and held them close.

I cleared my throat. I was loathe to let her go but knew I should, lest Max get antsy. "Go finish your date, then you can call me tonight."

"I will. Thanks, Cade." She sniffed.

Wolf snarled inside. "If he makes you cry, I will jerk a knot in his tail so hard he'll never get it undone." It came out punctuated with a growl.

She giggled. "I tie excellent knots." I flashed back to the night she'd admirably trussed up Drew on the football field.

"I know," I replied, smile in my words. "You tie my insides up in knots every time we're together."

I could hear her smile. "In a good way, I hope."

"The best way."

"Bye, Cade. I'll call you tonight."

"I'll be here."

I sat looking at the phone for a minute after we

hung up. She loved me. She'd said it. Out loud. A delicious shiver worked its way over my shoulders down my back. A goofy grin spread across my face. Glancing back at the basketball footage on my screen, I knew I couldn't concentrate on it anymore right now. I closed my laptop and bounded down the stairs.

"Cade? You finish with the footage?" Dad asked. He was pouring hot water over a teabag. "You want tea?"

"Thanks, I'm good. I've been over the footage. I think it's imprinted on the back of my eyelids." Right next to an image of Sarah.

Dad smiled as he put the kettle down and looked at my face. "Something tells me you've been talking to Sarah." His lips twitched.

My grin grew. "Possibly."

"Things are still going well? What's she up to tonight?"

"She's on a date with Max," I blurted.

Dad pulled up, eyebrows hiking to his forehead. "I wouldn't expect you to be this pleased about that."

"Yeah, Max sucks." I finished my rummaging in the cookie jar, snagged a few out onto a paper towel, and stilled. "Dad, I love her," I confessed quietly. *Love* wasn't a word werewolves bandied around casually when speaking of the opposite sex.

Dad's eyebrows really did disappear into his hairline then. "Yeah?" Dad let the word dangle, waiting for me to elaborate if I wanted to.

My gaze met my dad's, blue like mine. "She said it back." Wolf practically danced inside me.

Dad smiled wide and pulled me in for a quick hug. "You're *that* serious about this girl?" he asked as he released me.

I nodded and stuffed a bite of cookie into my mouth, a silly grin taking over my face once more.

Chapter 19

Sarah

Max was looking bored and tapping his fingers on the tabletop when I finally exited the bathroom. Sean beat me to the table by a few paces with our food.

"Finally," Max said, although I wasn't sure if he was saying it to me or Sean. I'd taken longer than I should have in the bathroom.

"Here we are," Sean said, ever-present smile on his face. I scooted into the booth right as he leaned toward me to put my Caesar salad down.

"Did you seriously just check out my girlfriend's chest?" Max's voice snapped.

Sean's head popped up, a bewildered expression on his face at the same time I gasped, "What?" at Max.

"You are not allowed to look at her. Do you understand me?" Max growled.

I'd had enough of this.

"Max, are you serious?"

He turned to me, a testosterone-infused flush climbing his cheeks. "Of course, I'm serious."

"Knock it off. Now." I let just a hint of my wolf seep into my words. Sean wisely set the plates down and vanished.

"What? I can't defend your honor?" Max was getting good and worked up now. So was I. I was steaming mad.

"No. Not like that. Not like this. This is ridiculous. Look. I appreciate you bringing me here to dinner, and I appreciate that you are interested in me, but this attitude is not okay with me. I am not a thing. I am not yours. I do not belong to you." And I never would.

His eyes slit, but he kept his mouth shut, turning his attention to the food. He sneered. "This is medium. Not medium rare." He glanced up, and I could tell he was geared up to give Sean an earful.

"Don't you dare. You eat that steak the way it is, and don't you even think about harassing the waiter." My eyes blazed as Wolf bared her teeth in disgust.

Max's chin came up, debating whether he'd try to assert his dominance again. Holding my gaze, he put a piece of red meat into his mouth and chewed defiantly. My nostrils flared.

We ate in tense silence.

At last we were finished eating, and Sean dropped by, carefully speaking to both of us without letting his gaze linger anywhere overlong. "Can I get you all any dessert this evening?"

"No thanks," I answered before Max could speak.

"I'm done," Max said with a touch of revulsion.

"All right. I'll just leave this here, then. No rush." He pushed a black padded folder onto the table and left.

Max grabbed it and fished out his wallet. As he cracked the folder open for the receipt, his eyebrows drew together. Then his face paled. Quickly, he opened his wallet as an uncomfortable slithering sensation started in my belly.

Max cleared his throat. "I, um, I thought I had more money with me."

Wolf snorted in disgust. I said nothing, letting him

squirm until the silence grew intolerable and he met my eyes. I lifted an eyebrow. "How much?"

"I—" He cleared his throat again. "I'm about sixty short."

I was utterly speechless.

"Well, Max, I don't carry that kind of cash on me. You're going to owe my dad the cost of dinner tonight." I angrily dug out my credit card, stuck it in the folder, and held out my hand for Max's cash.

Having the decency to blush, he handed over a wad of bills. "This is going to be the tip. You're going to pay my dad back the full amount of dinner." I was done. So very, very done with this date. It was painfully obvious we were not in any way compatible. Max nodded and swallowed.

The silence was thick with tension on the way back to the subdivision.

"I'm sorry about dinner," Max finally said abashedly.

I sighed. "It's done."

"No. I'm sorry about how I acted, too. Not just being short on cash. I wanted to take you out on a nice date and treat you properly. But you didn't like it," he said, the end coming out as a question.

"Max," I started, feeling irritated sympathy for him, "I do appreciate that you wanted to take me to a nice dinner. And I appreciate that you're here because our bloodlines are compatible. But you don't know *me*. *I'm* the one that is going to call the shots, because I'm the one that's going to be the Alpha." I sighed. "I admit, it's not an easy position to be in. There aren't a lot of females that ascend to Alphaship, and it puts everyone in an awkward position. It's going to take some learning on all parts."

He nodded. "I'll do better. I still have the best bloodlines." He smiled, his earlier shame seemingly forgotten. I resisted the urge to groan. He was like an innocent little puppy, sure of himself, trying to figure out the world around him, and blissfully unaware of how irritatingly arrogant he was.

Chapter 20

Cade

"Cade, it looks like Coach is calling." Mom handed me my phone as we were finishing dinner Tuesday night.

"Hey, Coach, what's up?" I asked as I put my napkin on the table beside my plate.

"Cade, I hope this isn't a bad time," Coach Watson started.

"No, it's fine."

"Good. I just wanted to call because I got wind that there will be scouts coming to the state playoffs. We're one game away from it. I don't say this to put undue pressure on you, but you are one of the most talented players we've had come through in years. You have a real shot at getting good scholarship money. Now I've got all my feelers out, and I'm making contacts where I can. I'm behind you. I want you to really buckle down and give it your all this next game."

"I will, Coach," I said, breathless with excitement.

"I know. You always do. You hold this team together, Cade. You're going to do some great things this Friday night at the game."

"I hope so. Are their scouts looking at Bowen?" I couldn't help but ask. Bowen loved basketball as much as I did. It had been his one outlet the past few years. He deserved a scholarship somewhere.

"They'll be looking at everyone on the floor, but I've put your name and Bowen's out specifically. I shouldn't really be telling you about Bowen. You all won't be up for the same things as you play different positions."

"Oh, I know. I'm not worried about that. I just hope there are scouts specifically looking at him, too."

"We'll see how it goes. I'll let you get back to your evening. See you at practice tomorrow."

"Thanks, Coach. See you then." I hung up and looked wide-eyed at my parents, who were staring at me, waiting impatiently for me to spill the details. "Coach said there's for sure going to be scouts at the state games. We're one game away."

"Cade, that's fabulous!" Mom said.

"We'll be cheering you on the whole time," Dad said.

****

I waited impatiently for Sarah to call me later that night. I wanted to call her, but we had decided it would be safer if my name didn't flash across her screen if she was with her suitors.

She finally called about ten. "Hey, Alpha Girl," I answered.

"Hey, Wolf Dude." Even her teasing sounded tired.

"What happened? It's late. You sound exhausted."

"I am. Having the other Betas here just feels like an obscene amount of pressure. Which is stupid, because I don't have to choose any of them, but keeping up appearances and playing nice so as not to offend everyone is hard. And I have more dates this week. But tell me your news first. I can tell something good happened."

"It did." I smiled wide. "Scouts are coming to the state games. We just have to win Friday." My smile fell. "Do you have a date Friday night?" Would she be able to come to my game? I wanted her there. Wolf played harder when she watched.

"Kind of. I've got the movies with Greyson Wednesday, and Donovan wanted to take me to dinner Friday, but I told him I already had plans. That everyone who was anyone would be at the game Friday. I just didn't tell him my eyes would be glued to you the entire evening. He's taking me out for ice cream after. I want to be at your game, Cade. I want to watch you win and take your team to state."

Relief that she'd be there gusted through me even as anxiety rustled Wolf regarding Donovan. "Me, too." Something creaked through the phone line. "What was that?"

She groaned. "I think it was my neck. I need one of your famous massages."

Heat curled inside me as Wolf poked his head up.

"Just name the time and place." Images of her bare shoulders in her swimsuit flooded my brain. The way her skin felt under my thumbs as I rubbed circles against her tight muscles.

"Just as soon as all this is over," she said softly.

"As soon as this is over, I'm cashing in on that offer to kiss for a few hours. My lips are feeling majorly deprived." So were my hands. They needed to touch her.

"I don't think you'll have to remind me."

"Yeah? You like kissing your secret boyfriend?" A smirk slid into my words.

"As much as he likes kissing his secret girlfriend,"

she teased me back.

I chuckled. "You must really, really like kissing me, then."

I could hear the smile in her words. "I do."

"I'm an excellent kisser," I baited her.

"Mmm. I know. And I can't help but think how different those words would sound coming out of Max's mouth."

"Girl. Way to kill it." I grimaced at the thought.

She laughed. "Part of me really does feel sorry for him. I think his pack customs are just a lot different than mine—than ours. It's like a communication barrier with him."

"I know a couple of guys," I started, only half teasing.

"Yeah? What, you and Sam are going to go incite a pack war because Max doesn't have proper social skills?"

"What? Pshaw. Nah. We'd bring Bowen and Kyp, too."

She laughed again. "And what exactly would you plan to do?"

I snorted. "Nothing. As your dad pointed out last week, you'd have already disemboweled him by then. There'd be no need for our services."

"I love you." Her tone was light, and my spirits lifted with it.

"I love you, too."

"Keep your phone handy tomorrow. Date with Greyson. I may need a bathroom chat again if it's horrible."

"Always."

Chapter 21

Sarah

Greyson and I had decided to meet at the movie theater since he and Tate were staying on the other side of town while they were in the area.

Imagine my shock when I opened the doors to the theater and found not only Greyson, but Tate waiting for me.

"Hi, Sarah," they said together.

"Um, hi," I said tentatively, quickly searching eyebrows to figure out which one was which.

"Tate, you get tickets, I'll get snacks. Sarah, do you want popcorn?" Greyson said as Tate loped off to the ticket kiosk. No preamble, just a quick hi, and let's get to things.

"Popcorn sounds great," I said with a shrug. He politely guided me by the elbow toward the snack counter.

"Awesome. You want anything else? Soda, candy?" He smiled, and a little dimple appeared on his right side. It was kind of cute.

"I'm all right, but thank you."

Greyson ordered as I stood to the side, hands clasped in front of me, trying to calm my anxiousness as I breathed in the scent of salty, buttery popcorn and the unmistakable aroma of old theater—dust, people, sticky sweetness left behind.

"Here you go, Sarah," Tate said and handed me a ticket.

"Thanks. So," I said after a slightly awkward pause. Tate's gaze followed his brother. "You guys do pretty much everything together?" I had no idea why both of them had shown up for my date.

"Oh, yeah. Greyson may take over things one day, but I'll still be his Beta." He dropped his voice so only the two of us would hear. "We figure either of us would be a great match for you, and either way, both our packs would benefit."

"We're a two-for-one deal," Greyson said with a wink as he carried a giant bucket of popcorn and an extra-large soda.

I wasn't sure how I felt about that. Or what exactly was being implied. A shudder worked over my shoulders.

We made our way into our theater. Previews were just starting, and the lights were beginning to dim over the sparsely populated rows.

"This row?" Greyson asked.

"That's fine," I whispered back. An explosion on the screen highlighted the row of seats in orange and yellow as Greyson plopped into a center seat. I sat next to him, and Tate brought up the rear on my other side. I was a werewolf sandwich.

The giant tub of popcorn was on my lap, two hungry wolf boys on either side of me, and one mammoth soda in Tate's far cupholder. As a girl ran shrieking from a dilapidated house on the big screen, I glanced down. Feeling like *that girl* in the movies, I glanced at Greyson's hand palm up on my left armrest, and Tate's hand palm up on my right one. Each boy reached all the way across his body to grab the popcorn.

And they chewed. Loudly. Rhythmically. In time with each other. It was bizarre and started grating on my nerves about two minutes in.

Tate passed the soda over my body, coming within an inch of brushing over my chest, as he passed the cup to his brother.

"Do you want some?" Greyson asked, the smell of cola heavy on his breath as he whispered near my ear.

I shook my head and forced a smile. Greyson passed it back to Tate with slightly more room between his arm and my body than the first pass.

Focusing all my attention on the movie, I tried to block out the crunch of popcorn and the smothery feeling I got sitting between the two of them as they reached into the popcorn bucket on my lap and passed the drink back and forth, always just shy of brushing against me.

By the time the popcorn was nearly gone, my tolerance level was about shredded. Greyson reached his hand into the bucket for the last kernels. His hand ran the length of the bottom of the bucket—deliberately or just looking for one last mouthful, I wasn't sure. But I felt the stroke of his fingers through the bucket all along my thigh, and I knew I needed air.

"Sorry, bathroom," I muttered as I handed Greyson the bucket, snatched my purse, wiggled around Tate's long legs, and beat a retreat to the ladies' room.

Noting a few feet, I entered a stall and shut the door, just to have a moment of privacy. I shivered as Wolf shook herself out. I tried to reason with myself. Would I be this put out about this behavior if I wasn't already so emotionally invested in Cade? Like a drug, thinking about him spiked a craving.

Snatching my phone from my purse, I texted him.

—*Bathroom break.*—

—*As bad as the last date?*—

—*No. But I wish I was with you.*—

—*Me too.*—

I smiled, a quick flash of Cade's hand brushing the bottom of the popcorn bucket going through my mind. He'd definitely do it deliberately.

—*What are you doing?*— I texted, trying not to dwell on the thought of Cade's hand on my thigh. That wasn't a helpful train of thought.

—*Taking a break from science homework to text my girl.*—

Another smile spread over my lips. I liked being his girl.

He texted again. —*We're one date closer to those hours of kissing.*—

—*I'm remembering the last kiss right now.*—

—*Now I can't think of anything else.*—

—*I should get back.*—

—*Still thinking about kissing you.*—

—*Me too.*—

Chapter 22

Cade

Friday night came. I was nervous. Nervous like I hadn't been since my first varsity game as a freshman.

"Boys, huddle up!" Coach called. Wolf was jittery like I'd consumed a gallon of espresso. I needed to chill. Bad. I knew part of my problem was knowing that the other Betas were going to be at the game. Where Sarah went, they followed. Wolf growled at the thought. I knew Sarah was still mine, but the part of me that knew other males were sniffing around her trying to stake a claim nearly made me momentarily insane. And I couldn't shake the foreboding that came when I thought about her having ice cream with Donovan. He bothered me more than the others—probably because in the short amount of time I'd observed him, I thought he could be a wolf I respected.

Bowen punched me, and the sharp pain in my shoulder righted my focus. I nodded at him, took a deep inhale, and slowly blew it out my mouth.

"This is it, guys. We play hard tonight. We can beat the Bears. We've done it before. We can do it again. But don't get cocky on me. You watch out for their post—number seventeen. He's a beast. Bowen, he's your man tonight. Don't let anything past you." Bowen nodded beside me as Coach continued. "Cade, we're gonna need some three pointers tonight. Wings,

Eric, Chase, that's your job. Clear him for a shot when you can. All right. Let's do this, Wolves!" Coach Watson looked at me, expectation clear in his gaze.

"On three, men!" I hollered. Hands piled into the middle. "One, two, three!" And then howls broke out in the locker room. Wolf exulted in the noise, and I felt the two sides of me righting together, syncing.

We ran out of the locker room, tumbling through the line of cheerleaders and pom-poms.

"Get 'em, Cade! Yeah, Bowen!" I caught Raven's voice among the shouts and cheers. Catching her eye, I winked, glad to have her back on the floor now that her toe was fine.

Grabbing a ball and running my fingers over the tiny bumps grounded me more. Unable to help myself, I glanced at the stands. Mom's ear-shattering whistle pierced the air and drew a smile from me, but my gaze fastened on Sarah. She was here.

I'm here, she mouthed. Tension released as adrenaline replaced it. Donovan sat on one side of her, Max on the other, the twins in front, and Sam and Megan behind her. It wasn't ideal, but I'd take it. Max met my eyes; his narrowed. I winked at him.

My shot sliced in a perfect arc through the net.

****

It was a tough game. By halftime, I had long since sweat through my jersey, and even Wolf was panting with the exertion. We were tied. It was going to be a close game.

"All right, guys. We've got to pull out all the stops on this one," I told the team as we huddled in the locker room, guzzling drinks and wiping sweat.

"Cade, you up for some threes this half?" Coach

asked.

"Always." I didn't miss if I had a clear shot. And we needed the points. We needed a lead.

"All right. Boys, here's what we're going to do." Coach outlined his strategy, code Blue. We'd run this play in practice. I'd check the ball, make a long pass to Chase, dash around, get a pass back, and sink a three. Simple enough if it worked.

We filed out of the locker room, the dance squad still on the floor. Flashes of red and purple sequins danced around the room as the colored spotlights hit the dancer's costumes. We waited on the sidelines for them to finish.

My gaze trained to my section in the stands. Max and Donovan weren't sitting by Sarah. I wondered if they'd hit the concession stand. Sarah smiled at me, and Wolf caught a second wind. The twins were still sitting in front of her. Sam tipped his head to me behind her. I nodded back. Megan smiled, too, as she leaned against Sam.

"Kill 'em!" I turned quickly at Rachel's whispered words behind me as she and Kyp stood on the walkway between the bleachers and the gym floor. Kyp tipped his cup of soda in salute and glanced at Bowen with a grin. They nodded, and then the dancers' music ended, signaling the start of the warm-up before the second half of the game.

Spirits buoyed, we took the floor, dribbling, shooting, passing.

Second half started well. We had possession. Bowen got a pass under the net and was a few scant inches from dunking the ball as he made a basket. The stands roared.

But then the Bears got a breakaway and got an embarrassingly easy lay-up. Coach swore and tossed his clipboard onto the floor. The referee glared at him. Coach held up his hands in surrender.

"Run Blue!" Coach Watson shouted. That was it. My turn to sink a three and climb ahead.

Just as I got out of bounds, I heard Max's unmistakable arrogance coming down the walkway behind me.

"How can you not want to be all over that? When we had dinner, she had this low-cut shirt on. I got a great glimpse."

Blood boiled behind my eyeballs, and my anger momentarily blinded me, but then the ref's whistle broke through the haze of rage building up, and I slung the ball hard to Chase. Sprinting to my designated spot, I got a pass back before my man even caught up with me. I jumped, shooting the ball as I seethed. Our goal was now facing Sarah. Glancing up at her, I saw that Max and Donovan were just sitting back down. My gaze was jerked to the backboard as a collective gasp rose from the stands. The ball circled the rim, teetering on the brink. The air froze in my lungs.

A harsh exhale blasted through me as the ball tipped through the net. That had been too close. I had to get my anger under control.

"Get your head in the game." Bowen growled as we ran down the court. Shaking my head to clear it and slinging sweat with the movement, I focused again, heart pounding with adrenaline and a lingering desire to rip Max's tonsils out.

The Bear's point guard ripped it down the court, and I met him, ready to release the pent-up energy into focus. He barreled into me, and I let him, relishing the pain of the contact, letting it ground my focus.

Until the ref blew the whistle. Foul.

He sank both his shots. The Bears were up. And if we lost, state and scouts would slip through my grasp.

****

"All right, boys. We've got one minute to go. We're down by three. It's time to run Blue. Cade, you're the man. We've gotta get this game into overtime," Coach said as we huddled in our last time out. Grunts of approval circled our huddle, and a few guys slapped my back.

I could do this. I *had* to do this.

The whistle blew, and the countdown started. I threw the ball to Eric this time and dashed to my spot on the floor. But the Bears were onto us. My guard stuck to me like a second skin. Wheeling around him, I tore loose long enough to get a hard chest pass.

I planted to shoot. And saw Sarah focused on Donovan as he whispered something in her ear. She wasn't watching me. Wolf pulled up short.

My body froze.

"Cade! Shoot!" someone screamed.

Jolted back into action, I sprang and released the ball. With terror rising in my gut, time slowed as I watched the ball arc toward the net. Sarah turned to watch, her eyes huge in her face, the seconds on the clock disappeared.

Clang!

The ball bounced off the rim. I missed. I missed the shot.

Suddenly, a blur and a whiff of cedar whizzed past me.

Bowen leaped into the air, his shoes two feet off the ground. He snatched the ball out of midair, dribbled once, and launched toward the goal. Number seventeen drew his hand back to slap the ball down and out of Bowen's hands, but at the last second, Bowen twisted, slinging the ball up with his less dominant left hand and took the full force of seventeen's slap across the top of his head.

The ball went through the hoop.

The buzzer beeped right as the referee blew his whistle.

"Foul!"

The stands erupted as Bowen went to the free-throw line. The rest of us stood to the side. The timer was out. If Bowen sank these two shots, we'd win. If he didn't... Wolf whined. It'd be my fault that we lost. The gym quieted to a hush. Tension radiated through every muscle and sinew in my body.

Swish. The first one didn't even kiss the rim. Bowen bounced the ball twice, cocked his arm back, and with the confidence and grace of a wolf, let the ball sail.

Right through the hoop.

I nearly crumpled under the relief that rushed through my joints. Bowen did it. We were going to state. I was crushed in the throng of sweaty teammates as we merged in on each other to congratulate ourselves on going to state.

Outwardly, I crowed and pumped my fist with the rest of them. But inside, I was withering in shame. I let my team down tonight. I couldn't afford to do that. I'd almost cost them a chance at state championships.

I caught Bowen in the locker room later as we were

all heading out.

"You did it tonight, Bowen. You're why we're going to state." I swallowed. "Thanks for carrying my slack," I whispered around the invisible fist squeezing my throat.

Bowen looked steadily at me. "We're a team, Cade. We carry each other." He smiled and clapped my shoulder. "You coming over tonight?" he asked, referencing his hot tub.

"Nah." I shook my head. He and Raven would be in a celebratory mood, and I didn't think I could stomach it tonight. "But thanks. See you soon."

Bowen nodded, slung his bag over his shoulder, and headed out.

"Chase, Jamie, Eric, great job tonight, guys. Chase, some of those passes were excellent," I said to the last of the guys as they trickled out.

"Thanks, Cade. Have a good weekend, man."

"You, too." I sank onto a bench and tiredly undid my laces and jammed my feet into my slides. I needed to be alone for a while. Too many emotions were bottled up inside me. Even Wolf felt exhausted with the influx of uncertainty with Sarah, the way she'd looked at Donovan, and the way I'd nearly blown the game.

Chapter 23

Sarah

I looked for Cade as the players streamed out of the locker room, but his black hair never emerged.

"You ready?" Donovan asked politely, noting my searching. Knowing I'd have to wait to talk to Cade until later, I pasted a smile on my face.

"Yep. I was just watching for Bowen and Cade to congratulate them."

"We can wait if you want," he offered.

"That's okay," I said as I bit back a sigh. I was too afraid that Donovan would see something between me and Cade if we were together.

Looping my purse strap cross-body style, I tucked my hands in my jacket pockets, too keyed up at the thought Donovan might try to hold one.

"I've heard that Dutch Dairy makes a fantastic ice cream sundae," Donovan offered as he walked through the doors. He didn't let me go first but did hold it open for me once he was outside. The nippy February air pricked my nose.

"They do. I had a caramel one with pecans and chocolate chunks there once that was amazing," I answered. My mouth watered, remembering that delicious dessert. My dad and I had stopped by for ice cream after school one day.

"Is it okay if we go there?"

"That's fine." At least eating ice cream was something I could draw out, make last awhile so I had something to do with my hands.

"Here, this is me, green rental car." He pointed and clicked a key fob. "Here you go." He did hold the car door open for me.

"Thanks." I'd come with Megan and Sam, so Donovan could just drop me off back at my house when we were done.

"It's cold out tonight," he said as he brought the car to life.

"It is. We get a lot of cold weather in New York. How about Oregon?" Did I really just ask him about the weather?

"Lots of rain. But some cold, too. Do I turn right here at the sign?"

"You can, but if you turn left, there's a shortcut."

"Awesome. Can you navigate?"

"Sure." We fell into an easy rhythm of conversation. It wasn't awkward, and I slowly found myself relaxing as we pulled into Dutch Dairy's parking lot.

"Oh. I didn't think about there being an after-game crowd. Want to go through their drive thru and eat at the park or something?" Donovan suggested. I glanced inside. Lots of kids from school were there, eating, talking, laughing, flirting.

I wasn't wild about the thought of everyone seeing me with Donovan when I wanted to be with Cade. "That sounds good." Though now that I'd committed, being around other people instead of being alone at the park might have been preferrable. Wolf paced inside me.

We got our ice cream and headed to the park. We ended up eating in the car as it was too cold to be comfortable eating ice cream outside in skin. With dusk having since fallen, the wind was picking up, and a few stray leaves blew across the grassy area.

"This is great," Donovan commented around a mouthful of black cherry chocolate chip ice cream.

"Mm, so is this." I savored a bite of the dark chocolate ice cream slathered in fudge sauce, caramel, pecans, whipped cream, and three extra cherries. "Tell me about your pack," I encouraged. Mostly so I could eat. But Donovan was easy to talk to, too.

"The Hazeltons have lived in Oregon for generations—much like most other established packs. We've got recorded family back in Romania, but we intermarried with some of the local wolves once we ended up in Oregon, so we've got native and European Alpha genes. At the last count, we're the third largest pack in the United States. Behind Max's family." He smiled with a rueful grin I couldn't quite interpret. "We've been in lots of historical skirmishes, and we've maintained a steady battle readiness. Every pack member goes through training and maneuvers in their teenage years, and there are regularly scheduled trainings for adults, too. A hundred years ago, once some of the savagery from the territory had faded, my pack was caught unawares, and a good number of us were wiped out. Though not directly aimed at us, we've witnessed savagery from other packs more recently. We have a long collective memory, and no one wants that history to repeat itself. So we keep ourselves ready. Even more so after hearing about Victor Atwood and his attacks on the Wolfe pack."

"Wow. That's admirable." Even though he was speaking conversationally enough, and I'd asked, I knew he was showing me his pedigree—and it was a good one—one any werewolf girl should be simpering over. "The Thornehills are a smaller pack, but I do know the consequences of a pack being caught unawares." Bitterness churned in my belly.

"What happened?" His tone was curious but gentle.

I glanced at him. His attention was on me, even though he was still spooning in his ice cream. Was he asking about Victor or the pain I carried deep inside? Taking a breath, I decided to tell him.

"My mother was killed in a raid by near-feral wolves that had been too long without a proper pack."

"Sarah, I'm so sorry." His hazel eyes shone with concern, his eyebrows drawing together.

I shrugged. "It was a long time ago. I don't remember any of it."

"Still. It sucks."

A harsh laugh escaped. Both at the truth of his words and because they sounded just like something Cade would say. And that brought a pang of guilt. Because I was honestly having a good time with Donovan. And on paper, Donovan was everything I needed in a mate.

A strong Beta with a strong pack behind him. Generations of pack solidity. Both native and European Alpha genes that made his bloodlines even more desirable.

"What are you going to school for?" I asked, trying to lighten the heaviness settling in my chest.

"IT. I'm good with computers. And it's a good type of job to have as an Alpha or Beta since most of those jobs can be done remotely."

I nodded. "Dad works from home and sets his own schedule. It's been incredibly useful being a single parent and an Alpha."

"I can imagine. Was it hard, growing up the daughter of an Alpha?"

I blinked at him. He was the first of the Betas to ask me something so personal and so genuine. Wolf perked her ears up.

Slowly, I spooned another bite into my mouth. "In short, yes. Werewolves are a world dominated by bloodlines and male leadership. Not that a woman can't do it, and I fully intend to, but the old prejudices die hard. Has your pack ever had a female Alpha?" I studied him, gauging his response.

He pursed his lips, thinking. "Once. Way back. About the time of the Civil War, actually, I think. She wasn't Alpha long, though. She was killed in a battle. Her son was old enough and took over." Donovan shrugged.

"Pretty rare," I commented and swirled some whipped cream into chocolate fudge sauce.

"It is. But your dad has been training you. It's not like you won't know how to be an Alpha."

"I'm every bit as prepared as I'd be if I'd been a son." I kept the snarl behind my teeth. Donovan was trying to be complimentary, but it was a sore spot. I fought harder for the respect I got than I would have if I'd been born a boy.

Donovan nodded and popped another spoonful of ice cream in his mouth.

"What are your expectations?" I asked, leaving the question vague, but curious what it was he wanted out of things.

"I'm my father's Beta. I'm poised to take over my pack. It would be mutually advantageous for both of us to become mates. Your pack and my pack would grow equally stronger. So would our bloodlines."

"True. But what of our packs? You're set to become Alpha. How does that work with my becoming an Alpha, too?" I asked. Because I would not give up my position as Alpha of my pack. They were mine. My responsibility.

"Couldn't we both become Alphas? You'd lead your pack, and I'd lead mine? We could combine packs, but still hold equal Alpha."

I felt wrinkles folding into my forehead as I thought about what he said. It was an interesting proposition, but one that would have plenty of hurdles to overcome. I couldn't deny that his blood would make any offspring I bore that much stronger. I resisted the urge to shudder and tried to shut down the rational part of my brain before it tore my spirit apart. Because I didn't love Donovan. "How would you propose we join packs? We're on opposite sides of the country."

"True. Some from each would probably be happy to relocate one place or the other. It would take some rearranging, some compromise, and some work, but I think the benefits in the long term outweigh the discomfort of getting there."

My eyebrows lifted. I appreciated that he had put some thought into the long term. Not that it mattered. Because I wanted Cade. The rational part of my brain piped back up that Donovan brought more to the table and more opportunity and benefit to my pack. Wolf whined inside me as my ice cream suddenly seemed to curdle in my belly.

"How do you see things working? What are your expectations of me?" Donovan asked.

"I'm not sure yet," I answered honestly. "Regardless of how things pan out, I would like to remain on friendly terms with your pack," I offered—which was completely true.

"Agreed. But for the record, I like you, Sarah. You have fire in your veins. Not only are you pretty, but you're smart, too. That's a tempting combination." He smiled easily as he scraped the last of his ice cream from his foam cup.

"Thank you," I replied. Donovan was certainly my choice of the Betas presented with desirable bloodlines, but my heart ached at the thought. Would I be doing a disservice to my pack if I chose Cade? How could I not choose Cade?

My heart twisted up with my insides.

****

Donovan dropped me home not too late. He got out and opened the car door for me again but thankfully didn't try to kiss me good night.

"Sarah?" Dad called from back in the den.

"It's me," I called back as I flipped the lock, shrugged out of my coat and purse, and plopped them in a chair.

"How was your date?"

My hand went to my stomach, still tied in knots.

"It was fine," I said as Dad came fully into the room and leaned against the wall. He tilted his head to the side, studying me.

"What's wrong?" Concern etched lines in his forehead.

"I think I'm just feeling stressed about all of it." I hesitated while my belly churned, and Dad raised his eyebrows, waiting. "Dad," I started, "you approve of Cade. Right? Like, you're behind me pursuing him one hundred percent, right?"

"I am."

Wolf wiggled inside, and my shoulders relaxed. "Okay. I just needed to hear that."

"How come?" Dad came farther into the room and propped his hip against the table, loosely crossing his arms, settling in for a talk.

"Because on paper, Donovan is perfect. He has everything I should want," I said miserably.

"He'd be a solid choice," Dad confirmed. "But don't underestimate what *you* want. What the pack needs is important. But you have to lead them. You need to choose someone that completes you. Someone who will support you and let you be the Alpha. If that happens to be Donovan, you'd have my blessing. His bloodlines are strong, but not so strong that they trump everything else."

I was feeling marginally better, but guilt that I'd enjoyed myself with Donovan at all still ate at me.

"I think I'm going to go for a run. I haven't spent much time in fur lately. I think that'd help."

"Sure. Take your time. Sort through things. No one says this has to be on a deadline," Dad reminded me. Although it was pretty common for werewolves to marry and mate younger than the human population— even with Dad's reminder, it still felt like an addition to the burden I was already struggling under. And the sooner I decided, the sooner I could be with Cade…couldn't I?

Dad patted my shoulder and smiled down at me. I waited until he'd left the room, then opened the door a fraction, stripped off in the shadows, and glanced out the door. Seeing no one, I let my shift fall over me. It felt so good to let my fur burst through my skin, let my ears come out, the swish of my tail through the air, the crack of my bones and ligaments as they realigned. Shaking to rid myself of the last of my human vestiges, I nudged the door the rest of the way open and darted outside. Dad would shut the door behind me.

Dashing into the trees, I let go of everything and gave myself over to the wolf. I ran. Muscles bunched and corded, power thrummed through my veins as brush crumpled under my paws. The barest hint of green tanged the air as the cold blasted into my face. I relished its sharp bite as I leaped over a log.

With no conscious intention to go in that direction, I realized I was near the river. Not amazingly far from Cade's house. Wolf whined as guilt stirred afresh. I need absolution. I hated the way guilt erected an invisible barrier between me and Cade. It made me feel weak. Weakness was something I could not tolerate in myself.

The miniscule crack of a twig had me immediately crouching to the ground near some dead scrubby bushes. Wolf pricked her ears forward. We listened for long moments, but finally, hearing nothing else out of place and scenting nothing but the forest around us, I rose and trotted to the edge of the woods toward a meadow not far from the river.

Chapter 24

Cade

I stared up at the stars in the bed of my truck parked in the middle of a meadow near the river. I sat, freshly showered and in sweats and a hoodie, propped up against the back window of the cab. White plumes fogged in front of my face as I opened my mouth and exhaled.

Fresh air did wonders to clear my head. Usually. After tonight's game, even Wolf was too tired to go for a run. Physically, I was tired. Mentally, I was exhausted. Emotionally, I was wrung out. I didn't know what bothered me more. The way Donovan had captured Sarah's attention at a crucial moment, or the fact that I'd let her distract me enough that I could have easily lost the entire game—lost one of the futures I desperately wanted. Without state championships, the possibility of any more scouts checking me out was gone. Without that, a full basketball scholarship was out. I didn't *need* a full scholarship—not that I'd turn one down. I had ridiculous amounts of money saved up from a silly prank Sam and I had pulled, recorded, and uploaded to the internet years ago. Ad money had poured in. That money was for my future. College if needed. But one thing my bank account couldn't buy was visibility. I needed that. I needed scouts for college entrance and college basketball teams.

I sighed, breath fogging again as I stared at the sky. Stars twinkled in the black night. My head rested against the cab.

Suddenly, a flash of white at the edge of the woods snagged my vision. Sitting straight up, I squinted, then my heart pounded. It was a white wolf.

It was Sarah.

Her head swung to me. She startled, walked a few paces, then ran to the truck. Without hesitation, her flanks bunched, and she sprang into the bed of the truck, rocking it slightly under her heavy paws.

And then her silky fur was under my fingers as she nuzzled her head against my chest. I breathed in her scent of wild honey and citrus mixed with freshly churned dirt and undergrowth.

"Hey, Alpha Girl," I whispered, my eyes closing as her head rubbed under my chin. My fingers stroked down her ruff, the fluffy fur of her neck, sliding down her forelegs. Her cold nose skimmed my neck, and I shivered.

She sat back on her haunches, still touching me, and I wrapped an arm around her.

"I've got a robe in my bag. Want to be in skin for a while?" My heart picked up another notch. I wanted to talk to her. Badly. Feel her skin against mine, but she'd be totally naked under a robe. And that thought sent my pulse spiking. Her wolf chuffed a nod, and I moved away from her only far enough to reach my arm through the slightly open window to widen it farther and snatch the gray robe I had in my bag of extra clothes.

"Okay if I turn, or do you want me to get out of the back while you shift?" Nudity to a werewolf wasn't a huge deal normally, but hormones made a difference. She turned around, so I saw her back. She looked at me over her shoulder, her pale-green eyes slitting. I cracked a grin. "All right. I'll turn."

I faced away but was acutely aware of the sounds of her shift and the rustle of the robe on the bed of the truck. I swallowed.

"Hey, Wolf Dude," she said softly. I turned and drank in the perfect skin of her face and neck, the moonlight streaming down and making it glow softly. Her celery-green eyes were wide, though her eyebrows pinched more than they should have if she'd been totally relaxed. Anxiety coiled inside me like a spring.

We stared at each other a full minute as uncertainty stretched between us. Emotions roiled through me. Desire mixed with insecurity, leaving a bitter taste at the back of my mouth. Were we still secret boyfriend and girlfriend? The other Betas were still here. I should still keep my distance.

"How was your date tonight?" I asked, my voice breaking at the end. Embarrassment slid in next to the desire and insecurity.

Sarah took a deep inhale and leaned her back against the cab window, her fingers searching for mine. I grasped them, desperate for sure footing. She looked up at the stars and was quiet another minute.

"It was good."

My stomach dropped like a block of lead.

"Good how?" I hated that I had to ask.

She squeezed my fingers and glanced at me. "Good as in confusing." She sighed but continued before Wolf could start frothing in despair. "Donovan is practically perfect on paper. He's everything I should want in a mate. But I don't. I only want you."

"Then how is that confusing?" I whispered as I let my gaze slide from hers down the curve of her neck to the dip of her shoulder visible in the robe.

"It makes me question what is best for the pack," she replied honestly. My gaze jerked back to her eyes.

"Because I'm just a nice middle-of-the-pack guy," I finished flatly as uncertainty reared its head again.

"My dad said something tonight that I found helpful."

I lifted an eyebrow, still trapped in a quagmire of insecurity.

"He told me I needed to choose the one who best completes *me*. Not the pack. The one who will let me lead. You've always let me lead, never tried to supersede my authority. You've never once tried to hold me back from that." She studied me a minute, her eyes narrowing in thought. "Cade, if I rescinded my Alphaship, would you still want me?"

Air left me like I'd been punched. "You can't give that up for me." I gasped, shock and horror leaving me in a cloud of concern. Was she serious?

"But if I did, would you still want me?"

"Sarah, I'll *never* not want you. *Yes, I'd still want you.*"

A grin tipped the corner of her mouth, and the realization of what she'd just asked me settled over me, and the haze of concern cleared. To me, Sarah was Sarah. To the others, she was a Beta, a would-be Alpha. Desirable genes and a way to keep politics.

"That's why I want you, Cade. You don't care. You see *me*. You want *me*."

Heat started building in my middle. She was still

choosing me.

"I thought maybe I'd lost you tonight." The words passed my lips without my permission.

She shook her head as her gaze darted to my mouth.

Pheromones teased my nose, and I swallowed as my eyes dilated slightly.

"We can't," I strangled over the want rising in me.

"I know." She breathed heavily.

But we did.

Our lips crashed against each other's, her tongue, my tongue, gasping, wanting, tasting, teasing. Her hands snaked around, pulling my face closer, her body pressed against me. My hands moved over her back, a groan escaping when they moved up her shoulders and felt nothing but smoothness beneath the gray robe, reminding me with a sudden jolt that she was wearing zero clothes underneath. Hot blood rushed through me at a staggering pace.

Her lips gave no quarter against my mouth as her hand slid down my chest, my heart thundering under my hoodie and the pressure of her fingers. Kissing her harder, I crushed her against me, my hands sliding down her back to the curve of her waist. Breaking from her lips, I kissed her cheek, trailing along her jaw, down her throat. She tipped her head back with a breathy noise that only encouraged me. She moved, her body arching against me, and a corner of the robe slipped off her shoulder. I kissed that, too.

"Cade." She gasped as her fingers fisted into my sweatshirt, pulling me, dragging my lips back toward her mouth. She tasted like the wild honey she smelled like. I inhaled as my mouth worked up the inside of her throat, back to her lips where she pressed hers hard against mine, her leg knocking against mine as we swayed together.

Intimacy I'd never experienced spread from my middle to my extremities, kindling something in me that soon consumed me. I desperately wanted to pull her onto my lap, but if I did, her robe was sure to come loose, and I would absolutely come unglued if I saw any more of her skin right now.

Suddenly, rough hands clamped down on my shoulders, yanking me back with enough force that my body lifted from the truck. Shifting mid-air, I landed heavily on the grass beside the truck, terror and anger warring for prominence as I staggered to my paws and took in my attacker.

No.

Chapter 25

Sarah

Panic engulfed me as Cade was torn from me and a snarled shriek nearly busted my eardrums.

Screaming, growling rage shattered the night air as Max's face elongated, back and forth between his fur and his skin, caught between a shift in his anger. Enraged anguish ripped from him as spittle flew from his mouth where his canines threatened to burst through his gums. His arm jerked back like he was going to hit me.

My blood iced in horror at what he must have seen between me and Cade, and then flaming anger took over.

My shift was instantaneous as my Beta blood kicked in and Wolf took over.

Springing up, I caught Max around the throat, and took him thrashing down to the bed of the truck, my teeth squeezing, but not yet breaking the skin of his smooth neck.

Max whimpered and snarled as rage radiated off him like claws shredding down my belly.

"*Recompense.*" He spat the word around my teeth closing on his throat. I froze.

Recompense. Repayment for a wrong. Legal werewolf rights to blood. I had committed a grievous wrong. I had no business kissing Cade while other

Betas were here for courting.

"He has sullied you. He will pay for this. *I demand his blood in recompense*," Max gritted as his thrashing stilled. His eyes were dilated in hatred. A giant fist squeezed around my heart. He was blaming Cade for this. Not me. My bloodlines were still too desirable—despite what he must have seen and assumed, he still needed me. I clamped around the whimper that tried to rise.

Cade snarled on the ground beside the truck, clearing the metal walls in one leap. He landed beside Max's quivering form on the bed of the truck. Cade's lips drew back, moonlight reflecting off the white of his fangs as he growled at Max.

Time stopped as a thousand scenarios pounded through my mind. Recompense. Grounds for war. Grounds for blood. Rights to it. Images of blood running over the ground with members of my pack scattered, broken, bleeding, dying at the hands of the Fieldings—the largest, proudest pack in America. But *recompense*. Max claimed Cade's blood—the only way to avoid a war between our two packs was to let Max have his recompense—let him kill Cade. I would not allow that. I'd die first.

Thoughts of snapping Max's neck between my teeth surfaced, but I immediately pushed them away. I would not become a murderess, but neither would I let Max murder the wolf I loved.

A sick pit of dread formed in my gut as a shadowy idea flitted to the surface of my brain. There was one way to save Cade's life. I'd lose him forever just the same. But he'd live.

Slowly, I released Max's neck, backing up and

morphing back to my skin. I stood tall and proud, the gray robe swishing around me like oil and sending a wave of Cade's watercress and mint scent to my nose as it broke my heart afresh. I refused to let Max or Cade see how my insides crumbled.

Max wheezed and stood, his hands shaking with the effort to control his rage.

"You've made her a whoring bi—"

His words directed at Cade were cut off with a mighty snarl and snap of Cade's teeth.

Max whirled on him, gleeful malice tripping over his face. "You keep it to yourself. I've claimed recompense. You have taken what should have been mine. You have committed evil. If I don't get satisfaction, you'll have started a war." Max smirked, gaining the upper hand. "Your blood is *mine*. And you will face excruciating pain at my hands." Max's face took a haughty look as he glanced back at me. "But I will spare this dog's life if you choose me as your mate."

Fury erupted in my veins as Wolf gnashed her teeth inside, nearly angry enough to forget my earlier decision not to rip out Max's throat. "Your claim will not matter," I told him, ice in my words. My heart faltered. I swallowed and continued, my voice strong. "*Lacessere*." Silence reigned the clearing. "*Lacessere*," I repeated. "It trumps your claim of recompense and excludes Cade. You can have your chance to win my hand, but I will *never* give it to you willingly."

Max faltered. My eyes narrowed as my insides shattered. I stared him down, willing him to cower before me.

"You, you claim *Lacessere?*"

"Yes." I spat the word. "You, Greyson, Tate, and Donovan will have to fight it out. The trials for *Lacessere* will be announced tomorrow." Bitterness swallowed me. "I'm leaving now. I'd suggest you do the same as I'd put my money on Cade as the better fighter. You may have called for recompense, but who knows what would happen if it were just the two of you alone."

I stalked to the end of the truck bed, sparing Cade's wolf one last anguished glace, then leaped off the truck, shifting in mid-air and dashing, robe and all, into the trees before my heart bled straight from my chest.

Chapter 26

Cade

Agony pulsed where my heart should have been. Wolf growled menacingly at Max as he beat a hasty retreat, jumping off and sprinting across the meadow like the hounds of hell were after him. I watched as the last bits of Sarah's white fur disappeared into the woods along with every dream and desire I had to make her mine.

Without realizing it, I'd shifted back to my skin. Tears wet my cheeks, and I doubled over as a wave of grief struck me, piercing me with talons of pain. Pitching over the side of the truck, I retched into the grass as tears tracked down my cheeks.

What had I done?

I'd lost her. I'd known I shouldn't kiss her, but I had anyway. I'd let her kiss me, and I'd kissed her back. And Max—who already bore a grudge against me—found us. And if Sarah hadn't claimed *Lacessere*, I'd probably have Max's fangs sunk in my throat right now. If she hadn't, she'd have opened the Thornehill pack to a certain war with the Fieldings. She'd given me up in order to save me. And now she was lost to me forever. I'd never kiss her. Never touch her. Could love her only from a distance. Because I couldn't turn it off. Every cell inside me pulsed with it.

I heaved again, bile coming up and burning my

throat as tears choked me. Wind blew, suddenly biting on my skin, already covered in a cold sweat. Shuddering violently, I wiped my mouth on the back of my arm, and in a daze of stupefied horror, I got my spare jeans and wrinkled shirt out of my bag.

Cranking the truck into gear, I drove on autopilot. It was only when I realized I'd pulled in and parked at Sam's cabin that I acknowledged Wolf's insistence that I seek my Beta—my best friend. Parts of me were too numb to feel while the other parts of me were being raked over with fiery claws that set despair in my soul and left me adrift in a sea of anguish.

Stumbling barefooted to the door, I knocked, shivering in the wind that had picked up. I jammed my hands into my pockets, my fists clenched hard enough my nails left indentations on my palms.

"Cade?" Sam's shocked voice reached my ears through the pain that clouded them.

"Sam. I messed up. I messed up so bad." The words came out with a sob. "*I'm* messed up so bad."

Sam didn't say anything else, just dragged me into the cabin and to the couch where I sank, my legs suddenly like jelly, and cradled my face in my hands as tears squeezed out of my eyes, even as I screwed them tight shut.

"Sam?" Megan whispered from the doorway of their bedroom. Sam moved slightly beside me, probably shaking his head.

"Cade, is Sarah…?" Sam asked.

A moan rose in my throat, but at that moment, I was incapable of anything else. The front door opened quietly, and a gust of frigid air slid in, sweeping across my clammy skin before it clicked shut. Megan's sunshine and roses scent lightened. Her car started in the driveway.

"Cade, what happened?" Sam squeezed my shoulder, and I willed myself to rein in the sobs that were tearing me up inside.

"I messed up. She's gone. Forever," I told him brokenly.

"Messed up how?" Sam asked. "Did you guys..." He didn't finish as I shook my head.

"No. We didn't do *that*." If we had, it wouldn't have mattered if she'd claimed *Lacessere* or not. I'd probably be figuratively—maybe literally—dead at either Max or Austin's hands, and Sarah would have been forever tainted. Maybe even removed from Alpha succession.

"She claimed *Lacessere*."

"She *what*?" Sam said. "Why would she do that?"

"Because Max caught us kissing. She did it to save me. He wanted recompense. Was entitled to it." My stomach rolled again at the mere thought of it. "And now I've lost her forever. There is nothing I can do because I'm not a Beta. I'm not an Alpha. I'm just a guy in the pack who loves her more than anything." I shoved the heels of my hands in my eye sockets, trying to quell the tears that gathered and threatened to stream again.

Sam groaned and rubbed his hands over his face. "So now you're both stuck without the other, with no way around it. Because if Sarah recants *Lacessere*, Max will demand your head on a platter."

I nodded miserably.

Sam leaned back on the couch with a heavy sigh.

"What can I do, Cade? How can I help?"

I gave a mirthless laugh. "Unless you can turn me into a Beta overnight, there's nothing anyone can do."

Sam sat straight up. "What'd you say?"

I pulled my tear-streaked face from my hands and speared my friend with a scathing look. "I said, 'unless you can turn me into a Beta overnight, there's nothing you can do.' "

Sam's face animated. His gaze flitted from one side of the room to the other as his eyebrows drew together as he concentrated.

"What?" I rasped.

"Cade. Trust me."

"What are you thinking?" I asked, trying not to let hope burst to life.

"Let me text my dad."

My belly writhed as I thought about my Alpha hearing all about my misdeeds and the way I was kissing the Beta of another pack when I shouldn't have been. Grimacing, I suppressed a howl as Wolf thrashed in misery and anxiety.

Sam punched buttons on his phone before looking up and concentrating. He was using his link to his dad.

My heart ached dully, beating dismally against my rib cage.

"Okay. We're going to go talk to Dad. We're going to tell him what happened. I think he can help."

Hope erupted in my chest. Would Dominic still help after hearing how I'd majorly messed up?

"Help how?" I asked desperately.

"Come on. You want a hoodie?" He tossed me a red one.

"Help how?" I repeated as I struggled with the sleeves.

"You might not have lost her for good. There might be the slimmest possible chance you can get Sarah back."

"Anything. I'll do anything." Wolf yipped in desperation.

Chapter 27

Sarah

I held my composure until I reached my house. Shifting into my skin, still covered in the robe that smelled torturously of watercress and mint—like Cade—I let myself into the house. My face cracked as great heaving sobs wracked my chest, and I thought I might fly into a thousand pieces.

"Sarah?" Dad's alarmed voice carried down the hallway along with his pounding footfalls. Without waiting for an explanation, he scooped me up in his arms, holding me against his big chest like he had when I was a little girl.

I burrowed my face into my father's shirt, my tears soaking into the soft material.

"What happened? Are you hurt?"

Yes. My insides were flayed wide open. "I claimed *Lacessere.*"

"*Lacessere?*" Dad gaped, pulling back to search my face. "Why? You, I thought you *loved* Cade?"

"I do," I choked. "I had to. *Because* I love him." With that admission, I ripped myself from my father's arms and ran up the stairs to my room, shutting the door and sinking to the floor, letting my sobs and alternating howls out without holding back.

****

I don't know how long I sat there in a puddle of

misery on my floor, but sometime later, a soft knock sounded at my door. It was too light to be my dad's. I'd cried so hard my whole face was swollen, including my nose—I couldn't even smell enough to scent who might be behind my door.

"Sarah, it's me."

Megan. My heart cracked all over again. For the first time in my life, I had a friend close enough to let behind the walls I erected around myself.

I scooted back enough and wrenched the doorknob open, still huddled in Cade's robe on the floor, face wet with tears.

"Oh, Sarah," Megan said as she softly closed the door. She didn't say anything else, just sank down next to me, put a steaming mug of tea to the side, and hugged me hard. Fresh tears dripped down my cheeks, but the wracking sobs had stopped, though I felt my heart would never beat wholly again.

"Did, did he tell you?" I hiccupped, assuming Cade had gone to Sam and Megan and told them what happened. Not only was Sam Cade's best friend, but he was his Beta—that was our job as Betas—to take care of our pack. My heart clenched. In trying to take care of my pack, I'd lost so much. I knew leading required sacrifice. But I never thought I'd have to sacrifice my heart on the altar of my pack's well-being. I was willing to make the sacrifice, but I was angry. So angry. At myself. Because if I'd not kissed him, if I'd not encouraged him, if I'd not let things go where we'd agreed they wouldn't, we wouldn't be in this predicament.

"No. He got to our house in bad shape. I left so he and Sam could talk alone, but I came down here right away."

"Thank you for coming." I sniffed, my swollen nose running and stuffy at the same time.

Megan scooted back and sat cross-legged next to me, our knees touching. "Do you want to talk about it?"

"I was so stupid," I muttered. I was stupid in love. Wasn't that how the saying went? It was true. Being in love with Cade made me *utterly stupid* to act the way I had tonight. The whole story came tumbling out—my frustration with the Betas, my inability to stay away from Cade. How much I loved him. How much it didn't matter, because *Lacessere* was binding. I'd uttered the words. And Max's pack would take his word over mine. "If I refuse to go through with it, it'd be war. A slight this big wouldn't go unchecked. In the end, it was either war and Cade's blood, or my marriage to Max, Greyson, Tate, or Donovan." I wiped my eyes on the edge of the robe and caught the faintest whiff of watercress and mint as my nose slowly lost some swelling.

"We'll think of something. We have to," Megan said urgently. I glance up at her. Her eyes were anguished, determined. "No one should have their choices taken from them like this. You and Cade belong together. We've got to make it happen."

I sighed heavily. "You're a good friend, Megan. But I don't think there's anything that can be done."

She sighed and nudged the now cool mug toward me. "Your dad said it was your favorite tea. I thought it might help. Do you want me to stay over tonight?"

"Thanks." I sniffed and took a lukewarm gulp. "I'm kind of a tea snob," I said. "Tangerine loose leaf." I nodded to the cup and took another sip. "No. You don't have to stay over. That's okay. I think I'm just going to go to bed. It's got to be crazy late. I just want to shut it all out for a few hours." I'd sleep. Right after I planned with Dad what the three trials of the *Lacessere* would entail.

"You sure? I don't mind." Megan looked at me intently, her face a picture of sincerity.

I gave her a watery smile. "I know you don't. And thank you. Really. I've never had a friend for the tough stuff like this before. It's nice not to feel so alone." Wolf whined inside me as I forced my chin to stop wobbling.

"Call me if you need anything. *Anything*. I mean that. I don't care what time it is." Megan nodded as she rose from the floor.

"Thanks, Meg."

I shut the door quietly behind her and stood for a moment, my nose buried in the folds of Cade's robe. Eventually, I took it off and laid it on my bed and put on my pajamas. I had a battle strategy to plan. I chose *Lacessere*. I also chose the three trials the Betas would go through. The winner would win my hand and become my mate. I refused to marry Max or Greyson or Tate. I needed to stack the deck so Donovan came out the winner.

Even so, he was a poor substitute for the wolf I wanted.

Chapter 28

Cade

We took Sam's car the scant mile or so down to his parents' house below the cabin. I had every line of the house memorized. I'd spent almost as much time at it as I had my own house growing up. I was probably more comfortable with Dominic and Mary Wolfe than most of the wolves in the pack. Though the thought of telling Dominic what I'd done still burned the back of my throat and had shame crawling through my gut.

"We're good, Cade. Dad already knows the basics," Sam said as he put the car in park.

"I haven't heard him howling on the warpath just yet, so I'll take that as a good sign," I quipped. Hope that my Alpha could do something—anything—to help me win back Sarah had rooted firmly in my heart, and I was clinging to it for dear life. I rubbed my arm under my nose and scrubbed my hands over my face once more.

Losing Sarah tonight had shown me how badly I needed her and to what lengths I'd go to fight for her.

Sam killed the engine, and we got out. The cold concrete of the driveway and sidewalk stung my bare feet. I'd have to go back to the meadow at some point and see if my shoes had survived.

Sam didn't knock but opened the unlocked door and ushered me into his parents' living room. The clock on the mantel chimed softly. Two o'clock. Crap. My parents were probably starting to get concerned.

"Sam, my phone is back in my truck. I need to text my parents."

"Sure." Sam passed his phone over, and I shot a quick text to let my parents know where I was. I was just finishing as Dominic came into the room, a mug of steaming hot chocolate in his hand. He had on gray sweatpants and a plaid bathrobe, half tied and hanging off his large frame.

"Well, boys, I kind of thought these sorts of shenanigans would stop once you got a bit older," Dominic said with a note of sarcasm as he settled into an armchair. Wolf squirmed in embarrassment as flashes of other mischievous things Sam and I had done together flashed through my brain. We plopped on the couch. "Austin called. I think I'm pretty well in the know." Dominic gusted a sigh. "Cade, this comes at a very opportune time for you, because I'd already made my decision this morning, but now my decision could have a life-changing effect for you." Dominic took a sip of his hot chocolate. "That being said, I am not pleased with the way you've conducted yourself. Not only was it foolish timing to act on your hormones, but you've also put a target on your back and, by extension, the pack's."

I felt my Alpha's disapproval down to my toes. I knew I deserved his disapproval—I deserved more than that. I nodded, thoroughly abashed. "I'm sorry," I squeezed past the shame lodged in my throat.

"I figured as much," Dominic said. "You're not the first wolf to fall in love and do something rash." He glanced at Sam, a hidden twinkle momentarily shining in his eye. Dominic took another sip and cleared his throat as he turned back to me. "Sam has convinced me to go ahead with my scheduled plans despite what happened tonight. Now, Cade, I need you to think long and hard about this. Because what we're about to discuss is nearly unprecedented. It's a loophole. You're going to take heat from the other packs. You better decide if Sarah is worth the trouble it's going to cause if you upset *Lacessere*."

My ears perked forward. "Upset it how?" I ventured.

Dominic squinted at the clock and frowned. "I'm leaving for law firm business in California in about five hours."

"You're leaving?" I tried to wrap my brain around what Dominic was saying.

My Alpha nodded. "I believe it's about time I let Sam take on more responsibility. This seemed like an okay time to do that." Dominic speared me with a hard look. My gaze flicked to Sam.

"You'll be acting Alpha," I said dumbly, excited for my friend, but still not seeing where this was going.

"Yeah. And I'll need my Beta," Sam replied slowly. Understanding dawned, and a hot rush sped through me, making me momentarily light-headed.

"You'd...you'd let me...choose me?" I stammered as ramifications of what this meant crashed through my chest and stole my breath.

"You've always been my second." Sam smiled. "You act like my Beta anyway—you always have my back. If we make it official, I don't see why you can't enter the *Lacessere*. You'd be a Beta. You'd have every right to try and claim Sarah."

I sat in stunned silence for a moment, trying to wrap my head around what my Alpha and Beta were doing for me.

"This is a slippery slope, isn't it?" I asked. Hope pounded through my veins.

Dominic nodded. "It's legal. But only by a hair. I checked the legalities myself. I haven't said anything to Austin, though. I wanted to make sure you were absolutely, one hundred percent certain that Sarah is your chosen mate. Because that's what happens if you win. This can't be a teenage crush. This is a game for keeps. You win, you keep Sarah forever. You lose, and she's gone forever."

My belly tightened. "I think we've already started forming a mate bond," I confessed. Saying the words out loud confirmed what I'd been feeling. Sarah and I were meant to be together. I loved her. More than I loved myself.

Sam and Dominic raised their eyebrows simultaneously in an eerily similar gesture.

"In that case, we'd best do everything possible to see that you win the *Lacessere,*" Dominic said, a twinkle appearing at the corner of his eye again.

Chapter 29

Sarah

"Dad, what three challenges are going to best show me who a good leader is? And if I'm being totally honest, which of these is going to let Donovan win?" Bitterness tinged my words, and I scrubbed a hand over my eyes for the thousandth time as yet more water trickled from their corners. After Megan had gone, Dad and I had sat at the table and had a long talk. We were now up brainstorming trials and challenges. We had a whole list of notes scribbled on paper. Chocolate wrappers littered the table near my chair, and only crumbs remained of the cookies Dad had put on a plate near our two mugs of tea.

"I would suggest each wolf show proof of leadership abilities. You also need to know if they have any monetary sense. As Alpha, you are in charge of pack funds and making sure those in the pack who have less are properly cared for. Your mate will help with that. And then I'd choose a paired tournament-style fight. You need a strong fighter who can work with others and who has good sense, as well as leadership abilities that aren't going to overshadow yours." Dad searched my face, his reflecting the pain he saw on mine. "Donovan has a good shot of winning. He's older, and he's more experienced. Sarah—" He paused.

I glanced up at him, my eyeballs stinging. "I know,

Dad. It's my mess, and I know you'd help me out of it if there was any way you could."

Dad closed his mouth and nodded tightly. His hand reached over the table and squeezed mine. We sat there for a full minute in silence, Dad letting me have my pain. I held it close against me—the only thing reminding me that what I had with Cade was—had been—real. Because it was over now.

"If you're happy with this list of trials, why don't you go on up to bed. Try to get at least a little rest. I'll make calls once the hour is decent. We need to have an unbiased judge for the winner. Dominic mentioned that there was one last Lenape Native left who still carries the wolf gene. He's probably the best unbiased possibility."

"Okay." I didn't have energy for anything else. Trudging up the stairs, I fell across my bed, fisting Cade's robe to my chest and inhaling his scent once more before my eyes slid shut, tears cementing them closed.

****

I woke mid-morning. For long minutes, I lay there, my head pounding, my chest aching, my eyelashes crusted with the vestiges of my grief. Cade's robe and his scent were draped around me. Closing my eyes again, I pretended they were his arms. I relived every second of last night's kisses. The way his lips moved against mine, how they'd caressed the sides of my neck, throat, the top of my shoulder. How his hands had held me.

With a shuddering sigh, I sat up. I couldn't dwell on this. Because if I did, I was going to fly into a thousand pieces. And today, I had to have my mask firmly in place. I could let no chink in my armor show. Max would pounce if it did.

As I was just finishing my scalding-hot shower, I heard a heavy knock at the door downstairs. Quickly wrapping a towel around my middle, I cracked the door and strained my ears.

"Morning, Austin." Max's grating voice carried up the stairs. Wolf seethed within, and for a second, red swam before my vision. My anger at him had not faded.

"Max." Dad's wary tone was not lost on me.

"Your daughter has claimed *Lacessere.* I've spread the word, and we'll all be waiting, gathered behind Sam's cabin, for her to make her proclamation of the trials." I could just picture him standing back, crossing his arms with an arrogant smirk on his face. Maybe they'd let me in the ring to fight during the trials, and I'd swipe that smirk literally *off* his face.

"I'll let her know. When she's ready, we'll come." Dad's voice, tinged with Alpha, left no room for argument, and it helped buoy my spirits that at least Dad was supporting me as well as he could, despite what I'd done.

Knowing it was unavoidable and that the longer I postponed, the more time my mask would have to crack, I got dressed. I chose jeans, boots, and an oversized sweater—clothes I was comfortable in that still made me look presentable.

Giving my hair a quick blow dry, I glanced at my reflection when I whipped my head back up after I turned the blower off. Dark shadows cupped my bloodshot eyes. I looked a wreck.

Shoving down the emotions I couldn't deal with that second, I dug out my concealer and plastered it over my face so my despair was hidden from the world.

"You ready?" Dad asked as I hit the bottom of the stairs.

"No. But let's go anyway." My stomach grumbled, but the thought of eating made me queasy, so I shoved a granola bar in my purse, and we headed out the door. Dad drove, and long before I was ready, he parked in front of Sam's cabin. Other cars were parked there, too. Dread clawed my belly, squeezing painfully with its sharp nails.

We said nothing as we exited the car, and the dark, tangy musk of *wolf* met my nose. I could feel Dad's protective hackles raise as we rounded the corner of the cabin to see the assembled wolves around the communal fire pit. Dozens—some human, some wolf— milled around, but everyone stopped and stared as I came into focus. I made an easy target with the afternoon sun hitting my light-blonde hair and my white sweater. I might as well have been a lit beacon. Wolf snorted as I realized my white sweater not only made me stand out, but probably screamed *virginal werewolf up for highest bidder* to the waiting crowd.

Scanning, I found familiar faces. Kyp, Rachel, Bowen, Raven and her parents—my heart stuttered painfully seeing the physical reminders of Cade—Jake and Cindy from Sam's pack, a few others I knew from my time in Rock Falls. Megan stood beside Rachel, both of them smiling encouragingly. But Dominic, Mary, Sam, and Cade were absent. My heart constricted. I hadn't expected Cade to be here, but part of me had hoped. And hope was doubly excruciating when it was crushed.

Max, the twins, and Donovan had gathered over to

one side. Max stepped forward.

"You're finally here," he said loud enough it echoed, a slightly haughty note in his voice that nearly sent Wolf ripping through my skin.

"I come at my own pleasure," I replied, the barest hint of a growl backing my words, reminding him that I still held the power. Even if he told everyone what he stumbled upon last night, *Lacessere* rendered his words impotent. It would probably damage my reputation some if he did tell—not that kissing Cade was wrong, I'd just kissed him at the wrong time, and the wrong person had seen.

"Where is our third Alpha and Beta? We're on Wolfe lands; we will not proceed until the Wolfes are present." Dad nodded to Kyp and Bowen, standing to my right where the cluster of my friends stood to support me. Wolf rubbed her head against me inside, reminding me that I wasn't alone.

And then it hit me.

Watercress and mint, and snow and pine. Sam and Cade must have just come out of the front door. They came into view around the side of the cabin, and my heart skipped a beat. Cade's gaze locked on mine, and the barest hint of a twinkle shone in their blue depths. Wolf pulled up short.

Something was going on.

"Wolfe representation is here," Sam said confidently as he and Cade stood to the left of the gathered group.

"Very good." Dad nodded to Sam in deference. Scents swirled around me, muddying them together, as a light breeze picked up. Wolf scented. There was a slight smack of *different*, but there were too many others near for me to get a clear scent.

Dad continued. "My daughter has claimed *Lacessere.* We have decided the three trials. There will be proof of leadership abilities, examples of monetary sense, and a showing of strength by paired fights. Would each of the eligible young men step forward?"

Max swaggered up so he was a few feet in front of us. Greyson and Tate walked up in step with each other, stopping beside Max and a foot apart from each other. Donovan, slightly taller than the others, stood beside Max.

And then to my utter shock, Cade stepped up confidently next to Greyson.

"You can't be here. You do not belong. You are not *eligible*," Max spat.

"I think you'll find that I am," Cade replied evenly. Cade held Max's gaze as the younger wolf's eyes narrowed and his nostrils flared.

"It should be noted that my father, Alpha of the Wolfe pack, left the state early this morning on business. I am left Alpha in his stead. Cade is my Beta," Sam said evenly as his wolf's power rang in his words.

Blood pounded in my ears, and for a second, I thought my heart might explode. My fingers twitched once with the sudden desire to whoop and shout in a most unbecoming fashion.

Murmurs rumbled through the crowd. Some shocked, some pleased, a few confused. Greyson and Tate wore identical expressions of irritation while Donovan, his mouth set in a grim line, looked determined. Max's face was turning red.

"His claim is accepted," I answered, proud my voice held no tremor of excitement. That was the difference. Cade's scent had an added layer of power to it.

Wolf lurched inside me. *Lacessere,* once my death sentence, could now be the way my heart attained everything it desired.

If Cade won.

Chapter 30

Cade

My brain buzzed as Sarah carefully met my gaze from where she stood next to her father. Wolf lifted his chin proudly. We were here. We would fight for her. She understood that now. I could see hope shining in her eyes. Our time wasn't over yet. We could still be together.

Beside me, raging heat quivered off Max as he seethed at my presence—my barely legal presence—for the *Lacessere*. I'd always been his competition, but now he knew how deep that competition ran. Last night he'd been so sure of himself, but now there was nothing he could do. I was here. I was going to win.

I *had* to win.

Before I could do something supremely stupid, like add insult to injury by running my mouth, the crackle of car tires on gravel sounded from the front. As a large group, we collectively moved to the front of Sam's cabin.

Stooped with age and a nearly tangible scent of wisdom floating off him, an ancient Lenape man, his skin bronzed and crisscrossed with wrinkles, with two fat gray braids dangling over his shoulders, exited a white car.

"Tishcohan. You honor us with your presence," Austin said as he, Sam, and Kyp broke away from the mass of us and politely went to exchange scents with the old man.

"Welcome to Wolfe lands, and thank you for presiding over the *Lacessere*," Sam offered as he straightened from scenting the old man's neck.

Tishcohan, possibly the oldest werewolf I'd ever seen with my own eyes, nodded his head. "I have come to satisfy the ancient rites. Where are the young men?" His voice was both rich and reedy. Tired and strong. Wolf shivered inside me in the presence of this native man of the land. The Lenape had been in Delaware long before European werewolves filtered in. In some places, like in Donovan's Hazelton pack, newcomers had mingled with the native blood, producing well-balanced wolves with the strengths of both lines. The Wolfe pack and the Lenape had always been friendly but had never intermingled. I'd heard Tishcohan was the last of his people that carried an active werewolf gene.

Max, Donovan, Greyson, Tate, and I all stepped forward so that we were a line between Tishcohan and the rest of the gathered packs. His onyx eyes rested on each of us in turn. Max was first. He stood straight, confidently meeting the old man's eyes. Greyson and Tate were next, standing shoulder to shoulder. Tishcohan raised a gray eyebrow as he assessed the two of them. I was next.

Wolf squirmed with anxiety as the ancient gaze landed on us. Swallowing hard, I stood as still as I could, meeting his eyes, not with challenge but with reverence. I tipped my chin back slightly, exposing a sliver of my throat in the ultimate show of werewolf trust in human skin. His gaze slid from us to Donovan, who also tipped his chin back.

"You have many paramours, little she-wolf. It will be my honor to preside over such a gathering. It has been many years since the last *Lacessere*." He turned from speaking to Sarah to the rest of us. "It is my sacred duty to uphold the traditions and laws of the wolf. For each of the challenges set forth by the Thornehill she-wolf, I will choose the paramour that best fulfills each challenge."

The stakes had just been raised. This man was completely impartial. If I won, I'd have to do it on my own merits alone. There would be no quarter given. Wolf puffed his chest, rising to the challenge.

Sarah met my eyes.

Win.

"Paramours, go now and plan how you will fulfill the first challenge. Proof of leadership." With that, Tishcohan leaned heavily on a cane and turned to converse with the three Alphas still gathered near him. The rest of us were dismissed.

Bowen nudged me. "Come with me," he said softly. The other wolves were dispersing. Mom and Dad were coming toward me, and Raven suddenly appeared at my elbow. Megan and Rachel weren't far behind her.

"Into the cabin," Megan whispered, tipping her head toward her house.

Megan shut the door firmly behind her once we'd all piled into the cabin.

"Cade, we're behind you," Mom wasted no time in saying. I'd only had the barest conversation with my parents about why I was suddenly their Beta, and why Sarah had claimed *Lacessere*. There had been some shock, anger, and sorrow, all directed at me and my actions, but now that things were done and couldn't be undone, we were moving forward.

"As soon as Sam and Kyp get in here, we need to do some serious planning," Rachel said as she grabbed a platter of cookies off the counter of the newly expanded kitchen. "Cookie, anyone?"

"Are these the rejects for the catered dessert for this week?" Raven asked with a smile as she snagged a purple, orange, and turquoise iced cookie with a smudge down the middle.

"They still taste good," Rachel said with a touch of sass in her easy smile.

Wolf paced. He was keyed up, anxious, excited.

"Thanks," I said as the cookies were passed to me. I grabbed a plain chocolate chip with one edge slightly darker than the rest.

Just then the door opened, and Sam and Kyp came in, a whiff of pipe tobacco with them. "Austin is taking Tishcohan back to his house to settle," Sam said. He shrugged out of his jacket.

"Now we plan," Kyp finished as he light-fingered a cookie.

"Basketball," Bowen said. I glanced at him.

"State is this week," I said, even though everyone in the room was painfully aware that the biggest basketball game of my life was coming up. Bowen's too.

"Yeah. And there is no better way to show your leadership than to have them watch you lead the team. The team is your pack. You're our Alpha. You should use that," Bowen said with a serious nod, his dark eyes intent. I found myself humbled by his earnest support—

everyone's complete support.

Since we'd only just found out what the challenges were, I hadn't had time to think about it yet. I'd been preoccupied making sure Sarah knew I was still a viable option and making sure I didn't shoot my mouth off at Max.

"I agree," Sam chimed. "I can't think of any better way for you to demonstrate your leadership."

"Not to put things too bluntly, but you've only been a Beta a few hours. You've been captain of that basketball team for years. You've played varsity since you were a freshman. That team belongs to you," Dad said sincerely.

Their confidence warmed me, and Wolf settled slightly.

"So what do we do? Just have Tishcohan come to the game?" I asked, unsure what else we could do for that.

"Absolutely. We have him sit close enough his wolf ears can pick up the behind-the-scenes stuff—how you encourage the team, how you lead them, how you call the plays," Sam said. Mom nodded enthusiastically. Hope burned in my chest.

"All right. Game on."

Chapter 31

Sarah

It was strange having Tishcohan living in the guestroom of our borrowed house for the duration of *Lacessere.* He was an interesting old man, and I would have loved to listen to some of his stories and his history. I needed to be sure I asked him while he was here. If I could focus enough. Wolf was thrumming. Anxiety, excitement, terror, and hope all crashed through my veins.

Monday evening, after a blessed break from my would-be suitors (though I still saw Cade in the hallways) at school, Tishcohan informed Dad and me that he had a list of the ways each Beta planned to express his leadership abilities. Several were ready to show their leadership that night.

At five thirty on the dot, there was a knock. Dad nodded to me. I left my plate by the sink and went to the door.

"Hi, Sarah. We're here to show our leadership skills," Max said, a challenging gleam in his eye.

I said nothing, keeping my snarl of irritation behind my teeth, but stepped back so they could come in. Max, the twins, and Donovan came into the kitchen. Tishcohan wiped his mouth on a napkin at the table. We were just finishing baked chicken, roasted potatoes, and green beans.

"Sorry, sir, would you like us to come back?" Donovan asked, a crease forming between his brows as he glanced at the remains of dinner on the table. Greyson and Tate looked uncomfortable while Max leaned against the counter.

"No, no. It is all right. But where is the fifth?" Tishcohan asked.

"We are not his keeper," Max said with a scowl.

The old man leveled his gaze at Max, and a tiny spark of triumph raced through my heart. It couldn't hurt Cade's chances if Max offended the judge.

"It is his right to see his competition," Tishcohan reprimanded.

Max wilted some under the admonishment.

"He's probably still on his way home from basketball practice," I offered. Max glared at me. I lifted a brow at him in silent challenge.

"Would you like me to give him a call?" Dad asked, probably feeling the mounting tension.

"We will wait for now," Tishcohan answered.

"Can I get you anything to drink?" I asked him, needing something to do with my hands. There was a lot of building testosterone in the kitchen.

"I would love some of that tea you made last night." The old man smiled at me as he said it.

"Anything I can help with?" Donovan asked.

"That's all right. Thanks, though." I glanced up at him, pleased that he'd offered. I turned back to the counter and reached for my tin of tangerine tea.

Just as I was taking the hot water off the stove, I heard Cade's truck pull into the driveway. I couldn't help the way my heart sped up and the way Wolf did a little flip inside me.

Greyson opened the door, and Cade's face, still flushed, his hair damp with sweat, popped through the doorway.

"I'm sorry I'm late. Practice ran long. I got here as quick as I could." The fresh scent of watercress, mint, and the salty odor of sweat filtered into the kitchen. Sweat wasn't a smell I was fond of, but Wolf found Cade's scent, even after a two-hour practice, appealing, unlike anything else.

I stopped myself short of an obvious inhale that wouldn't have done anything to help the swelling tension in the room.

"You are here now," Tishcohan said as he rose stiffly from the table. I handed him a steaming mug of tea. He nodded to me as he took it, then turned back to the boys. "Let us discuss your leadership abilities. Max, you have requested to go first." Tishcohan's braids swung as he nodded for us to come into the living room.

"Can I get you a pillow for your back?" Dad asked as the old man sank into an armchair. He held up a weathered hand, indicating he was content enough for the moment. He put the tea on the side table where fragrant steam wafted into the crackle of testosterone clogging the air.

Greyson and Tate sat close together on the end of the couch. I lingered, wanting to sit next to Cade if I could. I craved him. Craved his touch, his scent, his attention. I wanted him. I *needed* him to win.

Donovan sat in the middle of the couch, squished enough there was space for one more. He glanced at me and tipped his head, asking if I'd like to sit.

I sighed. I sat. Then squirmed in elation when Cade

perched on the arm of the couch next to me. His hip pressed against my shoulder, his thigh alongside my arm. My other side was pressed against Donovan, but I didn't care. I was touching Cade. Wolf quieted.

Max strode to the middle of the room and produced a folded paper from his pocket.

"Thank you," he said with a slight bow to Tishcohan—the most deference Max had shown to anyone that I'd seen.

"What do you have, little wolf?" Tishcohan asked as he pulled spectacles from his shirt pocket, put them on, and unfolded the paper.

"I have here the record of all the Fieldings. You can clearly see how my pack has retained power for generations. Leadership has been bred into my family for hundreds of years. There's a reason we are the biggest pack in America. It is because of our leadership," Max finished proudly. He pointed to the top of an impressively complex family tree. "Our time in America starts with Eric Fielding. His family tree starts in Germany." Max continued, tracing his finger down the tree, giving little snippets about impressive things certain members of his family tree had done. When he was finished, he stood back, a smug look on his face. Cade shifted beside me, intentionally rubbing against my arm. Sparks sailed through my veins.

"This is an impressive lineage," Tishcohan remarked as he studied the paper. Max nodded. "But this shows me who your ancestors were. Not how you will lead."

Triumph sprang to life inside me. That was one strike against Max.

"But," Max spluttered, "this is how leadership

works! I am the product of all these generations of leadership—of all this power!" he protested.

"Yes. But it does not tell me how *you* will lead. You cannot rely on the power of your pack to make decisions for you. You must do that yourself." A weathered hand slid down a silver braid. "Thank you. Your claim will be considered against the others."

****

Tuesday night, once we were all assembled again, Greyson and Tate had their chance to demonstrate their leadership abilities. In the darkening twilight of the woods, I stood to the side, again flanked by Cade and Donovan, with Max standing close enough at my back I could feel his hot breath against my neck. Wolf pulled her lips back but held her peace because as I was, I could also feel Cade's heat radiating from his skin. Donovan stood just as close on my other side. We were a tight little ball of nerves and hormones.

Dad and Tishcohan sat together on a fallen log while Greyson and Tate emerged from the woods in their wolf forms. With silent communication only to each other, they were off, one to the left, one to the right. They moved with hardly any sound, but by some unspoken communication—or link—between them, they wove between trees, zig-zagging around each other, working even better in tandem in fur than they did in skin.

After several truly impressive maneuvers, they shifted back to skin and came back to the rest of us.

"Because we are twins, our link is twice as strong. We can anticipate each other. Not only will I be Alpha, but with Tate as my Beta, we can co-lead. Because our thoughts and actions are so in tune, it gives the pack an added layer of protection. It will help us lead as in some ways, Tate is like an extension of me," Greyson explained.

"It's like they *are* the same person sometimes," Donovan murmured.

"You have to admit, it would be helpful in terms of running a pack together," Cade said softly from my other side. I longed to reach out and take his hand.

"Right?" Donovan agreed.

Max said nothing behind me, but his breathing changed. I could practically hear his muscles tightening in irritation.

****

Thursday, Donovan took center stage. We gathered again around my dinner table.

"I wanted to show a battle strategy I was in charge of planning a few months ago. I've been studying werewolf battle tactics and fighting methods since I was too young to shift. As Beta who will someday accede to Alpha, learning how to best protect my pack has been one of my top priorities. We haven't had any raids on Hazelton land in recent memory, but there are still packs of feral wolves that roam up north of our Oregon territory. We have taken in several wolves who have been left bereft because of those attacks. That keeps us on edge."

I shivered, thinking of the stories I'd heard of the night our own pack was attacked. The night my mom was killed. Cade's ankle brushed against mine under the table. He sat opposite me tonight, as I'd been sandwiched in between the twins at the table before Cade could get to my side.

Even the minor contact with him both calmed and

excited me. I willed my heart rate to hold steady and not give away my heightened emotions to the rest of the room full of sensitive wolf ears. Donovan laid out a map of his pack territory.

"Your pack has extensive woodlands," Tishcohan commented, perusing the map and nodding approvingly.

"They weren't always this extended. My ancestors came and settled in Oregon territory long before it was granted statehood in the 1840s, but when we came, we mixed with the local natives. They had the wolf gene, much like the Lenape," Donovan explained as he drew his finger over the middle of the map. "Everything from here up to the border of our lands right before Washington State begins originally belonged to the tribes. But over the years, we banded together and formed one pack: the Hazeltons. We're the product of generations of smaller pack conglomerates combining, intermarrying, joining forces, and working together."

"Your lineage is also impressive," Tishcohan said. He leaned over the table where he could better see the markers Donovan set up.

"Thank you. We've taken what our native brothers used in their fighting and applied it to our own methods. Combined, it's produced something we've honed over the past century into useful, well-thought-out, and maintained strategy. Here. Follow this blue piece here, and I'll show you how we operate to protect our territory."

I hated to admit it, but I was intrigued by Donovan's strategy. He moved pieces on the map, explaining what they were, and how each part of his pack functioned. I was impressed that Donovan had come up with this himself. He understood battle strategy and mechanics far better than I did. It left me feeling oddly lacking. Fear tightened my belly, and Wolf whined inside as the thought that Donovan would bring an impressive array of skills to our pack if he won the *Lacessere*. A shudder rippled over my skin at the thought. Regardless, my heart beat for Cade. I knew Cade didn't have as much experience, but I was in love with him. He was who I wanted to wake next to. He was the one I wanted to spend my days with. He was the one who I knew would support me as I led and became Alpha of the Thornehills.

Chapter 32

Cade

Saturday morning, the team loaded onto the bus, and we drove two hours to the college campus where the Rock Falls Wolves would battle it out against the Marion High Warriors for state basketball champion.

My palms were sweating as I exited the bus, and the crisp air tickled my nose. Trees dotted the fringes of the courtyard and the parking lot. I stared at the giant multiplex building. Inside that building, my dreams would be made or shattered—whether by winning the game, or by impressing Tishcohan. I needed to do both.

Bowen bumped my shoulder as we crossed the pavement. "You can do this," he said quietly. Bowen and I had grown close during the past few months—not only had he married my sister, but we'd bonded on the basketball court. And his confidence boosted mine. Wolf was edgy. Impatient, anxious, elated. The direction for the rest of my life rode on today's game.

We entered the building. The smell of sweat, floor polish, and those little unique smells that made up the scent of every gym washed over me. I brought the scents in, letting them settle me. Instead of going straight into the locker room, I dropped my bag on the sidelines and walked a few paces into the silent cavernous room—far larger than any other gym we'd played in. My slides made the faintest hush of noise against the polished wood floor. A huge cubed scoreboard dangled from the high ceiling. I paced slowly to the arc of the three-point line—my domain.

"Cade!" Coach Watson yelled into the silence.

Wolf startled. I whirled, only to catch the basketball Coach sent rocketing toward me. Without another thought, I turned, jumped, and shot.

Swish.

My shot sliced through the net in a perfect three-pointer.

Coach smiled as my team broke out in applause. We rallied together, right there on the court.

"Guys, this court is the same size as any other. You see that shot Cade just sank? That's what we're here for," Bowen said. He met my gaze as his brown eyes sparkled with excitement. This was my team. I needed to lead them. Wolf stretched authoritatively inside me, and I felt my new Beta power rush through my limbs, setting them quivering in anticipation.

"This is it. Everything we've worked for. All those hours of sweat. All those thousands of sprints and millions of practice shots. All the time spent together. Knowing each other. Playing together. It's for this. We made it here, and we're going to dominate. But I want to say one other thing." I met the gazes of every one of my teammates. Both Coach Watson and Assistant Coach Young beamed at me. "Guys, let's have fun today. Let's win, but let's remember why we all started playing. We love the game. And we're good at it."

"Howls on three, then beat it to the locker room," Coach said as he stuck his hand in the middle of the huddle.

"One, two, three!"

We howled, the noise bouncing off the walls and echoing weirdly in the otherwise quiet gymnasium. It filled me with a giddy sort of expectancy. I was ready to show the world what I was made of.

****

An hour later, people were filtering in. Music was playing, and my blood was thrumming. We'd warmed up. My muscles were loose. My head was clear. Wolf and I were in sync. We were having some time just to warm up our shots before the formal warm-up began. I sank another three, then glanced around. The gym was filling up, and I expected to see several wolves coming in soon.

One wolf in particular.

And she didn't disappoint. There. Right through the double doors, I caught sight of her light-blonde hair. A stupid silly grin stretched across my face. I couldn't have wiped it off if I'd tried.

She met my gaze and smiled back, her green eyes sparkling, even from across the large room. She tugged the bottom of her blue shirt, emblazoned with a yellow wolf head, showing me she was wearing Rock Falls team spirit gear and letting me know she was doing it for me.

I'm here, Wolf Dude, she mouthed. Her expression turned sly, and quick as lightning, she puckered up her lips and blew me a little air kiss. Finishing with a wink, she turned to the stairs, the rest of the Betas trailing her.

My heart skipped a beat, and Wolf preened. Wolf puffed his chest up higher as the rest of the Rock Falls cheering section started tumbling in. Mom and Dad, Raven, Sam and Megan, Rachel and Kyp, Rachel's parents, and Kyp's mom, among others. Austin

Thornehill came with Tishcohan leaning on his cane and Austin's arm. I nodded to them. Austin gave me a quick thumbs-up of encouragement before leading the ancient Lenape to the seating right behind the Rock Falls' side of the bench. His sensitive wolf ears shouldn't have trouble overhearing things from that vantage.

****

It was nearly time for the game to start. I took one more glance at Sarah, my parents, and my friends. Risked one more at Tishcohan and Austin. Austin smiled encouragingly. Tishcohan sat, his face unreadable, but nodded to me.

"This is it, Wolves," I said as I pulled my thoughts in and centered them. Putting my hand in the middle of our team huddle, I met every pair of eyes around the circle. "We can do this. We know how to play the game. We know how each other plays the game. Watch your man, watch your team." We were silent a second, the weight of what we'd already achieved and what we were setting out to do settling over us. "Regardless of what happens here today, we're winners. We've made it this far. It's been my honor to play basketball with you all." It suddenly hit me that this was the last time I'd formally play with this team. These guys who had become like brothers in our own pack.

"You, too," Jamie said. "No one could have led us better than you have, Cade."

I nodded to him, grateful for his vote of confidence.

"Take us there one more time," Micah said.

"Call the shots. We're with you and behind you," Bowen said.

My throat suddenly clogged. "Coach?" I got the word out without betraying how close my emotions were to the surface. Wolf rubbed his head against me, and my emotions settled.

"Gentlemen, let us play some ball." Coach winked. "Stick to your man. Let's not let anything by that we can help. Howl on three."

"One, two, three!"

We broke into howls, and the hair on the back of my neck rose as I realized the whole of the Rock Falls portion of the stands were on their feet and howling with us. A wild, deep undercurrent of *wolf* echoed around the gym and set Wolf dancing inside me. Energy coursed through my veins, and a flush of excitement filled me, sharpening my focus. Glancing up, I met Sarah's gaze, a secret smile on her face. Her gaze lasered in on me.

The Warriors didn't stand a chance.

****

Bowen got the tip-off and flicked the ball straight to me. Pounding down the court, I got a breakaway, stopped at the three-point line, shot, and *swished*.

Even though we got off to a good start, the game was tough. The Warriors were stiff competition, and we were giving it everything we had.

At the end of first quarter, a round of howls echoed around the gym and brought a smile to my lips. We were down by two. One basket. We weren't out yet. Not by a long shot.

"Guys. You're doing an awesome job. Eric, keep on that wing—number nine. He keeps trying to slide down. Jamie, if he does, peg him, then Bowen, you switch to zone and cover the deep paint. He's got too many shots off tonight. He's good, and we need to compensate. Questions? Everyone good?" I glanced at Coach. He nodded.

"Let them try to get a basket inside my territory." Bowen growled the words.

Jamie, the other post, high-fived him across the circle.

"Just watch your fouls," I said. Bowen nodded. He already had two.

"Get out there and play some ball," Coach said as we piled our hands in again.

The game continued, and we were starting to take some heavy hits. We were holding, but things were starting to get ugly.

At about one minute before halftime, Eric swished a shot from the corner. I gave his shoulder a quick thump of encouragement on the way back down the court, but I didn't have the breath for words, because just at that second, the Warrior's point came barreling down the court. I pivoted to pick him up, but as I did, he came right up on top of me, and his foot came down on my pivoting ankle.

I heard a quick pop, and then pain flared up my ankle into my calf. Swearing under my breath as I lost my balance, I hit the floor right as the buzzer went off, signaling half the game was up. He'd made his shot. We were tied, sixty-seven to sixty-seven. And my ankle was throbbing.

Terror bloomed in my chest as I tried to move my foot back and forth. Hissing as the tendon pulled painfully, I stopped trying to move it and instead focused all my energy on trying to get my butt up off the floor.

"You okay?" Bowen asked as he and the team crowded around me. I cringed as I realized people were watching me now. I had to be okay. Because I had to play the rest of the game. I couldn't let my team down, and I had to finish—because if Tishcohan gave this *Lacessere* point to Donovan, I might lose my mind.

"I'm fine," I growled through clenched teeth. White-hot slivers of lightning spiked up my leg as I let Bowen grasp my forearm and help heave me from the ground. Locking my jaw, I let go of Bowen and did my best not to limp to the sidelines. My team flanked me, insulating me within their folds.

Coach's eyes were crinkled at the edges, and Coach Young already had the med bag out.

"Can you make it into the locker room?" he asked anxiously. "Jamie, Bowen, help him if he needs it."

Limping more once I was out of view of the crowd and the specific audience I needed to impress, I slumped onto a bench in the locker room.

"How bad is it?" Coach asked as the team gathered around me. Cringing again at all the attention, but knowing I was hurt, I gritted my teeth.

"Tape it. It'll be fine." I could already feel the tissues knitting back together, but it was going to be tender for a while. I'd be all right to play. I wouldn't be quite peak, but I could make do. *I had to*.

"You sure?" Coach Watson narrowed his eyes at me.

Coach Young sidled up. "Take your shoe off. Let's look."

I gingerly wriggled my shoe off and kept my face impassive as he poked gently at the sweaty skin of my ankle. Fortunately, there was hardly any swelling, although I could already tell there'd be blood pooled into a nasty bruise at the bottom of my foot come evening.

"Well, it doesn't look near as bad as I was expecting," Coach Young said as he finished his examination.

Wolf clenched his jaws to keep us from responding to the pain as he carefully moved my foot up and down. Already the slicing pain was replaced by a dull ripping ache.

"Tape it. I'm okay," I repeated. The coaches looked at each other.

"You're sure?" Coach Watson asked again. "You tell me—it's not worth risking your future career by pushing too hard now. This game is important, but not important enough to wreck your foot over."

He had no idea how much of my future hinged on my performance in this game.

I nodded. "I'm good."

Coach Watson pursed his lips. "All right. Tape it up." A collective sigh went up from the team.

I could do this. I *would* do this. I had to.

****

I played. But it *hurt*. The constant pressure, rolling, moving, jumping was taking its toll on my foot. My ankle was taped well, but I couldn't heal properly without letting my foot rest. I could feel the tendon tear over and over as I thundered up and down the court.

Wolf had his tongue out. We were flagging, in pain, and still neck and neck with the Warriors.

Two minutes to go. We were still tied. I'd never seen a game, let alone played in one, where the teams were so evenly matched in all the years I'd played basketball.

We had the ball. We had to score this possession, or we could lose everything in overtime. My heart pounded as adrenaline rushed through me. Wolf examined the floor, the placement of players, calculating the best move.

The referee blew the whistle, and they were on us. Heavy. I got the ball passed in to Eric, who passed it back almost as soon as my feet were in bounds. Shoving with my shoulder, I dribbled low to the ground, desperately trying to make it over the half-court point.

They double-teamed me, crowding me, making it impossible to see, let alone make any headway.

There. The line. A menacing growl sounded in my chest, more animal than human, as I plowed my way down the court. I crossed. The timer was dropping fast.

An involuntary grunt escaped as one of the players guarding me hit my ankle with the side of his foot. Limping a step, I nearly lost control of the ball.

Eyes dilating, leg on fire, I desperately searched for my team—anyone I could get the ball to. I couldn't take a shot. I couldn't do anything. There were two men on me, so someone had to be open.

The gymnasium was so loud, even my wolf ears couldn't pick out individual noise. The teams shouted; the stands were in uproar. My heart thundered in my ears.

Eleven seconds.

I had to pass the ball *now*.

Gripping the ball in both my hands, elbows out, I crouched. Clenching my teeth, Wolf bunched his muscles, preparing for a last-ditch effort to win the game. Springing with everything I had left in me, there was a *pop* that echoed around me as the two guys guarding me wavered through a haze of pain. My feet left the ground, the force of my jump ripping my flesh, even inside the tape. Fire rushed up my leg, and agony radiated off me as Wolf howled inside. I jumped high enough I cleared the Warrior guards.

Faster than a strike of lightning, I scanned the floor. Jamie. Jamie was open under the basket. Seemingly hanging in mid-air, I launched the ball to Jamie with everything I had left.

And then I descended. I didn't see what happened. I had no idea if my pass had been completed or what happened in the next few seconds.

I hit the ground, a groan of pain exploding up my throat as my ankle crumpled under the impact of my weight against the floor. My body slammed against the wooden planks of the floor as the gym erupted in noise loud enough it nearly drowned out the buzzer.

Jerking my arm under me, I propped myself up to see my team rushing toward me—skipping, leaping, yelling—red-faced and triumphant.

We won.

We won the state championship. Jamie had made his shot.

I don't know who grabbed me, but as pain, relief, awe, and euphoria struggled for prominence, someone grabbed me from the floor, yanking me up. I was crushed in a dozen sweaty arms as the entire team hugged each other. Someone started our team howl, and before long, our throats were raw from howling, long, loud, and proud.

Searching the bleachers from my team huddle, I

found Sarah. Her hands were clasped under her chin, a smile lighting her whole face. I pumped my fist in her direction, my parents, sister, and best friends gathered with her.

Last, I glanced at Tishcohan. He sat, weathered and ancient, a smile wrinkling his face. Relief that I'd done as well as I could shuttled through me. There was nothing else I could have done. I didn't know if I'd impressed him enough to award me the point, but he wasn't displeased. I'd given it everything I had.

But right then, my ankle needed some attention. I cringed, realizing I might actually need crutches.

Chapter 33

Sarah

He did it. They won. Even though Cade hadn't made the winning shot, he made the winning pass. If he hadn't, they'd have gone into overtime—and who knows what might have happened then.

Heat bloomed in my chest as he met my gaze. I knew he was hurting. I could see it etched between his eyebrows, but I could also see his elation, his joy. I loved him so much. Wolf sighed in contentment, basking in his attention as he pumped his fist in the air in my general direction.

"Excuse me, are you Mr. and Mrs. Rivers? Cade's parents?" A man in a striped polo shirt and khakis sauntered up next to Cade's parents a few rows behind.

"Yes. I'm Steve, and this is my wife, Amalie. What can we do for you?"

"I'm Mike Mims. I represent New York State University's athletic department. Your son is one heck of a player. Coach Young passed Cade's name on to me early in the season, and I've been keeping tabs on him. I was wondering if we could set up a time to discuss the possibility of Cade coming to play for us next year."

"Yes! We'd be happy to." Steve's answer came enthusiastically as Amalie's eyes shone, and she nodded her head.

New York State University. Wolf leaped inside me.

****

Once everyone was back in town, the whole basketball team, their girlfriends, their friends—basically the majority of the teenage population of Rock Falls—flocked to the roller-skating rink and pizza parlor a few miles outside town.

I hadn't been there since I'd been living in Rock Falls, but it was the only restaurant in the area large enough to hold so many people. The team had been forbidden by coaches and parents alike from doing anything stupid, so this was where they all herded. I was sure there'd be plenty of stupidity going on later, but for now, we were all here. And by the looks of things as I entered, it was going to be a fun night.

Colored lights beamed down on the roller rink floor, already dotted with people zipping around it. Tables with retro red-and-white-checked tablecloths were lined around the outside of the rink several tables deep. Already pizzas were being dished out and placed on tables, and drinks lined the counters. Music blasted from speakers up in the rafters of the giant room, and the bass drummed under my feet. I hoped they turned the music down at some point.

"Wow," Greyson and Tate said simultaneously on either side of me as they stood beside me.

"Ever been to a roller rink?" I asked.

"Nope," they both answered.

"But it can't be that hard. If uncoordinated humans can do it, we should be able to, right?" Tate said, with no derogatory tone in his voice, only curious comparison.

I shrugged. "I'll watch you the first few rounds and see how you do." I chuckled to myself. I had been to a roller rink. Admittedly, it had been quite some time ago, but I remembered how it took a while to get my legs under me with the rollers strapped on my feet. Even with my wolf's natural athletic grace.

Donovan smirked as he joined us.

Max was sullen. "I don't get why we have to be here for this. It's just some stupid basketball game," he muttered.

Donovan's nostrils flared, and he turned on Max before I could utter a retort. "You do *not* have to be here. You are welcome to go. But if you stay, please be civil. Don't share the misery. Your misery may love company, but the rest of us don't. And it's not 'just some basketball game.' The Wolves just won the state championship. There is no higher title for them to win. They are the best high school basketball team *in the state*. Cade was highly instrumental in that achievement. The world does not revolve around you, Max. Be happy for someone else, even if you don't like him and he's your competition. Grow a pair and act like a man."

My eyes were round, and I had to keep my mouth from dropping open. Max seemed to shrivel under the harsh words from the older wolf.

"Donovan, it's a shame *we're* competition. I think we could be friends."

My blood turned to lava, and Wolf leaped inside me at the voice behind me.

An amused expression flitted across Donovan's face as Max's eye twitched. Greyson and Tate stood back, watching the scene unfolding around us.

"Well played, Cade," Donovan said as his amused expression morphed into a smile as respect lit his eyes.

He stuck his arm out, and Cade clasped his hand.

Turning, I took in Cade's trademarked cocky expression and casual stance draped across crutches, his foot wrapped and sticking out oddly behind him. He was freshly showered, and watercress and mint engulfed me, making Wolf jelly-legged.

"Thanks," he said and tipped his head back toward Donovan before letting his blue gaze land on me, quickly taking me in and setting my insides on fire.

Fortunately, Sam and Megan weren't far behind Cade.

"Anyone want pizza?" Sam asked, his eyes missing none of the tension and amusement in our little knot.

"The more meat, the better," Greyson chimed. Tate nodded enthusiastically and smacked his lips.

"Everyone else is on the way. We should snag a table before they're all gone," Megan said sensibly. We started moving as a group, and I realized I'd never even congratulated Cade on his big win.

"Cade, you did an *amazing* job today. Congratulations!" I hoped he heard the meaning behind my words. I was *so* proud of him.

He gave me a cheeky smile. "And not only that, but a scout came and talked to Mom and Dad at the game about setting up a meeting." His excitement was practically bleeding through his pores. Wolf jumped inside.

"I heard. I was right there in the stands when he talked to them." I desperately wanted to throw myself at him and feel his arms snake around my waist as I planted the world's biggest kiss right on his mouth, but the crutches and the company weren't working in my favor. I tried to convey with my eyes that I knew *where* the scout was from, too.

A crooked grin broke across his face. He knew I knew.

We settled at a table after putting in our orders. I wedged myself in last, next to the end where Cade lowered himself, his foot stretched out and his crutches propped against the end of the table. Our legs touched from hip to knee, and bubbles erupted in my belly. I hadn't had physical contact with him in days, and I only then realized how much I needed it. Unable to help myself, I let my hand run down the top of his leg under the table. I felt him shudder against me, and it broke goose bumps out on my own arms and set a twinge in the pit of my stomach that had nothing to do with my growling belly.

"Cade!" Rachel called exuberantly over the din of noise as she and Kyp moved through the throngs of people to our table. "I am *so* impressed. You guys did it! You won *state*!" She squealed as she gave him a high five. Cade chuckled. "How's your foot?" Rachel went on, hardly stopping to draw breath. "Can you scoot over? I need to talk to Sarah," she politely asked Tate who was smooshed up against my other side. Donovan's eyes slit slightly as he watched us across the table, and I willed my cheeks not to flush, as both my hands were still under the table. One of them still wrapped around Cade's leg. I couldn't seem to drag my hand back. It was like a part of me had been missing, and I couldn't let it go now that I had it in my literal grasp.

Slightly flummoxed, Tate scooted down, and Wolf breathed deeply as his body heat left my side. Rachel wiggled down into his vacated spot, Kyp beside her, shoving my would-be mates farther down the table.

Megan's eyes shone across the table from me, and I had to make sure none of my inner smile showed on my face. These girls were the best.

We made small talk while we waited for our food, and every few minutes, someone new would stop by, congratulating Cade and sharing the general excitement. Cade's happiness was infectious, and Wolf smiled with him.

****

Bowen and Raven were the last to the party, and the pheromones that came in with them were almost strong enough to cover the aroma of the sausage, chicken, and bacon pizza on my plate.

"You guys are late," Max commented obliviously.

"Yep," Bowen said matter-of-factly as Raven blushed.

Cade coughed and turned a slight shade of green beside me. Donovan snorted, and then the whole table erupted into grunts and choked laughter. I took the opportunity to pat Cade on the back under the pretext of dislodging his mozzarella stick.

His hand squeezed my knee under the table and sent my heart tripping. It was good the rink was noisy. The other wolves at the table would probably have been able to hear its increased rhythm otherwise.

"Wow. You don't miss much, do you, Max?" Cade said, leaning over to see Max at the other end of the table. Cade sat back, cleared his throat, and took a long pull of his lemonade. Reluctantly, I let my fingers graze over his back as I stopped patting him.

Max just looked disgusted and put out as he ate another bite of his pizza. Cade's hand was still on the top of my knee, but he slid it over so it rested on the inside, his fingers cupping just behind the bend in my leg. My insides were tying themselves up in knots like they hadn't been in weeks. Cade's thumb stroked over the top of my knee. Wolf whimpered inside.

"Rachel, what are you eating?" Cade asked. Megan and Rachel were sharing a pale pizza with little dots of chicken and stringy green things.

"It's a Blanca pizza. It's *so* good. The roller rink is the only place around here that makes them," Rachel said.

"Here, try a piece," Megan said and nudged the tray toward him. With a shrug, Cade snagged a piece and sniffed.

"What exactly is on this?" He raised a skeptical eyebrow.

"Girly food," Bowen retorted.

"It's white sauce, chicken, and spinach," Megan said after she speared Bowen with mock offense.

"Spinach," Cade said dubiously.

"I like spinach," I offered. Cade glanced at me from the corner of his eye and very deliberately took a slow bite, holding my gaze. He was practically smoldering at me in front of everyone under the guise of eating spinach. Only Cade could possibly pull that off. And he did. Because my insides melted as he licked his lips, then glanced at the pizza. Then his eyes screwed shut, and he made a face.

"You try it, Miss I-like-spinach." He put the offending slice on my plate, squeezing my leg again under the table.

Lifting an eyebrow at his teasing challenge, I picked up the slice and took a bite. It was delicious.

And it had the faintest taste of Cade on it. Wolf was breathing heavily, and it took everything in me not to throw the pizza across the room and yank Cade down to kiss him right there.

"This is *really* good," I said instead. My toes wrapped around his leg as his hand squeezed and slid an inch higher up my leg.

I needed to get control of myself.

"Do you guys know where the restroom is?" I asked, suddenly needing space to right my mask before it slipped off completely.

"Sure. Come on. I'll go with," Rachel said with a pointed look at Megan.

Rachel and I squished out of our spots. I might have leaned on Cade and brushed myself against him more than was absolutely necessary on the way out.

"It's way on the other side over here," Rachel said, her wild riot of red curls bouncing as her green eyes held a secret amusement.

We traipsed through the rows of tables, through an arcade, and over to the far side of the building. I could hardly even see our table from where we were, and I could only just make out the neon red restroom sign hanging in a back hallway.

Mercifully, the bathroom was quiet, and the only person in there was finishing applying her lipstick. She was a girl I faintly recognized from school, but I didn't know her name. Rachel gave her a cheerful smile and a wave as the girl left, leaving us alone in the bathroom.

"I'm guessing you don't really have to go," Rachel said, a grin in her voice.

I sighed and ran my hands over my face. "No. I just needed a minute before I attacked Cade right there at the table."

Rachel giggled. "Did you know my sister Clary used to work here?" she asked a little too innocently.

"Really? She's your oldest sister?" I clarified.

"Mmhmm. Megan and I spent ridiculous amounts of time here when we were kids up into middle school." Rachel flicked her fingers, examining her bright purple nails and neat cuticles nonchalantly.

"Why do I get the feeling you're about to drop something on me here?" Wolf perked up.

"Well, it just so happens that there's a supply closet down at the very end of this dark hall. And that it's accessible from both sides. So no one would know if, say, two people were to secretly meet there for a few minutes." Rachel glanced up at me, her eyes shining. "It also just so happens that I know both of those doors are unlocked right now, and that Megan is talking the boys into a game of roller dodgeball. It'll take at least fifteen or twenty minutes. And people on crutches really shouldn't be roller skating."

Wolf leaped inside while my heart pounded against my ribs. "Rachel, you are the *best*." I gave her shoulders a quick hug as she giggled. "Show me this supply closet?" Hope was like a wild animal unleashed in my chest cavity. My head spun, and for a second, I was dizzy.

"Just be smart, okay? Everyone's suspicions are going to be up if you all are both missing once the game is done. I'll call your phone when you need to get back. Good?"

"Yes!" I breathed, my voice hitching slightly in excitement. I needed to see Cade. Feel him. Touch him. Be touched by him.

"Enjoy," Rachel said with a wink as she checked that the coast was clear, then popped the supply closet door open. "Light is right there to the side. Don't turn it on until Cade is inside. Someone might see the light and get suspicious," she whispered. "Better yet, just use the flashlight on your phone."

"Got it."

"Okay. See you in a few." She nodded with one more conspiratorial smile.

And then I was left in darkness. But only for a moment or so.

The opposite door creaked open, and watercress and mint mingled with the astringent dusty smell of the closet.

"Cade." I breathed. The door clicked shut and my eyes dilated again in the darkness.

"Alpha Girl?" My blood went all fizzy.

"I'm turning on my phone light; squint." I flipped on my screen and harsh white light shot up to the ceiling and filtered down. The light bathed us in a gray beacon. We just stood there on opposite sides of the closet, drinking each other in.

"Cade, I am *so* proud of you," I whispered.

"I miss you," he whispered back. His crutches were leaned against the wall. I took two giant steps, hesitating in front of him as the light played strange shadows over him. His gaze roved over my face, his breathing shorter than normal. "Are you still mine?" he whispered with a hard swallow. My heart ached at his words.

"*Yes.*" I propped my phone on a box. Without waiting any longer, I reached out and grasped his hands. They trembled lightly against mine but stopped as I guided them around my waist. He didn't need any more encouragement. His arms came the rest the way around me, drawing me to his chest. My hands looped around his neck as I tilted my face toward him.

His lips met mine in a slow, wanting dance that sent Wolf flopping onto her back, her tongue lolling out. My fingers trailed up into the hair at the back of his head, tugging his mouth harder against mine.

His tongue teased me, darting into my mouth only to leap back out and trace my lower lip, then plunging back in and stroking against mine. My toes curled as a needy little noise escaped my throat.

Cade grunted, his hands clenching around my sides, right at the top of my jeans. His mouth moved more urgently, and I went up on my tiptoes to reach him better, my body pressed against the hard planes of his.

"You're killing me right now," he growled against my lips but didn't wait for a response, only kissed me deeper, his hands pulling me tighter and waking every nerve ending I possessed.

My lips left his mouth, trailing burning kisses over his square jaw, up to his ear. He turned, dragging his lips down my cheek and jaw as a breathy noise rose in my throat and broke my lips from his skin. His lips closed over mine once more, softer, less urgent, longing, and loving.

My phone buzzed on the box top.

Not yet.

I whimpered against his lips once more, kissing him frantically just one more second.

"I love you," Cade said as he crushed me against his chest.

"I love you, too," I whispered. He ran his finger down the side of my cheek and brushed his thumb over my trembling bottom lip.

And then we forced ourselves apart and left the sacred space of the supply closet.

Chapter 34

Cade

I lay in bed the next morning, a few birds rustling and fluttering near my window. I thought about yesterday. About winning state. About scouts. About Sarah. About her kisses in the closet. I sighed. For the moment, I was utterly content. Refusing to acknowledge my bubble of contentment might be busted later that afternoon when we met with Tishcohan for results of the first round of *Lacessere*, I dwelt instead on the warm sensation curling in my gut.

Eventually, I got up, wincing as my foot came in contact with the floor. It was mostly healed but still a little tender. I didn't think I'd need the crutches today if I was careful and didn't do anything stupid. I'd need to put off a run in fur for another day or two at least.

"Cade? You up?" Dad called on the other side of my door.

"Kind of," I replied, my voice still scratchy from sleep.

"Can I come in?"

"Sure."

Dad cracked the door open and popped his head in, a wide smile on his face. "Good morning, son. How are you feeling this morning?"

"Right now, pretty good. Lotta good things yesterday." A grin tipped my lips upward.

Dad nodded. "More good news. I just got a call from Mike Mims—the scout. We've got a meeting with him and your coaches Monday after school."

"Wow. That's fast."

"It is. They wanted to move on things. It's March. Time to get those rosters filled and all things allotted appropriately. Do you still have your college packet with your stats and essays and stuff together?"

"Yeah. I think the folder is in the top drawer of my desk." I pointed with my chin. Dad pulled the drawer open and found the orange folder while I heaved to my feet. Wolf growled as my injured ankle protested under my full weight.

"How's the foot?"

"Maybe a bit more injured than I thought before I stood on it." I wiggled it around, and it gave without issue. It was probably just stiff from being propped up and wrapped all night. My toes wiggled into the fluffy carpet. "It'll be all right. It's mostly healed."

"It was courageous of you to play with it hurt that bad yesterday. I'm not pleased you're hurt, but I am proud that you still led your team."

"Thanks. It wouldn't be so bad, but I kept retearing it after it was wrapped."

Dad's brows wrinkled. "Let me know if it's still hurting this evening. We'll have it looked at."

"All right. I'm heading to the shower before I look over my bank statements to make doubly sure everything is in order for this afternoon."

"Good idea. Only a few hours until Tishcohan gives his verdict on the first challenge, and you present for the second. We'll be there supporting you."

Excited unease slithered down my backbone.

****

That afternoon, a collection of us from all three packs gathered again behind the cabin at Sam's house. Tishcohan perched on a stump near the large fire pit and waited for the rest of us to gather. People trickled in—members from all the packs in the area, plus each of the suitors as they, too, joined in. Sam nodded to me as he passed to stand near Tishcohan. Max wore a dark expression, while Greyson and Tate were blank slates. Donovan looked confident and composed, but not arrogant. Anxiety churned in my gut.

Wolf paced inside, antsy and nervous now that we were all gathered, and the pronouncement was about to be made. My heart lurched against my ribs as Sarah rounded the corner of the cabin with Megan, Rachel, and my sister flanking her—for moral support?

"Thank you all for coming. I won't keep people waiting, as I'm sure everyone is anxious to hear who has won the first round of *Lacessere*." Tishcohan pulled to his feet using his cane as leverage. Sam stood behind him, ready to help if needed. "The five of you have presented admirably, some better than others. We shall go in the order of presentation. Max, you cannot rely too heavily on your heritage. It is a fine, strong heritage, but you must show me what is inside *you*."

Max's face tinged red, and his eyes slit, but he said nothing.

Tishcohan continued, "Greyson, Tate, I am both fascinated and intrigued by the added abilities your twinship seems to have given you. The two of you will make a fine pair as an Alpha and Beta with this kind of communication, but it did not show me how you can function independently of the other."

The twins remained impassive.

"Donovan, you have surpassed the others in your strategy. You will keep your pack safe."

My heart fell somewhere down around my ankles as Wolf whined, pawing at my insides. Tishcohan paused, hope lighting Donovan's features. I didn't dare look at Sarah. My jaw clenched as I forced my hands to keep still at my sides. Tishcohan nodded to Donovan, then turned to me. My heart beat loud enough for those near me to pick up its unsteady rhythm.

"Cade. While Donovan seems to surpass you in strategy, it is you who *showed* me *how* you lead. I saw your pack—human though they were—how they followed you, supported you, obeyed you. You encouraged them, you knew their strengths and let them use them. You did not stifle this, nor did you take glory for yourself. You put the needs of the pack above yourself. It is for this reason that I pronounce Cade Rivers the winner of the first *Lacessere* challenge."

Air *whooshed* from my lungs as relief weakened my knees.

"Thank you," I managed. I glanced at Sarah. Her celery-green eyes dilated just slightly as her nostrils flared. Her shoulders sagged. I was one up. I just had to win one more challenge, and I'd be declared the victor. Then I'd belong to Sarah just like she'd belong to me. It could happen this afternoon. Wolf jerked inside. Applause circled the gathered wolves as Tishcohan settled himself once more on the stump.

"We will now continue with the second *Lacessere* challenge—monetary sense. It will likely fall to the mate of the Alpha to regulate any pack funds that may accrue and will fall to their discretion how to spend them when the Alpha has other things to tend to. It would be foolish to put someone in charge of such things if he cannot do it wisely. We shall go in the same order."

I groaned inwardly and forced myself not to fidget. I was last. I wasn't sure I could gracefully stand the suspense of watching all the others go first. Although, it did give me the opportunity to watch them, and see how they presented themselves, and take note of Tishcohan's reactions.

"Max. You may come forward." Tishcohan motioned for Max to come up to the stump. A chilly breeze tinged with hints of spring moved silently around the wolves gathered. I caught traces of the forest I knew so well and tried to focus on keeping those scents close. Not on the way my heart refused to go back to its normal pace.

Max produced a folded piece of paper from his jacket pocket, unfolded it, and handed it to the old wolf.

I wasn't really sure what else we could present to Tishcohan aside from something like a bank statement. We were still young, and most of us hadn't yet had the need to handle more than gas money and going out with our friends. I'd brainstormed it with my parents, and they'd agreed that bank statements, or something similar, seemed the only logical thing to show. I gritted my teeth, thinking that Donovan probably had the most experience, even if only because he was one year older and had lived away from his parents while he attended his first year of college. He'd had more opportunity to flex his monetary muscles than the rest of us.

I was confident that I probably had the healthiest bank account—because a stupid stunt Sam and I had filmed when we were barely old enough to shift went viral. Our parents nearly murdered us, but ad money poured in. We'd both let it sit in our accounts and accrue. Neither of us had made any big purchases aside from a vehicle until Sam and Megan decided to add on to the cabin—enlarging the kitchen for Megan and Rachel's baking business and putting an actual bedroom and master bathroom on. I worried the inside of my lip as Wolf paced, wondering what the others had done or what they were going to show.

"This is all your access to pack funds?" Tishcohan raised an eyebrow.

"Yes," Max said proudly. Wolf pulled his lips back.

"Your parents have given you full access. Recently, it would seem. They must trust you implicitly," the old man said, his tone indecipherable.

Donovan's finger twitched in my peripheral.

"I have all the access." Max's voice held all the swagger he'd displayed at the diner that first day he'd come into town. My skin crawled.

"Have you contributed? Used the funds for anything?"

"Uh," Max stuttered as his cheeks flushed. "I use it when my dad tells me to go get stuff for pack gatherings."

Tate snickered, and Donovan's lips twitched. He hadn't come out and said it, but reading between the lines, Max only had access for his glorified errand runs. Max glared at us, sparks nearly shooting out his nostrils.

Tishcohan's face gave nothing away. "Thank you. Greyson?"

Max shuffled back to the clump of us as Greyson and Tate moved together to stand before Tishcohan.

They handed him a paper as well. Tishcohan's eyebrows rose as he scanned the document. "This is your joint account?" Was that a touch of surprise in his voice?

"Yes," they answered in unison. Wolf shivered. Their twin-ness was almost unsettling sometimes.

"How do you differentiate who has spent what on this statement?"

The boys shrugged. "We spend it. We do not track who uses it for what. But it's only the two of us," Greyson said. Tate nodded.

"Just us," Tate echoed.

"I see. And what do you do to earn this, or is this pack dispensed?"

"We have a yard business," Tate said.

"We mow lawns and do pool upkeep in the summer," Greyson added.

Tishcohan looked at the paper once more, then passed it back to Greyson. "Thank you. Donovan. You are next."

Donovan nodded and grabbed his backpack from near his feet. Taking a laptop out, he flipped it open and pulled up a chart. I was close enough to the side that if I squinted, I could see the graph.

"These are projections. I'm studying right now about investments and the market and how to make informed, wise decisions. Admittedly, I made a few foolish mistakes with money when I was younger, but I have learned from those and am doing everything I can to rectify that." Donovan pointed to the bottom of the screen. I was too far away to read the fine print, but judging by the way Tishcohan's eyebrows and lips were moving, he was both amused and horrified at what he saw. Perhaps the mistake was so grievous that Donovan would be disqualified on the spot.

I could only hope.

Because Donovan was stiff competition. He had more experience than me. And he was honestly a nice guy. I wanted to detest him for it, but he had earned my grudging respect instead. Wolf gnashed as anxiety burbled in my gut.

I risked a glance at Sarah. She was watching the computer screen, her lip tucked between her teeth and a concerned look in her eyes.

It didn't bode well if she was worried, too.

"Thank you," Tishcohan said at last. Donovan closed his laptop. Then it was my turn.

That burbling of anxiety suddenly exploded.

You've got this, echoed in my head. I stopped just short of jerking in surprise. Sam had just used our Alpha/Beta link. It was considered rude to use the link when in our skin, but he must have seen the worry on my face. Wolf soothed some under our current Alpha's words, and I tried to erase the tension from my forehead.

I got my own laptop out and brought it to Tishcohan.

Pulling up my bank statements, I showed him my current balance. His eyebrows had raised with the other documents, but they fairly flew up and buried themselves at his gray hairline.

"This is yours? Not the pack's account?"

I swallowed. "No, sir. It's mine. Here. This is the very beginning." I showed him the first deposits, smaller but then growing in size as our video attracted more and more attention. Finally, when I had scrolled up to the final balance number again, the number was sizeable.

"And what have you done by way of your purchases?"

"I did buy a car. I traded it for a truck not long ago. But otherwise, aside from a few small purchases here or there, it's all been saved to be used for college, or if there happens to be a bigger need that comes up."

"You have saved considerably," Tishcohan said. Hope lit in my chest. I wanted to look at Sarah, but I kept my gaze carefully trained on the old man.

"And how did he make so much money?" Greyson grumbled. A curl of unease fluttered in my middle. It wasn't the brightest of ideas that Sam and I had. It actually fringed on being punishable by pack law.

Tishcohan looked at me. "That is a valid question. How did you make so much money?"

I cleared my throat. "A video I helped make went viral several years ago. This is ad money."

Tishcohan shook his head, his gray braids sliding on his shoulders with the movement. "I do not understand all of these new things. In my day, a man did years of hard work to earn these kinds of numbers." He sighed heavily. "But the old ways are changing. The packs need new leadership and people who understand these new ways." Tishcohan looked up into my eyes, studying me. I held my breath. He was close. So close to declaring me the victor. Wolf thrashed, anxious, hopeful, desperate.

Tishcohan opened his mouth, still looking me in the eye. He gave me a slight nod of deference, and hope broke loose inside my chest. This was it. I willed my hands to stop shaking. "The winner of the *Lacessere*—"

"Wait!" Max shouted. Wolf growled, and the noise echoed in my chest for everyone gathered to hear. "Wait," he said again with a calculating gleam in his eye. "What video went viral? How do we know this isn't just some ploy—that you haven't had pack funds transferred into an account to make it look like it was something you earned? That this whole Beta scheme wasn't something you and your friend concocted? I don't believe you."

Chapter 35

Sarah

A wicked snarl ripped across the clearing as Sam bared his teeth, human still but elongating as his eyes dilated dangerously large. Angry noises rushed around the clearing as other wolves from the Wolfe and Kypson packs took offense. My own wolf begged for release so I could put Max in his place once and for all.

"It is only out of respect for the elder present here that I allow you to stay on Wolfe lands. Be careful who you insult, whelp. You do not have your pack here now. It is only you. On *my* land. With *my* allies." Sam growled the words and stalked a few menacing steps toward Max.

Max's eyes grew large, and the stench of his fear was acrid against the freshness of the forest. My heart thundered, both in rage and in anguish. Tishcohan had been about to declare Cade the victor—my mate. I was sure of it. But judging by the thoughtful look on the weathered face, I wasn't sure that was going to be the case now. I wanted to howl and thrash in frustration, but I kept my mask firmly in place. My fingers clenched into fists so hard, they left crescent marks on my palms.

"Your objection is untimely and ill phrased," Tishcohan said with a frown. "But to set all parties at ease, please show us the video. Then there will be no doubt."

A cold sweat broke out on my forehead. Not because I didn't believe Cade, but because I'd *seen* the video. Cade had shown it to me some time ago, and honestly, I'd fallen a little bit in love with him when he'd shown me his cocky twelve-year-old recorded self. While their stunt was impressive and hilarious, it was also a stupid thing for them to have done. With a small degree of horror, I met Cade's eyes, then Sam's. Dad's body tensed beside me at the general undercurrent of dread that saturated the wolves around us.

Sam's mouth tightened into a hard line. Megan clasped her hands around his arm. A general wave of unease slithered around the gathered wolves. It was my understanding that everyone in the Wolfe pack knew about the video, but that it had happened so long ago that it was just a brief flash of memory.

Max, Greyson, Tate, and Donovan all came forward at Tishcohan's nod. They gathered around the stump where the old man sat and stared at the computer screen.

Cade swallowed, and I think his dad was the one that gusted a sigh as Cade connected to Sam's Wi-Fi, pulled up a web browser, and typed a few words. With a final glance at me that had his heart in his eyes, he clicked *play*.

Silence reigned the clearing as Tishcohan watched young human Sam and young wolf Cade play around, doing stunts, and obviously being werewolves, if one knew what to look for.

"That comes awfully close to breaking wolf law." Donovan breathed the words, mostly to himself as the video ended.

Tishcohan shut the laptop and sat still, a concerned, pensive expression on his lined face, the folds of his forehead wrinkling deeply. For long, intolerable moments, the silence stretched on.

Tears burned the backs of my eyes, and my heart alternated between galloping in my chest and coming to a dead stop as Wolf thrashed, and my anxiety nearly cracked my façade I held to like a lifeline.

"I am afraid I must agree. While you have shown remarkable fortitude in keeping this money you have earned, Cade, it seems ill-gotten. This does come too close to revealing the existence of werewolves. For this reason, I must choose Donovan Hazelton the victor of the second *Lacessere* challenge."

Growls and a few curses spun among the wolves at Tishcohan's pronouncement as my heart cracked down the middle.

Sam cursed, and Bowen's growl was audible as Cade's eyes slid shut and his head bowed. He wouldn't look at me. But Max did. His eyes glowed triumphant with his unexpected victory. He still likely wouldn't get me—but Cade might not now either. It couldn't have gone better if he'd planned it. I didn't think he'd known about the video beforehand, but if he had, so help me, I'd make sure he paid for it one way or the other. At least he stood very little chance of winning since Donovan had won the second *Lacessere*.

Bile rose in my throat, and I thought I might be sick. Without any of the niceties I should have given, I turned on my heel, and as soon as I was at the front of the house without prying eyes, I stripped, shifted, scooped my clothes into my mouth, and ran for all I was worth. Tears streamed from my wolf's eyes into my white fur as anger and despair mixed into a giant ball of misery in my chest.

One more. There was one more challenge. If Cade could win, then it would be fine. But it galled me to no end that everything I'd wanted had been ripped away a second time from me. Twice, Cade had been within my reach. And twice, he'd been snatched away by some cruel twist of fate.

Fate's other name was Max.

Chapter 36

Cade

I tried not to be an absolute bear the rest of the weekend, but by Monday, I was still feeling pretty morose and melancholy. Excitement in the halls was still high from the win at state. The guys all paused for fist bumps or more congratulations when we ran into each other. My cheeks ached from all the forced smiling I'd done, and my tongue felt thick in my mouth. I was still hugely disappointed by the weekend's *Lacessere* events. Had Max not opened his big, fat mouth, I'd be bound to Sarah right now.

As lunchtime approached, I perked up some, realizing that as the basketball season was over, we'd all be filtering back to different tables in the lunchroom. That meant I'd be at a table with Sarah.

Sure enough, she was already there, watching for me. Her green eyes lit when she saw me coming with my tray. A smile ghosted at the corners of her lips as she scooted over closer to Raven, making room for me. I squeezed my sister's shoulder on the way to my seat. She flashed me a smile. But not as big as the one Sarah gave me as I slid onto the bench next to her. Our legs touched like they had at the roller rink, and my blood pressure immediately spiked.

"Hey, Alpha Girl," I whispered unevenly.

"Hey, Wolf Dude," she whispered back. Her hand

found my knee under the table, and I covered her hand with mine.

"You all going to eat or just stare at each other for lunch?" Rachel said, her eyes laughing at us from across the table.

I was good with staring.

Sarah's belly rumbled. "I should probably eat," she quipped as she turned her attention to the sandwich in front of her. I glanced at the tacos on my tray but quickly forgot all about them as Sarah dragged her hand up from my knee along the top of my leg before picking up her food.

I took a long drink from my water bottle, trying to will my heart to slow back down. I'm fairly certain there was a sudden influx of pheromones at the table, but everyone was polite enough not to say anything. I considered forgiving Raven and Bowen for all the pheromones they brought with them everywhere they went. It was easier to ignore the chemicals my other paired-off friends released. It was an involuntary action when Sarah's fingers sparked a sudden wave of lust. I cleared my throat and tried to focus on the conversation.

Oddly, there were none of our human friends at the table today. I didn't know if maybe a club had a trip or people were out sick. But it was just us wolves.

"I think we need a girls' night," Rachel was saying.

"I've been baking like a mad woman. Someone needs to come eat some of it," Megan said with a rueful smile.

"You can save the double fudge chocolate chunk ones. I'll eat all of those," Sam said. His eyes twinkled at his wife, and my stomach tightened. I took a bite of my taco and tried not to think about Sarah's leg still pressed against mine.

"You guys want to come over to my place while the girls do their thing?" Kyp offered. "Mom works nights this week, so it'd just be us. Rich and Lucy have both moved out. No one else needs the house right now." Kyp had inherited a huge house from Victor, and he used it like a halfway house for any pack members who needed it. I admired him for it.

"Sure," I said around my mouth of lunch. I could use the distraction before the last *Lacessere* challenge. Tonight, I had the meeting with the scout. Wolf rubbed his head against me. If I didn't win the *Lacessere*, did I want to be that close to Sarah's pack? Could I be that close to Sarah if she belonged to someone else? If they offered me a scholarship, it would be stupid to turn it down... Would it be worth it to pay thousands more not to have my heart ripped out every day if Sarah married someone else?

The mere thought of someone else touching Sarah, kissing her, taking her clothes off... Wolf gnashed inside me, and I shook my head.

"Cade, are you okay?" Sarah asked. She nudged me with her shoulder, sending little ripples of pleasure through me to mix with the murky feelings already brewing.

I shook my head again, trying to clear it. "Sorry. I'm fine." It was a lie, and we both knew it.

"I know," she whispered. For just a second, I heard the raw pain behind her words. I wanted to hold her—tell her I'd never leave unless they dragged me from her. But we were in the middle of the lunchroom.

"What day do we want to hang out? Tonight?"

Megan was saying.

"Cade's got a meeting with the scout tonight," Sam said, satisfaction in his voice.

"Oh my gosh, I forgot that's tonight!" Rachel squealed in excitement for me. I grinned, her enthusiasm smoothing some of my fears. Raven reached around Sarah and patted my shoulder. I smiled at her. Pride shone in her eyes. It was nice that, in most ways, I was still her older brother, who basically hung the moon and stars.

"We should plan for Thursday night," Bowen said quietly. He was right. We all knew Thursday was the start of the last of the *Lacessere* challenges. My tiny semblance of peace fled.

"Tuesday," I said. "Let's meet Tuesday." The words felt raw as they scraped my throat on the way out. Tonight, I needed to focus on basketball and that possible future. But tomorrow, I'd focus on the other possible future.

Plans for girls' night commenced. Sarah leaned close, her wild honey and citrus scent wrapping around me like I wanted her arms to. "You can do this," she whispered close enough her lips brushed my ear. Her tongue flicked my earlobe, and I had to clench my teeth as my hands gripped the underside of the table to keep from groaning out loud. Tendons stood out on my forearms as my muscles bulged with tension.

Sarah leaned back and raised an eyebrow. She glanced down at my straining muscles as Wolf tried to erupt into fur in his excitement.

Sexy, she mouthed.

This girl was going to be the death of me, one way or the other.

Chapter 37

Sarah

Girls' night was a welcome relief from Tishcohan and my house. I genuinely liked the old man, but I was still bitter that he had handed the second *Lacessere* victory to Donovan. I understood his reasoning, but my heart only wanted one outcome. And Donovan, perfect as he seemed, wasn't it.

I knocked on the door of Megan's cabin, and she opened, her eyes happy.

"Sarah, come in. Rachel has nail polish. I've got dinner in the slow cooker and enough cookies to sustain a small third-world country."

I grinned and entered, the mouth-watering scent of seasoned pork roast and vegetables swirling around, mixing with the yeasty smell of fresh bread Rachel had probably baked. Sugary sweetness wafted from the boxes of treats stacked on an extra table that I knew must hold several varieties of cookies. Wolf rumbled in approval.

"It all smells delicious," I said, inhaling appreciatively.

"Hey, Sarah!" Rachel called as she grabbed a pitcher of tea from the fridge. She sniffed it. "Ooh, Meg, is this that new tea you were telling me about the other day?"

"Yes. It's this amazing peach blend. I stirred it with

a sprig of fresh lavender right after I brewed it, and it gave it this little extra kick that is just fabulous. Sarah, can I get you a glass?"

"Please. I've learned to just go with anything you make."

"Ah, you're sweet. Trust me. You wouldn't have wanted to try some of our earliest experiments. Rachel, do you remember those German apple pancakes we tried to make?" Rachel laughed as she handed Megan a glass. I shrugged out of my jacket, hung it on the hook on the wall, and put my purse beneath it on the floor.

"They were the most disgusting tough, rubbery blobs. You could have used them for frisbees," Rachel quipped.

"What happened? I've never eaten anything of yours that wasn't delicious," I said.

"Rachel was mixing part of the recipe up while I mixed the other part. We were supposed to each be making half the recipe, then we were going to combine them into the final product. We miscommunicated who was mixing what. We ended up with double some ingredients and not enough of others. It was a disaster." Megan laughed.

I smiled, my mood lightening already. I took a sip of the tea, and flavor exploded across my tongue. "Wow. This is amazing."

Meg beamed. "So, not to get all heavy, but how are you doing, Sarah?"

Megan always cut right to the chase of things. It was nice to have someone who came right out and said something, rather than beating around the bush, concerned about my Beta status.

"I mean, we can wait for Raven if you want. I just

214

wasn't sure how comfortable you'd be talking about her brother. She'll be here in about a half an hour. She had a few things she had to do first," Meg said.

I set the glass on an end table and sank down onto the couch. Running my hands over my face, I collected my thoughts. Wolf nudged me. It would be good to have someone to vent my frustrations—my fears—to.

"Honestly, I'm pretty disgusted right now. Cade has been mine twice. And either a stupid mistake or a stupid werewolf with a chip on his shoulder the size of the greater Atlantic has ruined it. The first time was my fault. I kissed him when I shouldn't have. That's what got me into this whole mess. I only claimed *Lacessere* to keep Max from ripping out Cade's throat. But after this weekend—" I growled in disgust.

"Cade is still yours. He's going to be yours even if someone else wins," Rachel said sadly as she sat down on the other side. Megan perched on a love seat opposite us.

"Which is another problem in and of itself." I sighed. "I know we're not true mates, but I think we've started forming a mate bond—which shouldn't happen until after we're literally mated." Wolf squirmed as color flooded my face. "And now I'm stuck with whoever wins the *Lacessere*. There is literally nothing I can do about it." I buried my face in my hands, frustration trying to leak out through my eyes.

"I don't know. I mean, Kyp and I are Claimed, but we are waiting until the actual human wedding for the real mating part, but I have every belief that we've already got a mate bond," Rachel said with a shrug.

Ice lanced through my heart. What if I did have the beginnings of a mate bond with Cade? Could that change the outcome of the *Lacessere*? I wasn't aware of anything that trumped *Lacessere* rules, but if anything could, it would be a mate bond. Those sorts of things were taken to the extreme in the wolf world.

It couldn't hurt to ask Tishcohan. If there was any way I could be with Cade, I'd move heaven and earth to do it.

Chapter 38

Cade

"The fights are paired fighting," Kyp said as he brought a few boxes of pizzas to the table the delivery guy had just dropped off. "You need to pick your second."

I glanced at Sam. Sam and I had been fighting partners for as long as we could remember.

"Sam? I've always been your second," I said.

Sam nodded seriously, his blue eyes intense. "Absolutely. And if you want me, I'm there, one hundred percent." He chewed the inside of his cheek and Wolf wiggled in unease.

"But?" I hedged. Kyp paused by the counter.

"But I might not be the best fighter you can choose from." Sam glanced to Bowen and Kyp. Both wore a surprised expression at Sam's words. "No one wants you to win more than I do," Sam said.

"I'm not sure about that. I'm married to his sister. I need Cade to get the girl for purely selfish reasons," Bowen quipped, his words teasing but his eyes serious. Wolf puffed his chest.

"We *all* want Cade to win. Any of us would be honored to stand as your second," Kyp said.

I glanced at them—Sam, Bowen, and Kyp. My closest friends, my brothers. Wolf acknowledged their support, reveling in it.

"Though I hate to say it, I think you would be better prepared if Bowen or Kyp were your second." Sam turned to the brothers. "Both of you have more experience fighting like this than I do—fighting two on two, specifically. We don't know who the other Betas are choosing as their seconds either. Most likely family members from their own packs—who we've never seen."

Kyp nodded, agreeing with Sam's assessment before turning to me. "And only Sarah, Austin, and Tishcohan are allowed to watch the fights until the very last one that will mark the winner of the whole *Lacessere*."

"Wouldn't want anyone to have an unfair advantage, observing fighting techniques, now would we?" I groaned. Sam grunted.

Kyp smirked and opened a pizza box before speaking again. "Cade, you're fast. What skills do you need to round out your own?"

I thought for a minute. I was fast, it was true. I wasn't a wimp, but if it came down to muscle on muscle, an older, more seasoned wolf could outmatch me. Like had almost happened on the football field. If Sam hadn't come when he had, Sarah and I might have been goners. I quelled a shudder at the thought. In an enclosed space where we'd be fighting, my speed would only take me so far. I couldn't run, hide, and then ambush, which was what wolf speed like mine was best for.

"I need brute strength."

All eyes swung to Bowen. His wolf was half the size of an ox, and he was stout as one, too.

He quirked one side of his lips. "Brute strength

I've got." He cracked his knuckles, his impressive biceps flexing and driving home his point.

"Bowen, will you stand with me?" I felt the need to ask him formally.

"To the death."

"Let's hope it doesn't come to that," Sam quipped. "Also, I'm starving."

"Plates are here," Kyp said as he put a stack of green plates on the counter.

We gorged on pizza and played a few rounds of some race-car video game that Kyp beat everyone at, surprising all of us—Kyp included.

"You want to go do some practice rounds?" Bowen asked once we'd digested some.

"Definitely. Sam, Kyp, you up for some practice, too?" I asked.

They nodded. It was time to hone those skills that were going to win my fights and win me my girl.

Chapter 39

Sarah

Bouncing on the balls of my feet to calm my nerves, I counted to three and begged Wolf to settle. My heart was jumping around like a jackhammer. I was going to talk to Tishcohan while I offered him some of the cookies Megan had sent home with me. Girls' night had done wonders to boost my spirits, but now I was all keyed up again at the thought of approaching the ancient Lenape to all but beg him to break the *Lacessere* in lieu of the mate bond I thought I was forging with Cade.

Gripping the plate with both hands, I took a quick breath and went down the hallway to the living room. Tishcohan was nestled in an armchair, a book in his hands. His weathered face wrinkled more as he smiled at my entry.

"Ah, you come bearing gifts, little she-wolf. This is much appreciated."

"Good. Megan—Sam's mate—made them. I thought you might like an evening snack," I offered.

"They look tempting. Sit little one, tell me what troubles you."

I wasn't going to get another opening like that. I sat as Tishcohan selected a praline cookie with caramel and toffee bits. I hoped he didn't have dentures. He'd never get the sticky, sweet deliciousness out of his teeth without taking teeth out of his mouth if he did. He chewed and grunted appreciatively, and I was relieved when his teeth all stayed where they were supposed to.

"Tishcohan," I started, wanting to choose just the right words. "Has...has there ever been a *Lacessere* that has been broken?"

"Broken?" He raised an eyebrow. "Broken how?"

"Are there any wolf laws that trump a *Lacessere*?"

His wide lips pursed, sending more wrinkles around them. "No. *Lacessere* is one of the most sacred institutions of the werewolf."

"Aren't mate bonds sacred, too?" I whispered.

"A true mate bond, yes. But a mate bond cannot be completed unless the couple...couples." He looked up sharply. "You have not done this, have you?"

My cheeks burned. "No," I answered quickly. "But I think I may be forming a mate bond." I swallowed, Wolf panting, waiting for his response.

His face gentled. "You cannot feel a mate bond until you are fully Claimed and mated. Fear not, little she-wolf. The winner of the *Lacessere* will take the place of he who holds your affections. You will forge a bond with the one you marry."

"Then nothing can be done?" I whispered. Anguish clogged my airways, and black dots spun at the edges of my vision.

"I am afraid not. *Lacessere* is final and binding. It may hurt now, but your feelings will fade once the Claiming ceremony is fulfilled."

"I see." I strangled over the word. "Thank you."

I couldn't wait for his reply but nearly sprinted from the room, up the stairs, and to my room. Shutting the door behind me, I collapsed, sliding down its wooden expanse. I was numb. Too numb to cry, too numb to scream the rage and helplessness that burbled inside me. I sat, huddled, my arms wrapped around my knees.

Cade *had* to win. I couldn't forge another bond like this. It might kill me. I didn't think I could withstand the pressure of having Cade ripped from me and replaced with someone else, no matter how noble or good he was, assuming Donovan won. It didn't matter. I was in love with Cade. I didn't want anyone besides Cade. I never would.

****

Wednesday afternoon after school, I came straight home. Today was the first day of the last *Lacessere* challenge. The fight.

"Dad, I'm home," I called.

"Hi, Sarah. How was your day?" Dad asked like he did every day as he came into the kitchen. He opened his arms wide, and I went into them. He knew how anxious I was about the coming fights. The stress of the *Lacessere* was about to tear me in two.

"School was fine. Did the other wolves get into town?" I mumbled against his chest. He ran a fatherly hand over my hair and plunked a kiss on the top of my head.

"They did. Max's older brother and Donovan's cousin."

"And?"

"I couldn't get a read on Max's brother—but he has the nickname Beefy Brutus for a reason."

I winced. "Is he as big as all that?" Did Cade stand any chance at all?

"He's not lacking in the muscular department." He

sighed as I pulled away to get a glass of water.

"And Donovan's cousin?" I swallowed the lukewarm tap water, needing something wet on my parched throat.

"Angus. He was raised in the Hazelton pack, too. He'll know strategy as well as Donovan."

"Who did the twins pick?" My eyes slid closed as I pinched the bridge of my nose.

"Each other." My father's tone implied his confusion and bewilderment.

"Each other?" I parroted. "They know that if they progress, only one of them will fight in the final round? How are they going to do that if they both want me? Or at least my bloodlines?" Bitterness seeped into my words.

Dad held up his hands. "I have no idea. But Tishcohan could find no rules against it, so they are each other's firsts—seconds—whatever." Dad shrugged.

"Is Tishcohan already wherever it is he decided the fights would be held?" I hadn't heard him since I'd come in, and my delicate wolf ears should have heard him moving by now.

"He is. Sam came down earlier to take him."

"He must have left school early, then. Hope he doesn't get in trouble for that."

"He cares about you. He wanted to make sure everything is just how it should be." Dad sighed. "We're all rooting for Cade, you know. Maybe not Tishcohan specifically, but we all want you to be happy and want the best candidate to win. For everyone's benefit."

I scrubbed a hand down my face. On paper,

Donovan was the best candidate. He was the full package. Even tied up with a pretty bow considering he was good looking to boot. But I felt nothing romantic for him. He sparked nothing aside from a polite interest in him as a friend. Much like I felt about Sam or Kyp or Bowen.

But Cade.

I got worked up at the barest thought of him. My soul sang for him. Wolf howled inside. My blood ignited with him. I felt complete when I was with him.

"We should go," I said suddenly, trying to stop the onslaught of feelings before I was buried under their avalanche.

Dad nodded and grabbed his keys off the hook by the door. "All right. Round one, here we come."

****

The fight ring was set up in a secluded meadow not far off the river. We were far enough away from the Wolfe subdivision that we wouldn't be overheard. Enough space separated us from civilization in the forest that we'd know anyone was coming long before they got to us, and we could melt back into the woods. It was secluded enough that nobody expected any humans to venture up this far.

Max stood with his brother. Beefy Brutus. I realized I had no idea what his real name was, but I didn't suppose it mattered that much. Everything about him was thick. His head, his neck, his shoulders, his arms, torso, legs—even his feet were thick. He and Max had similar facial features, but where Max was wiry and still bore the lean boyishness some sixteen-year-olds carried, his brother had left any trace of boyishness behind long ago. But thick and thin aside, their facial features were remarkably similar—and both arranged in arrogant disdain. Wolf whined. I felt sorry for Greyson and Tate. Beefcake would tear them to shreds without Max having to lift a claw.

Greyson and Tate stood to the other side of the makeshift ring. It was only a few sticks set in the ground with brightly colored ribbons tied around them. They stood, their faces impassive, shoulders nearly touching. Of all the Betas, I felt I understood them the least. Max was immature, young, and arrogant. Donovan was older, more experienced, kind, but firm. Cade…well, Cade was the exception. But Greyson and Tate had this connection I didn't understand. I didn't understand how they wanted me to fit into their dynamic either. It was like they were just in it to win me, but it didn't matter who. Maybe it didn't matter to them. I was surprised to realize that made me feel insulted. It might not matter to them—they might just want my bloodlines mingled into their pack, but it mattered to me. My whole life, my whole Alphaship, would be partly determined by who I Claimed, married, and mated. Shouldn't that matter to them, too?

I shook my head, clearing the unhelpful thoughts. Looking at Beefy Brutus stretching his corded muscles, forearms and biceps rippling, again I was struck by how little it would probably matter. I was dubious that the twins would fare well against the Fieldings.

The Betas and their seconds stepped up to an invisible line that seemed to be drawn in front of Tishcohan. Eyes slit, and low growls echoed in chests.

"This is the first round of the fight. This is a paired event. As soon as one member of the pair surrenders or is downed, the pair is excluded. Nothing is off-limits, but remember that this is not a fight to the death. Once a wolf surrenders, that is the end. Back away. Do not let your animal's bloodlust cloud your humanity." Tishcohan carefully looked at each pair and nodded.

The pairs dipped their heads to each other as Wolf paced inside me. Forcing my clenched hands to my sides, I tucked my fingers inside my fists so I wouldn't tear my nails down to the cuticles with my teeth.

The boys collectively morphed into their wolves. Beefy Brutus stood a foot taller and probably a foot thicker than either Greyson or Tate. Max's wolf was big enough. Both the Fielding wolves were brindled and speckled, their coats a variety of colors. Greyson and Tate were gray. Very dark gray. And identical in fur. The tiny eyebrow scar that separated them wasn't visible in their wolf forms. Tate was on the right. I'd just have to keep track.

The Betas padded to their spots inside the ring and faced each other.

"You may begin!" Tishcohan called loudly.

In a burst of turf, dirt, and fur punctuated by a loud growl, Max and Brutus lunged at Tate, attacking him with a ferocity that startled me. Wolf whined inside, and I wanted to take a step closer to Dad.

Max leaped, lunging on top of Tate and sinking his teeth into the top of his neck while Brutus snapped at Tate's then exposed chest.

Tate went down with a whine and bark of pain almost before Greyson had a chance to attempt dislodging Max.

Max hung on, viciously yanking his head back and forth, whipping poor Tate like a rag doll. Brutus sank his teeth in farther, and Tate stilled.

A short, desperate howl from Greyson stilled the fighters.

"Stop," Tishcohan ordered. It was over. Greyson had surrendered to keep his brother from further injury.

My stomach roiled, and Wolf recoiled from the way Max and Brutus strutted and preened. Greyson nosed Tate, who stood wobbling. They limped together into the woods.

"Max, you are the victor of this round."

My blood iced. Max won the round. With his brother, did any of the other wolves stand a chance of winning?

Cade had won a round. Donovan had won a round. And now Max had won a round. My skin crawled. There would be more challenges if Max won the fights. I didn't think I could bear to have the *Lacessere* stretch on forever. I clenched my jaw. I wasn't sure I had enough honor in me to force myself to Claim Max, either, if it came down to it.

Wolf whined.

Chapter 40

Cade

Thursday night was my fight against Donovan and his cousin Angus. Donovan and Angus who were practically steeped in battle tactics in the womb. I was more nervous than I could ever remember being.

"Chill. Your wolf is giving mine anxiety," Bowen commented dryly with a wry smile.

"Easy for you to say," I grumbled. We were driving together to the designated spot.

"Remember. We've got to be unexpected. That's the only way we're going to win this. You good with what we practiced?" Bowen glanced at me.

I blew a quick breath out. We'd brainstormed with Kyp and Sam and then practiced what we came up with nearly every spare second. "I have to be. I can't lose this, Bowen," I said, willing the desperation to stay out of my voice. Wolf whined and paced.

Bowen shifted uncomfortably. "You know, if we can't win this with our combined strength…I do have—" He swallowed hard. "—another ability."

I blinked, my own anxiety momentarily forgotten. I knew what it must have cost Bowen to offer to use his mind control—the gift his despicable father had unknowingly given him—that part of him that he hated more than anything. That he was willing to use it on my behalf rocked me to my middle. I knew we'd become close. But that was about as close as Bowen could come to laying himself on the line for me aside from literally doing it.

"No. Don't think I don't appreciate the offer. Because I do. I really do. But I won't have us accused of cheating and have this blow up in our faces and start a continental pack war. And I don't want that sitting on your conscience either." I glanced at him. His face relaxed, and his shoulders lost some of their tenseness.

He nodded. "Okay. We'll stick to our attempt at surprise, then."

"I hope it's enough."

"Me, too."

****

Too soon, we stood in the meadow, the colored ribbons fluttering in the slight breeze. Sarah was there. Wolf was acutely aware of her. And of Donovan and his cousin Angus. Both were similar in height and build. They looked to be about the same age—Angus might have been a year or so older. Brown hair, lightly bronzed skin, hazel eyes like Donovan. Keen eyes. Intelligent eyes. I gulped. Wolf paced in agitation inside me.

Tishcohan went over the rules. As pairs, we nodded to each other, and then it was time to shift to our fur. My ankle still gave the slightest twinge as I backed up a step and glanced at Sarah.

Her hands were rigid at her sides, her mask in place.

I'm here, she mouthed. Heat filled me and boosted my confidence. I had to do this. If I didn't win, I'd lose Sarah. And I couldn't do that.

Throwing my arms wide, I let my shift overtake

me. Silky black fur rippled along my arms as my jaw jutted out, sharp canines cutting through my gums as my snout changed shape, immediately picking up new information as scents increased and magnified. Ears pushed through the sides of my head, and my backbone cracked as my tail disengaged. I fell to all fours as my transformation finished. Wiggling out of my gray robe, I paced to Bowen where he was shrugging out of his robe, too.

With one last longing glance at Sarah, I took my place in the ring, my focus lasering in on what I had to do next. I'd only have one chance to do this. I stepped next to Bowen, praying that Donovan and Angus wouldn't rush us at once. I needed two seconds. Two seconds to wheel around and set our plan in motion.

"Fight!" Tishcohan yelled.

Waiting for nothing else, I turned tail, wheeled around, and kicked up dirt as I pivoted and launched toward the outer edge of the ring. My ankle twinged again, but I ignored it. I raced five paces to the end of the ring, turned again, and took in everything in one moment's glance.

Donovan and Angus paused in their rush to greet us, perplexed at my seemingly hasty exit. I took a giant launching step, gathering as much momentum as I could. Angus's eyes widened as I came thundering back toward them.

Bowen howled, shattering the silence of the meadow and drowning out some of Angus's warning bark to Donovan.

With a snarl, Angus reared back, coming up on his back paws. It was perfect. Whether he realized he'd walked right into our plan or not, I would take the opening.

Vaulting off Bowen's broad back, I sailed through the air, landing heavily on top of a surprised Angus. Sinking my teeth into his neck he'd unwittingly exposed when he went up on his hind legs, Wolf relished the feel of flesh and fur in our mouth. I had a good hold. I could easily puncture him if he thrashed, or if I wanted to. I clenched a fraction tighter around his windpipe and grunted as his paw caught a glancing blow in my midsection.

Shaking him lightly, I squeezed my teeth even harder. If I bit down any more, there'd be blood. Unless Donovan miraculously escaped Bowen's advances—and I highly doubted he would—and attacked me from behind, Angus had to eventually surrender. He was a bigger wolf, more experienced, and probably more skilled, but our one advantage of surprise had worked. We'd taken an unconventional move, and it had paid off.

"Do you surrender?" Tishcohan called from the sideline.

Angus snarled, thrashed, and clawed, but there was nothing he could do, and nowhere he could go. If he rolled to either side, I'd cut into his neck. The rest of my body had him well pinned under me.

Donovan yipped angrily somewhere just out of my line of sight. Bowen growled low and dark. Angus thrashed and kicked out again, catching my sore ankle. Wincing, my teeth shuttered against his windpipe. Blood trickled into my mouth.

Angus stilled.

"Do you surrender?" Tishcohan asked again. A furious whine escaped Angus.

Relief, excitement, and hope soared in my chest.

Yipping in triumph, I backed off and let Angus up. Wolf tossed his head back, and we howled into the swirling wind. Finished, I met Sarah's gaze across the field. Her hands were clasped under her chin, her face impassive, though her eyes sparkled.

Chapter 41

Sarah

He did it. Cade did it. He beat the great strategists with a moment of surprise. But now he had to fight Max. Elation and terror warred in my chest as I met his gaze from his spot in the rink.

Donovan and Angus returned to their robes, snatching them up in their mouths and heading to the fringe of forest to shift back in private.

He won, he won, he won, my heart seemed to pound to the rhythm of the words. We were one step closer to being together.

****

Friday night Donovan, Angus, and Greyson and Tate fought. It was a longer battle than when Max and Beefy Brutus had trounced them, but in the end, strategy prevailed in a much kinder way than the brutality of Max and Brutus' assault.

Greyson and Tate were out.

I called Megan later that night, needing someone to listen to me without judgment.

"Hey, Sarah. How are things? Are you allowed to tell me any details?"

"Hey, Meg. I'm not really supposed to. But it's common knowledge—or at least it will be by tomorrow morning, that Greyson and Tate are out."

"And you feel…?"

"Relieved." I scrubbed a hand down my face and pushed my head farther back into my pillow where I was laid out on my bed.

"You sound disappointed about that."

"No. I'm not disappointed, but I feel guilty that I feel so relieved. This whole thing is such a giant mess."

"Wanna come up to the cabin? Or I can come down there?"

I had planned on staying in. My emotions were in tatters, my temper was sharp, and my fuse short. "I'm not sure I'll be very good company," I said.

"I wouldn't be very good company if I were in your position either. That's okay. We'll do a movie if you want—no socializing necessary."

The kindness in her voice was nearly my undoing. Suddenly, I did not want to be alone. I'd spent most of my life alone in one way or another, and right now, I was sick of it.

"Be up in a few minutes? Okay if I come in my pajamas?"

"Absolutely. Sam mentioned he had some stuff he wanted to talk to Rev about. He may go do that this evening. It's not too late yet."

I glanced at the clock. Just past seven o'clock. "Okay. Be there soon."

****

The cabin was in sight by seven thirty, and Wolf relaxed some of her tension as I parked. Gravel made little noise as my fluffy house shoes padded to the front steps. Megan met me at the door.

"Hey," she said as she closed the door behind me.

"Hey back," I said. I rubbed my hands over my arms. It was cooler here than back at my house.

"Tea? Sam just left to go over to Rev's for a while. Rev is a night owl, so they may be there long enough for a movie. Or we can just sit and talk," she offered, glancing at my face.

A rueful smile twisted my lips. "Pretty much, I'm just a mess. And I will be until this is over. And it's going to be over this weekend." I sank into a chair. "I mean, whoever wins the fights will most likely win me. Unless Max wins. Then the *Lacessere* will drag out even longer because there will have to be another challenge." I wanted to bang my head against the table but traced a wood grain with the tip of my finger instead.

"You know, it's okay to just be a girl and feel things. I know you don't like to because it makes you feel weak. But you're a girl. You're put together differently than guys. And that's a good thing. What makes you, *you,* is unique and beautiful. You're made to function differently. When you take over your pack, things will change because *you* are the Alpha. Regardless of who your mate is or who your father is or who anyone else is. You are you. And it's okay to be a girl in a world of male Alphas."

"Are you channeling your inner Grandpa George tonight? Because I'm pretty sure I just got some major wisdom vibes off you." I smiled, her words warming me in a way I hadn't realized I'd missed. I *was* a girl. I'd tried so hard for so long to make sure I was living up to my would-be Alpha duties it was easy to forget that I was made to be different. In a good way.

"Sorry if it came off too strong. I know I sometimes feel like I need permission to feel a certain way. It's crazy but true. In fact, Cade actually gave me a similar permission speech about Sam once." Megan smiled at her memory.

"Yeah?"

"Yeah." She chuckled. "So tell me"—a conspiratorial twinkle lit her eyes—"what is Cade's most attractive feature? You need to just settle back and have girl talk."

I sighed. "I don't think there's a part of Cade I don't find attractive," I confessed. Megan arched an eyebrow. "Shut up," I quipped as we both burst into giggles.

Laughter bubbled up inside me, a weapon against the stress, and before long, I found myself laughing uncontrollably.

"Grandpa always says, 'laughter cures what ails,' " Meg said, wiping her eyes.

I sighed and sat back, lighter but still apprehensive. "It does help. Megan, can I ask you a personal question?" Wolf cringed inside. We weren't used to letting people inside and were even less used to asking others for help regarding personal matters. It had been just me and Dad for as long as I could remember. And there were some things I just didn't want to discuss with my father. The position of Beta separated me from most others, and having friends to share secrets with was still a new phenomenon to me in some ways.

"Of course, you can. Ask away. I'm pretty sure you won't ask anything Rachel hasn't already," Megan said with a smile.

My mind flitted to the coming weekend. Assuming the *Lacessere* didn't go into a fourth challenge, I'd be married to the victor by the end of the weekend. I swallowed. "What's it like?" I rasped. "Being married…the physical stuff?" I ended on a whisper. I'd never missed my mother more—I knew the science of things, but I desperately wished I had my mom to talk to about stuff like this. At least I had a friend now. Back in New York, I'm not sure I would have had anyone to ask something so personal.

Megan's eyes gentled. Not in pity, but sympathy. Wolf sagged inside me. It felt good to trust someone else.

"Well, it's less glamorous than the movies make it out to be. It was pretty awkward in the beginning. Don't get me wrong, it's good. *Really good* in a lot of different ways—not only the physical. But doing it cements you to that other person like you've never imagined anything could. Being with Sam was like literally taking my heart out of my chest and handing it to him. It's a level of vulnerability that I didn't know existed until that moment. Even though it's good, it takes work, trust, and some practice." She winked, and I cringed. "Sam and I were both virgins—and that made it easier for me in a lot of ways. It was more special—*sacred*—because it's just something only the two of us have done together. I wasn't worried that I was doing everything wrong because he didn't have any more experience than I did. Together, we have no other comparisons, no outside expectations, nothing but us. And we trust each other. Completely. I don't think a lot of people consider all the emotional ramifications of having sex with someone. It does stuff to your heart, too."

I nodded, digesting that.

"There's nothing that says you have to do *everything* this weekend, you know. You don't have to

237

do *anything* you don't want to," Meg said quietly. "Even if Cade wins. You don't have to do anything until *you* want to."

"Well, if Cade wins—and he really better, or so help me, I'm going to skin him—I don't think there will be any question of wanting to wait," I confessed, willing my blush to stay at bay. "He gives me that smirky smoldering flirty look, and my insides go crazy." But if someone else won? How could I stand to let anyone else even touch me, let alone be intimate with them? I didn't know how to be intimate—I didn't want to be intimate with anyone besides Cade. And trust? I might someday be able to trust Donovan. But not like I trusted Cade. If Max won...I didn't know what I'd do.

I swallowed as Wolf paced inside me.

Chapter 42

Cade

Saturday was an elimination match.

Bowen and I stood at the sidelines of the ring. It had been moved since the original ring was pretty churned up from the earlier fights.

Wolf stretched within me, ready and eager to have our fight with Max. He'd been a thorn in my side since he arrived in town, and—my own stupidity aside—he was the reason I was having to fight for Sarah at all. He growled at me from his place beside his impressively large brother.

Bowen slit his eyes, glaring at the pair of them. Brutus crossed his arms across his barrel-like chest. Bowen smirked, which seemed to enrage Max. His nostrils flared, and his face pinked. I could smell his irritation as it wafted strongly across the ring.

"You ready?" Bowen nudged me.

"Oh, more than ready." Wolf gnashed inside, pulling his lips back from his teeth.

"You know the rules. You may take your places," Tishcohan instructed.

We shifted quickly, all of us spoiling for a good fight. I could tell by the set of Max's shoulders he was out for blood. That was okay. I'd be happy to return the favor.

"Fight!" Tishcohan yelled.

In a crouch, I sank to spring up, ready to leap into Max and give him what for, while Bowen kept Beefy Brutus occupied.

But things didn't work out that way.

Max rushed me like I expected, but Brutus backed around Max, dancing nimbly out of the way of Bowen's reach, and stormed me from the opposite side.

I pulled up, coiling my muscles for another launch, ready to strike, but just then Brother Beefcake lunged as Max snapped an inch from my face. Lurching to the side, I only kept my chest from Max's incisors, but I wasn't fast enough to escape both Max and Brutus. Max sank teeth into my shoulder as Brutus landed hard across me, his teeth catching my ruff as he was aiming for my neck. I buckled under his weight, my still-tender ankle bending unnaturally under the strain.

I was in trouble. Bad trouble. Blood swelled out of my shoulder as Max exulted in his grip on my flesh. Wincing, I struggled, but it was in vain. I couldn't move.

And then the world spun as a roaring howl broke the night, and Max yelped. Bowen's scent of cedar and brown sugar cascaded over me along with the scent of my own blood as Bowen's head bulled into the front of Max's chest, then came up quick. Bowen gnashed his teeth, catching a full mouth of Max around his upper back, sinking teeth into flesh, and sending Max flailing and barking in pain. Bowen heaved and tossed Max's body like it weighed no more than a house cat.

Max went sailing through the air, landing in a heap of blood and tangled arms and legs, paws sticking out at odd angles.

Brutus yelped in alarm. His weight lifted, and

oxygen flooded my lungs as I watched in a daze as his neck extended above me in his mad dash to get to his brother. Knowing I wouldn't have another chance, wishing it was Max instead of his brother, I sprang from my crumpled crouch. I got a solid mouthful of the underside of Brutus' neck and bit down hard. Blood streamed into my mouth. Wolf relished it, the primal side of us in charge in that moment. I growled, tightening my teeth. Brutus whimpered and thrashed, but the harder he thrashed, the tighter I held, and the deeper my fangs punctured his neck. I growled again, warning him to be still. I refused to let him go, and if he kept wiggling, I was going to nick something he didn't want bleeding.

We struggled for dominance another minute, his brute strength far greater than my own, but my hold was too tight and in too dangerous a spot. Even though I was still half on the ground on my back, I had the upper hand.

"It is finished," Tishcohan said. His voice carried over the thrash and writhing of wolves, blood, and grass. "Cade and Bowen have won the fight."

Max set up a keening howl even as Beefy Brutus staggered away, slumping into the dirt, his head hanging.

I threw back my head to the moon. Every primal instinct of dominance, of power, came rushing over me, carrying my exuberant howl into the twilight sky. Blood trickled down my throat as my baser wolf instincts started to recede, and I shook my head, ready to be rid of the salty, metallic taste.

Knowing I had blood dripping down my shoulder and probably smeared all over my snout, I couldn't help but glance at Sarah. Our gaze connected, and I knew she wanted to howl with me.

One more fight. If I could beat Donovan, Sarah was mine for keeps.

Donovan. Who had always been my stiffest competition.

Chapter 43

Sarah

I woke Sunday morning to a gut churning with emotion. Hope and dread warred with each other, leaving me nauseated in a cold sweat.

Cade or Donovan. I'd Claim and marry one of them by sundown. My stomach tied itself in tighter knots, thinking about what might come after that.

It made me want to puke.

My phone dinged.

—How you doing today?— From Megan.

—Not great.—

—Hang in there. Need anything?—

Maybe a hole to go crawl into, never to reemerge.

—I'm going to run into town and get breakfast to distract myself and kill some time before the last fight.—

—Great idea. Let's all go. The girls.—

I glanced at the clock. Eight o'clock. The fight was set for ten thirty. Plenty of time.

—Meet you at Scrummies in half an hour or so?—

—I'll text Raven and Rachel! See you there!—

****

I was surprised to find I was the second one at *Scrummies*. Raven sat by a booth near the back corner and a large window where early spring sunshine dappled the sidewalk outside.

"Hey, Sarah," Raven said as I slid into the booth opposite her. I swung my purse off my shoulder and plopped it beside me, then wiggled out of my denim jacket.

"Hey. How are you? I haven't seen you in a few days," I replied.

"Yeah. I'm good. I was actually going to drop by and see you this morning, then Megan texted." Raven smiled.

"You were?" I was pleased but surprised.

"Yeah. I mean, without being weird about things, I'd *really* like you to be my sister-in-law," she finished quietly so we wouldn't be overheard.

Wolf chuffed a smile that reached my human features. "I'd really like that, too," I confessed.

"You're good for him, Sarah. And he'd be good for you. He's in love with you. For keeps. He's never been like this about anyone. I think you're it for him," she whispered. Her blue eyes, so much like her brother's, were large and luminous in her pale face.

Emotion rose in my throat. "I think he's it for me, too, whatever comes."

Raven nodded. "It's not over yet."

"No, not yet," I agreed.

Rachel and Megan bustled in right as our waitress was putting a pot of coffee on our table.

"Sorry we're a little late. We ran into each other in the parking lot." Rachel puffed as she slid in next to me and gave my hand a quick squeeze.

We ordered, chatted, ate, and drank way too much coffee. And before I was ready, it was time to go to the meadow.

For the final fight.

****

The last fight was again set on fresh turf in the meadow. The grasses were pristine. The midmorning sunshine glowed cheerily, casting the world in a golden glow while black storm clouds brewed inside me.

All that coffee I'd consumed was a bad idea. My jitters had jitters. At least I felt like I had support this time. Since this was the final fight, everyone was permitted to watch. I wouldn't have to stand feeling like I was alone in the universe while wolves fought over me, bleeding on the ground in front of me as I stared, face impassive, insides writhing. The girls had come with me from *Scrummies* and stood gathered around me like an insulating bubble trying to shield me from the rest of the world. At that moment, I needed their buffering presence desperately. I'd never underestimate my friends' mere presence again.

Just then Cade's truck rolled into the clearing. My heart leaped into my throat as his black hair emerged, his blue gaze cutting across the field and finding mine like I was the only thing worth looking at in the entire world.

"Steady," Dad whispered near my side where he stood opposite the gaggle of girls. "I can hear your heart."

I couldn't help it. Cade made my heart beat hard with a passion, and today, it beat in fear for him. Because if he didn't win today, I would be bound to Donovan Hazelton until the day I died.

Cade held my gaze a few moments longer than was probably entirely appropriate, but I didn't care. I didn't believe what Tishcohan had said either. There was no way what I felt for and with Cade wasn't the beginning of a mate bond.

With a herculean effort, I took a breath and schooled my face, letting my mask drop into place. Sam popped out of the other side of Cade's truck, nodded to me, again to Megan, and then moved to stand to one side where it was clear the rest of the members of the Wolfe pack were gathering. Cade's parents, Rev—who I realized with a sudden start would be marrying me to someone in a few hours—a few other wolves close to my age, and several other adults already clustered around Sam and Cade. More were coming. Cade was well-loved by his pack, even if he wasn't usually their Beta. Today he was, and they were coming out in force to support him.

Glancing at the opposite side of the clearing, I saw others were exiting vehicles and coming dressed in gray robes out of the fold of the woods. Kyp and Bowen, Kyp's mom Jennifer and her fiancé, Jonathan Stone, ten or twelve others from the Kypson pack gathered around them. I was grateful that the girls stayed near me and didn't go to their own respective packs. Today it was good not to feel alone.

A few wolves I didn't know filtered in. Some went to stand behind Max and Beefy Brutus, who still had a bandage wrapped around his neck. It must be pretty bruised or scabby still for him to keep a wrap over it yet. Greyson and Tate had left—they'd been eliminated. There was no hope of them winning. It was their right to stay as Max had elected to, but they'd gone instead. I wished Max and his ilk had, too. Instead, a few more had come to add to the Fielding numbers.

I'm glad the Wolfes and Kypsons stand with us and

far outnumber the Fieldings that have come, Dad said, using our link.

I was thinking the same thing, I said back. Because if it came right down to it, in a fight at least we had greater numbers with our allies present. After fighting battles with Victor and then his son, it would take something pretty drastic to break those alliances.

My heart seized for the second time as Donovan entered from the forest. He wore a dark gray robe and a somber expression. Wolf paced. I locked my fingers straight to keep them from curling into fists. I liked Donovan. I did. He was a gentleman, a great catch, had every possible credential a werewolf girl could want. I just didn't want *him*. Glancing again to Cade, I was only slightly surprised to find a look of respect on Cade's face. Donovan nodded to Cade, who returned the gesture. Several older wolves, Angus among them, stood behind Donovan.

"Ah, we're waiting on one more thing," Dad said, just a hint of a smile in his words. I glanced up at him, squinting slightly in the sunshine. Dad looked down at me and a full smile curled his lips.

Just then a loud, raucous honking burst from the forest road, scattering birds from the trees and even startling a deer across the top of the meadow.

Craning my head, I was shocked, delighted, and so pleasantly surprised that an uncharacteristic giggle escaped my throat. A hulking people mover lumbered up the path, nearly getting stuck in a rut before steaming to an undignified halt. The doors opened, and *my pack* burst through the door to swarm around me, gathered behind me, offering support by their presence.

"We couldn't let you go *Lacessering* and Claiming

247

without us here to witness and support you," Resha whispered as she stepped up behind me next to Rachel. Three faint scars covered her face where she'd been clawed at the end of the last battle. She squeezed my shoulder.

"Thank you," I whispered back, letting my gaze encompass my pack—my home—the reason I was doing all of this—gathered to stand with me. My throat tightened, and for just a minute, I was afraid my face would crack and all the pent-up emotion I'd been stuffing down for weeks would come flooding out. But seeing the faces of my pack family, their encouragement, their presence, I pulled it together, and with a grateful nod and smile to them, I turned back to face the ring—to face my future.

Tishcohan moved to take his place near the top of the ring. I stood opposite him at the bottom where I could see everything—all the gathered packs, all the fight. The ancient Lenape raised his arms. Cade and Donovan came forward.

Cade stuck his hand out to Donovan. I could just make out Donovan's raised eyebrows as he clasped Cade's hand in a sign of mutual respect and solidarity. Max spat to the side. One of his older pack members elbowed him, and he glared back at them.

"Good luck," Donovan said to Cade.

"You, too," Cade said back. I heard the sincerity in both voices. It drew my already knotted-up insides into a tight ball of impossible tangles.

Tishcohan nodded deeply to both boys, approving of their actions. "It is time," he said, his weathered voice having no trouble carrying over the clearing and the eighty or so gathered wolves.

Cade and Donovan began their shifts. One black wolf, and one a dark sable. Evenly matched in height and muscle. Only experience made them incompatible. I forced my hands to my sides, refusing to chew on my fingernails and show just how nervous I was. I glanced at the other Alphas. Dad was intently focused on the pair now taking position in the ring. Sam's brows were drawn in concentration. Kyp's finger moved over his thumb while Bowen stood resolutely with his arms crossed over his chest. Raven held her breath behind me. I reached back and tapped her arm without taking my gaze from the field.

Cade spared one more glance at me.

I'm here, I mouthed. I don't know if he saw or not as his head whipped back to face Donovan, concentration cloaking them both like a second skin.

"Fight!" Tishcohan yelled. Wolf startled within me, somehow still caught unprepared for this moment.

Chapter 44

Cade

Donovan didn't immediately lunge, and I hadn't expected him to. We circled each other, sizing each other up. We seemed fairly evenly matched, but I knew the Hazelton pack's obsession with battle strategy put me at a serious disadvantage. With Bowen's help, I'd been able to surprise them once, but there was only me this time. And my ankle was the slightest bit tender still. It had been reinjured too many times for it to heal completely yet.

We circled for what seemed like ages. At some point, I realized that this was a game of patience. My patience was frazzling. That was probably precisely what Donovan was waiting for. He was waiting for me to make the first move. Wolf growled, displeased with this.

After another five minutes of circling and several grunts and jeers from the gathered crowd, I knew Donovan would literally do this all day. He'd wait me out. My back ankle twitched, already tiring quicker than the rest of me with the constant motion of circling for minutes that each felt like an eternity. I had to make the first move.

Slowly, I began to tighten my circle. About three turns in, Donovan noticed, his eyes slitting the only indication he gave.

Without any further warning, I lunged, my back leg protesting. Raking my front claws across his face, I caught him soundly. He grunted as a line of blood welled over his muzzle but was fast enough that he danced out of range as my teeth snapped together, catching air instead of his neck.

Then the battle started in earnest. We held nothing back. Donovan sprang at me, his teeth locking together with mine, as we gnashed and pawed each other. Claws found flesh, teeth snapped, and blood oozed from several points on each of our bodies.

My flank had two punctures where his teeth had found purchase, and they blazed and throbbed in time with my injured ankle.

A snarl ripped through the air as Donovan tried to ram me. Leaping straight up, I narrowly missed Donovan's snout and deadly canines. My front paws came down hard across his back as my back paws smacked against the ground. Wincing at the impact, I immediately bit down on Donovan's back. Donovan swung around, so I only grazed him, but he knocked me off balance.

I whipped my tail in the air, desperately trying to regain my footing. My mouth shut around his ruff, but it wasn't deep enough. I tore a chunk of fur from his hide as he tossed his head. Howling as his fur came loose, he bucked backward, and my grip loosened.

In slow motion, I tumbled to the earth. Twisting, I scrabbled for purchase but found none. My back slammed into the earth, knocking the wind from me. Terror clawed at me as I stared up at Donovan's chest, his paw splayed to slash across my face, leaving my neck completely exposed for a winning bite.

No!

Sarah. I *had* to win. Because I could not live without Sarah.

With all my strength, I heaved forward. My forehead collided with Donovan's teeth as his paw whapped against the side of my neck instead of my face.

Gritting my teeth against the pain of his incisors burying themselves above my eyebrow, I felt his growl reverberate into my skull. He shook his head, dislodging his teeth and making my eyes jiggle in their sockets. Disengaging, I scampered back a few paces and wheeled to face him again. Blinking, I slung my head, flinging droplets of blood away, trying to keep it from running into my eyes.

With another snarl mixed with a growl, Donovan charged. Preparing to sidestep and catch him in the side, I crouched. My back leg throbbed as I bent at the ankle.

Donovan thundered nearer. Adrenaline kicked my heart up even higher. Donovan sprang on his hind legs. I pivoted, ready to bite, but Donovan changed tactics mid-air. Instead of going after my face like he was aiming for, he lunged to the left, and his paw swiped down my injured flank, claws raking through fur and hide, and pummeling my damaged ankle.

With a yelp of pain, I went down. My leg gave out. In a flash, Donovan was on me. His claws pushed into my exposed belly, and his teeth were clamped around my neck.

No. *No, no, no, no!*

I thrashed, I wiggled, I snarled, I might have even sobbed.

Donovan's grip was a steel trap. His teeth never tightened; his claws didn't puncture. But there was nowhere I could go. Nothing I could do.

Despair gripped me. Wolf whined, the noise wheezing through my lips. I tried to choke the noise off before it became an outright whimper, and I embarrassed myself and my pack.

"Donovan Hazelton has won the *Lacessere*. Rise," Tishcohan said.

My heart cracked right down the middle. Something snapped inside me, and for one wild, ferocious, horrifying moment, darkness rose up and overtook me. Blinded by agonizing anguish, I was only vaguely aware when Donovan's paw and teeth left me. Darkness eked out of me, covering me, strapping me in its torturous pain as on some base level I realized Sarah was gone from me forever. I felt the darkness swarm my heart and rip it from my chest. I didn't need it anymore. I'd never love again.

Chapter 45

Sarah

I stood next to Dad, dumfounded. I couldn't feel. Couldn't think. Couldn't react because my heart was lying in the middle of the ring, belly up, gasping for air like he was dying. Tears pooled in my eyes. Wolf howled inside me as my fingers curled into hard fists. I wanted to run. Become a wolf and run, and run, and run, and never look back.

Donovan cocked his head and stiffly paced back from Cade. They'd both received multiple injuries. Cade writhed noiselessly on the churned grass and dirt. Angus and Sam simultaneously brought gray robes so the wolves could shift back to skin.

Sam knelt beside Cade, whispering something low enough I couldn't pick it up. While my insides wept, I struggled to maintain my impassive façade, falling back on my mask to hide the pain that threatened to rip me asunder. Another moment as Sam covered Cade's fur with the robe, and then his black hair emerged, bowed over in a crouch on the ground.

My ragged heart leaped again—was he more hurt than I thought? Had Donovan jabbed his claws into Cade's soft underbelly? Wolf growled within me, ready to tear out Donovan's throat if he had seriously injured Cade. *Lacessere* or no.

"Donovan Hazelton has won the *Lacessere*,"

Tishcohan said again, driving a spike of misery through my middle. I bit the inside of my cheek to keep from audibly crying out. Pain shattered my insides into a thousand tiny fragments that would never fit back together properly. Cade struggled to his feet, Sam at his side. Tortured blue eyes met mine. Blood and dirt were smeared down the side of his face. His features were ragged, haggard.

Donovan cleared his throat, and my gaze jerked to him.

"No," Donovan said firmly. A collective gasp rose from the gathered packs.

"Donovan, what are you doing?" Angus hissed at his cousin. Donovan shot him a scathing look. Angus's brows drew down low over his eyes, his mouth set in a grim line.

"No," Donovan repeated, meeting my gaze. A spark of hope flamed to life, hot and vibrant against my breastbone. What did he mean, no? Donovan cleared his throat again before continuing. "I see now what Max tried to tell me earlier."

My hope turned to horror as my gaze cut to Max who crossed his arms, eyes slit, and a smug expression covering his features as his chin came up. Dread curdled with terror in the pit of my stomach. Donovan knew. Max told him an embellished tale of what he found when he caught Cade and me, and Donovan was going to expose it before all the packs. I suddenly felt faint and fought not to sway on my feet.

"Max tried to explain things to me, but I didn't understand at the time. I do now." Donovan gave Max a pointed look, then turned toward me. My gaze riveted on his face as he crossed the ring and came to stand in front of me. Wolf paced and frothed with anxiety. Donovan continued loud enough his voice carried to everyone gathered. "Sarah, you are a wonderful girl, and I would very much like to align our two packs. But I also don't want to be the cause of bitterness between the two of us, or between the other packs. It's clear now that your heart is already elsewhere. If it hadn't been for my careless remarks during the second challenge, Cade might already have been declared the winner of the *Lacessere*. I relinquish my rights as victor." He gave me a little bow, and hope surged like wildfire through my limbs, my fingers twitching as my gaze feverishly swung to Tishcohan.

The old man blinked twice, seemingly at a loss. He shrugged his shoulders. "Once rights are relinquished, they cannot be regained. Cade is the victor of the *Lacessere*."

Go now, Wolf demanded.

"Thank you," I said breathlessly to Donovan. I sprinted toward Cade, shifting mid-stride. Where I picked up my human foot to run, my paws hit the ground on the same pace.

Not caring what anyone thought, and knowing I had to make him mine before anyone could naysay or change their minds, I careened wildly into a stunned Cade, knocking him over. My wolf's muzzle closed gently over his human nose. I felt him shift even as I Claimed him. His nose became a snout inside my mouth, and I bit down again, just for good measure. Immediately, Cade wriggled under me, his mouth opening, and closing over my own snout, biting down hard enough I felt it, but not hard enough to hurt. I'd been Claimed back.

Threads of awareness buzzed in my head as a cord seemed to weave itself from Wolf straight to Cade. Emotional ties bound us together, sealing our Claimship.

Alpha Girl? Echoed inside my head as joy burst through me.

I'm here, Wolf Dude! Even my mental voice had happy tears in it.

It was over.

He belonged to me, and I belonged to him.

We were Claimed.

Chapter 46

Cade

I was ushered back to my own house in a daze. Donovan relinquished his rights. I was Claimed. Sarah Claimed me. I Claimed her back. I shook my head, trying to clear the shock and dizziness that persisted.

I was at my house to shower and to get patched up. Because I was a mess of scrapes, bruises, and had drying blood covering half my body. And because Rev would marry us officially in a ceremony before all the gathered packs in a couple of hours. My head was spinning. I was stupid-excited, crazy-sore, and reeling with everything that had happened this morning.

"Cade, snap out of it, buddy," Sam said, chuckling.

"What? Sorry. I might actually be in shock," I confessed. A sheepish grin slid over my face as I rubbed the back of my neck.

"Small wonder why," Mom said as she and Dad bustled in through the front door. They both converged on me, smothering me in hugs. I hugged them back, then winced as tendons and punctures protested the movement.

"Oh, Cade, you're practically eaten alive." Mom gasped. Her nose and eyebrows both wrinkled as she took in the visible scrapes, scratches, and blotches of blood coming through the robe.

"You need help patching anything?" Dad asked.

"I think I'll live. But I do need to wash off."

"Now that you're properly Claimed, I'm going to go call Dad," Sam said with a smile. "He and Mom have been waiting on standby at the airport in Chicago to make sure they didn't come home too early while you still needed to be the Beta. They might be able to make it back for your wedding."

"We'll wait for them," I rasped.

Sam winked, and a fresh wave of incredulity slipped over me. My entire pack had rallied behind me—my own Alpha had practically bent himself over backward to help me. Humbled and grateful, I nodded, incapable of saying anything at that second.

****

Two hours later, I was scrubbed, patched, healing, and only barely limping as I plopped at the kitchen table to have a quick bite to eat before heading out to the communal gathering spot behind Sam's cabin. My belly was trying to tie itself in nervous knots tight enough that I wasn't sure I'd be able to get anything down. I sipped a glass of ice water while Mom fluttered around the kitchen, her hands flapping, her brows drawn together as her dress swished around her legs.

"Mom?" I said, unsure how to even ask what I meant.

She stilled, then turned to face me. "I hoped this would happen. That you'd win the *Lacessere* and Claim Sarah. I want this for you. I know how much you love her. I…it's just going to take some getting used to. I wasn't expecting both you and Raven to leave the nest within the same few months."

"Oh. Mom, I'm sorry." Guilt niggled at me.

"No, Cade. There is nothing for you to be sorry

259

about. This is what your father and I have always wanted for both of our children—that you'd find the wolf you were destined to be with." Mom's light eyes shone with unshed tears even as she smiled.

"And you found her in Sarah," Dad said as he came in from the laundry room into the kitchen. He looped an arm around Mom's shoulders, and they both faced me. "Raven and Bowen are true mates, and you and Sarah have already started forging your mate bond together. Sarah is a fine young woman. As your parents, we couldn't have hoped for a better match."

"It just hasn't left us much room to prepare for having an empty nest so soon," Mom said with a shrug and a small watery smile.

Stiffly, I got up and went to my parents. The three of us shared a hug for long minutes together.

"You guys have always supported me. You've supported me every single step of the way in this—as strange, unexpected, and difficult as it's been. I don't know how to say thank you enough for that."

"You're our son. We love you," Mom said.

"We're always in your corner," Dad added.

Mom sniffed. "But if we don't hurry, you're going to be late for your own wedding." Mom laughed as she swiped under her left eye. "And your Claiming was already adorably rushed. Let's not make Sarah worry about the wedding."

****

As I got out of Dad's car in my freshly pressed suit, my gaze riveted on Rev. He stood by a large tree off to the side with Sam. My best friend's face was lit up with a wide smile. Wolf whined inside.

It wasn't until that moment that I realized I'd be

leaving Rock Falls. Once school was done, Sarah and I would go to New York. Her pack was there. Her life was there. And mine would be, too. I wanted that life with Sarah. More than anything. But a large part of me was suddenly sad to be leaving the life I'd known—my parents, my sister, my friends. I'd be changing pack allegiances. Someday Sarah would be my Alpha. But first, she'd be my mate.

A tingling awareness tickled the back of my neck. I turned, scanning the wolves gathering in the coming twilight.

Cade.

A grin tipped my lips as a hot rush swept over me. *Where are you, Alpha Girl?*

I'm still inside the cabin. But you look hot in your suit, Wolf Dude.

Glad you approve. When do I get to see you?

Soon. I love you.

I love you.

Sam motioned to me then, and I sauntered over to where he stood near Rev.

"Cade, congratulations," Rev said, his chocolaty skin dissolving into a mass of wrinkles. He smiled so hard his dark eyes nearly squinted shut. He pumped my hand and gave me a solid pat on the back.

"Thanks, Rev."

"Do you have any questions about the ceremony? You've officially Claimed each other. This is just the human formality part."

I shrugged. "I have no idea if I have questions or not." I gave a nervous chuckle.

Sam snorted. "You'll stand right over there, staring into Sarah's eyes. You'll repeat what Rev tells you to, and be sure to say, 'I do,' at the end."

"You're loads of help," I quipped.

"That does about sum things up, though," Rev said. "Do you have rings? I assumed you didn't but wanted to check."

"No. I wish I did." I resisted the urge to scuff the toe of my dress shoes in the dirt.

"You'll have time soon enough. I only got mine last week." Sam shrugged and flashed his hand, a simple gold band on his left ring finger. I'd been so preoccupied I hadn't even noticed. I grinned at him. I remembered his wedding well. He'd been so nervous. I could relate to that now.

"If you're okay, Cade, I'm going to go check in on Sarah before things start." Rev smiled again. "I'll see you in a few."

"Are you ready?" Sam asked me quietly as we found ourselves alone at the edge of the forest. I scanned the gathering wolves again. My own pack was gathered. Sarah's pack—soon to be my pack—was there. My sister's pack, even Donovan and Angus were all gathered to witness my marriage to the heir of the Thornehill pack.

I swallowed. "I think so?" My heart thumped erratically inside my chest, anxiety and excitement warring and leaving my blood pumping with an uneven cadence.

Sam smiled. "I'm so happy for you, Cade. I hope you don't have to wait as long to seal the deal as I did with Megan," he teased.

A shocked snort of laughter somersaulted up my throat. "Yeah, well, I don't think Sarah is the waiting type." I really hoped not. I had no desire to wait any longer than it took to get the human formalities over with. I was having a hard time wrapping my head around everything that had happened—and that was going to happen—all the massive changes my life was going to see in the next few hours, even, but I knew every part of me wanted Sarah.

"For your sake, I hope not. Man, one of the hardest things I've ever done."

"I'm going to let that joke slide," I said with a sideways glance at my best friend.

Sam snorted and elbowed me. For a minute, we were kids laughing together again about some stupid joke the other had told, just like we always had.

"Oh!" Sam pulled up suddenly, his gaze searching. "Dad's back."

Even as he said it, I felt the Beta power that had descended onto me recede. Like a sponge soaking up water, it left me dry. Not devoid but lacking the added essence being Beta had given me.

Dominic strode around the edge of the cabin, his gaze zeroing in on us and his face breaking into a huge smile.

"Well done, boys." Dominic whispered the words, but the wind carried them, directed at Sam and me, and my Alpha's assurance and praise wrapped around my heart and settled comfortably.

I had no time to dwell on it more because just then a hush fell over the crowd. Rev emerged, nodded to the crowd, then slowly walked to the stump at the head of the ring that surrounded the fire flickering into the darkening sky. Rev motioned to me.

"That's you," Sam whispered. He squeezed my arm and melted into the crowd as my feet took my body to the designated spot. Wolf's tongue lolled. We were jittery, excited, and slightly terrified.

Rev motioned with his hands, and all the assembled wolves parted into two groups and stood silently, saluting like an honor guard. A lone violin played somewhere in the background, but I didn't look to see who or where because just then Austin Thornehill's blond head poked around the side of the cabin.

And there.

Sarah stood beside him, her arm wrapped around his, dressed in a long white dress covered in simple lace. Tight lace sleeves tapered to her wrists, and a gauzy veil floated behind her on the evening breeze.

My heart both exploded and stopped as time stood still.

Chapter 47

Sarah

Cade's blue gaze locked on mine, a look of awe and adoration covering his features that sent all the girlish bits of me turning into mush. My breath caught as I looked at him. Dressed in a dark suit, crisp white shirt, and a dark tie, he was everything every girl dreamed of marrying. He was the whole package. He was my package. We were Claimed. Tied together until death separated us.

I hardly noticed the honor guard of wolves—all from mixed packs—as we slowly made our way down the makeshift aisle.

"I love you, Sarah," Dad whispered as we drew up next to Cade in front of Rev.

Glancing up at my father's face, I saw his eyes were rimmed in tears but full of joy. Wolf rubbed her head against me.

"Love you, too, Dad," I whispered back. I leaned up on my tiptoes and kissed his cheek. Dad grinned, nodded slightly, then gently took my hand and, with a shuddering breath, put it in Cade's.

"As it should be," Dad whispered once more before he squeezed our joined hands and stepped to the side to stand with Cade's parents.

I didn't hear much of what Rev said. But by the time it was my turn to say my vows, my heart felt full enough to burst.

"I do," Cade's strong voice rang out over the clearing with no hesitation.

"Sarah Thornehill, do you take this man you have Claimed to be your lawfully wedded husband? In sickness and in health, for richer or for poorer, to be your helper and your partner in all things?" Rev asked.

Wolf nodded. "I do."

"You may kiss your bride." There was no mistaking the smile in Rev's voice, even though my gaze hadn't left Cade's.

And Cade did. He smiled down at me, the slightest hint of a devilish smirk in his gaze. He slid his hands around my waist, one trailing up my back.

I'm going to dip you, Alpha Girl.

I was glad he gave me warning. He tipped me backward, his arms never wavering. Leaning back as gracefully as I could, I rested in his embrace, relishing the moment his lips covered mine.

The crowd erupted into howls of joyful celebration.

****

We had a reception right there after the wedding. Somehow, Megan and Rachel had pulled off catering dessert for a hundred—they had snacks, cookies, cupcakes, and a gorgeous three-tiered cake all done in white and silver.

As wonderful as it was, I was glad when it was late enough that we could leave. So many emotions filled me I needed a quiet moment. My heart was bursting with thankfulness, gratitude, and love.

Dad pulled me aside as we were saying our goodbyes. "Sarah, I'm going to stay with Rev the next few nights." He winked at me, and my face flushed.

"That's probably good, Dad," I said.

Dad made an exaggeratedly painful face. "Ah, please. No more!" I giggled as he pulled me into his broad chest. "I love you, Sarah. I'm so proud of you."

"Thanks, Dad. I love you, too." He held me tight for long moments, and I hugged him back. This man who had been my rock for all my life. We slowly pulled apart, and I swear there was a tear threatening at the corner of Dad's eye. He smiled and squeezed my hand once more before releasing me and stepping back.

"Are you ready?" Cade asked quietly as he came up next to us, his gaze landing on me but glancing to Dad, too.

I nodded once to Dad before turning to my *husband*. "Yes. These heels are killing me."

Cade snorted as he laced our fingers together.

****

We drove in silence in Cade's truck back to my house. I sat in the middle, Cade's hand comfortably resting on my knee. We pulled into the driveway, and Cade cut the engine.

"Hang on, I'll come get your door," he said, his gaze roving quickly over my face as a boyish smile crossed his lips.

He opened the passenger door, and I scooted over to the edge of the seat. Looping his hands around my waist, he lifted me down gently to the ground. With his hands still around me, he leaned forward and softly kissed my forehead. "Let me grab my bag," he said. Butterflies danced in my stomach.

I smiled and moved to the side as he dug a duffle out from behind the seat. I fished out my keys and unlocked the door. We entered the kitchen, and Cade set his bag on the floor. Unsure what exactly to do then—did I attack him right there in the kitchen?—I kicked off my heels and leaned back against the wall and let my eyes have their fill.

"Cade, you look tense all over," I said as my shoulders rested against the wall. My muscles weren't exactly loose either. Uncertainty had tension thrumming lightly beneath my skin. My cheeks flushed as I looked longer at the wolf I loved. The dim lighting produced shadows under the angles of his face. His cheekbones, his squared jaw. Delicious.

Cade rubbed a hand against the back of his neck inside the collar of his white shirt. "I guess I kind of am. Honestly, I hadn't really let myself think too much about what came after I won. I just focused on winning, because I knew that the rest of my life without you would be impossible. I'm not really sure what we're doing right now," he confessed with a slightly nervous laugh and a vulnerability I rarely saw in him.

My pulse picked up as a smile touched the corner of my lips. An idea struck. "I know you're famed for your great massages. Let's see how I do. I'm going to go change first, then I'll meet you in the living room."

"Deal. Want me to help you out of your dress?" he asked with a hint of his cocky arrogance. I glanced at him. His face was lit with laughter, and he let his gaze lazily rake over me from head to toe, lingering on a few areas longer than others.

Heat bloomed hot across my cheeks, and a sudden shyness overtook me. "I'll meet you on the couch," I said and popped down the hallway and up the stairs to my room before he could say anything else.

Bracing against the closed door of my bedroom for

a second, I let my lips quirk into a full smile. I took my time changing out of my simple dress. It had been my mother's. Resha had brought it back, cleaned and pressed, for me to wear today. It was strange to miss a woman I had no memory of, but I was glad of this connection to her today. Smoothing my hand over the white lace, I gently hung it in the closet. Going to my drawer, I snagged a plain tank top and pajama shorts. I wished I'd taken the time to buy something a little more wedding-nightish, but I hadn't. Because I couldn't bear the thought of having something like that, meant for Cade, if it wasn't Cade I married. And it had been so close. I shuddered and gratefully slipped into my pajamas.

Cade was already sitting on the couch in a T-shirt and his own pajama bottoms when I came down the stairs. He watched me cross the room, his gaze never leaving me as I sank down onto the couch next to him.

"Ready for the most relaxing massage you've ever had?" I asked, trying to calm the jitters that sprang to life in my belly.

"Mm-hmm," rumbled deep in his chest and sent pinwheels of excitement through me.

"Take your shirt off." The words dropped out of my mouth without my permission. My face flamed again, but Cade only raised an eyebrow, smirk hiding at the corner of his mouth as he reached back and pulled his shirt off, revealing toned abs and biceps that made my heart kick up yet another notch.

Not trusting my voice, I motioned with my finger for him to turn around. He did, and I was left with the broad expanse of his shoulders and back that tapered down to a trim waist, a few lingering bruises and bite marks marring his otherwise pale skin. His muscles quivered slightly as I tentatively put my hands on his shoulders. His breathing hitched, and it sent a shiver of power down my spine and the good kind of anxious flutters in my belly. The way he reacted to my touch. The way *I* reacted to it. That was special. Everything about him-and-me was extraordinary.

Genuinely wanting him to feel relaxed, and hoping it might relax some of my jitters, too, I shifted forward, my chest grazing his back as I rose on my knees so I could reach him better. I rubbed his shoulders, his upper back, loving the feel of his skin beneath my fingers. But his muscles never got any looser.

"Sarah?" he said after a few minutes.

"Yeah?" I leaned closer, my chest brushing his back again. I dropped a quick kiss where his neck met his shoulder, and he shivered.

"I hate to tell you this, but I'm not feeling relaxed."

I frowned. "Why not? Am I doing something wrong?" Uncertainty ate at me. Did he not like what I was doing?

"No, Alpha Girl, you're doing many, many things right. The first of which is that you're not wearing a bra. And as a red-blooded werewolf who is now your mate, can I just tell you that I've been dying to see your boobs pretty much since the second I first saw you? Feeling them rub up against me like this is the best form of torture imaginable, but it's not relaxing. *Very* exciting, but not relaxing."

I giggled. He grabbed my arm and tugged.

Chapter 48

Cade

I was going to combust if she kept on innocently teasing me like this. She had no idea what the feel of her curves against my skin did to me. I was practically sweating with the effort it took just to sit still enough for her to continue rubbing my skin—both with her hands and her chest.

Grabbing her arm gently, I pulled her around me and into my lap. Her celery-green eyes danced with laughter as she smiled up at me. Her legs dangled off the side of the couch, but the rest of her in that tiny tank top and short shorts was cradled in my lap.

We were silent a minute, just looking at each other. She reached up and pushed a piece of hair off my forehead. My thumb rubbed across her bottom lip.

"I love you," she whispered.

"I love you," I whispered back, my thumb moving to the side of her neck and lacing into her hair. Her hand feathered down my neck, over my shoulder, then her fingers lightly traced over the ridges of my arms. Wolf was panting inside, and my breathing grew more ragged.

"I'm not sure what I would have done if I'd had to marry Donovan," she said. A growl burned in my chest.

"The thought of him touching you is enough to make me see red. I understand why some men go feral after their mates die. If I'd lost you forever, I might have literally lost my mind." Her fingers grazed my chest. "I still might, but in a much more enjoyable way." I gasped. My fingers itched to explore her body, but I held them steady around her waist, cradling her, waiting for her indication she wanted me to.

A wicked grin twisted her lips. As if reading my mind, she took her fingers from my chest and grasped my hand. My heart pounded as she dragged it over her hip. I gulped.

"Kiss me, Wolf Dude."

"Anything you say, Alpha Girl."

Our lips met, slowly at first, then all the weeks of pent-up passion, the uncertainty, the worry, the love we shared, flowed between us. My lips and her lips. Her tongue and my tongue. My noises and her noises. Her hands and my hands.

She arched against me, her fingers raking across my back in an effort to draw me closer as my hands found places that sent blood thundering through me. Wolf howled inside, content and complete with our mate at last, desperately wanting to take this last step of togetherness.

At some point, Sarah leaned back out of my lap. My lips followed her as I shifted my own position, leaning with her. She gasped, and I kissed her again, eliciting a groan that sent the hairs on the back of my neck standing up.

"I think we should move upstairs," she said unevenly.

"Assuming that means to your bedroom, I'm all for it," I rasped back. I was wound tighter than I'd thought possible.

Skirting around the other clothes that had joined my shirt on the floor, we made it up the stairs and to her room. Slowing at the threshold, knowing we were crossing a sacred line, Sarah took my hand and led me to the bed. We sank down on the edge together, hands still clasped.

"Are you ready?" I asked her softly, my breathing still ragged.

"To be yours forever? In *all* the ways?" She smiled. "Definitely."

Chapter 49

Sarah

I woke slowly the next morning. Wolf stretched languidly inside me. Contentment like I'd never experienced filled me and put a silly grin on my face. I'd never felt so connected to another person. I rolled onto my side, letting my gaze drink Cade in as he still slept on the pillow next to me. His dark hair was swept messily across his forehead, his shoulders rising and falling softly as he lay on his front.

Megan was right. Neither of us had quite known what to do or expect last night, but it had been one of the most defining moments of my life. Intimacy—physical and that kind of emotional intimacy—was new to me, and Cade too, but the way my soul felt connected now to Cade's...I couldn't imagine sharing that with anyone else but Cade. And we were together for keeps now. It didn't matter that last night had been awkward. We had plenty of time to practice, as Megan said. Wolf chuffed.

Cade moved in his sleep, starting to wake.

"Why am I sore?" He groaned, squinting his eyes.

I chuckled. "I guess it depends on what parts of you are sore," I teased. "You did have a pretty intense fight yesterday. And then there was last night."

He peeked up at me from under his thick fringe of dark lashes. "I could do a repeat of last night. Those muscles are just fine." His cocky grin was only half visible as half his face was still buried in his pillow.

I giggled as he turned to face me fully. "Are you sore?" he asked, concern creasing his eyebrows.

I shook my head. "I'm all right." Accelerated healing was a wonderful werewolf perk.

"Good." His fingers skimmed up my arm, raising gooseflesh. "Good morning," he said softly, his thumb brushing against my lips.

"Good morning."

"What do you want to do today? I think we deserve a day off school." His thumb traced my chin.

"After the past two weeks, I'm inclined to agree. I think we need to be only *us* today," I said.

His face broke into a happy smile.

"You know, I distinctly remember that first afternoon we kissed—when you brought me home in your truck. You said you could kiss me for hours," I said as my fingers walked up the ridges in his arm.

"I distinctly remember you saying you were serious about *letting* me kiss you for hours," he countered with a smug tilt of an eyebrow.

"Don't get cocky," I said as a grin tugged my lips upward.

"Too late." He nudged me with his hips.

I snorted a laugh as a girlish flush bloomed in my cheeks. "Think we should try that kissing for a few hours?"

"Think you can *only* kiss me for a few hours?" He smirked. His eyes narrowed as a naughty smile covered his face. He reached for me under the covers.

"Probably not."

"Good. Shut up and kiss me, Alpha Girl."

****

The last weeks of school passed peaceably. Dad left to go back to New York and the rest of the pack. We'd been gone a long time. As promised, I was finishing my school year out at Rock Falls, surrounded by my friends. Tishcohan had gone back to his home the day after Cade and I married. Cade and I were trying to get the hang of being mates. We were doing an admirable job, and I'd never been more contented.

At the end-of-school assembly, when all the awards and scholarships were passed out, I was so proud I nearly burst when Principal Angelo announced that Cade had been awarded a full basketball scholarship to New York State. Not only because he was getting exactly what he wanted and deserved, but also because the university wasn't far from pack territory. I was planning to take a gap year and figure out what exactly I wanted to do while working for Dad and learning more about his business. I was leaning toward joining him both in his business and in running the pack more efficiently.

Bowen was offered two different basketball scholarships, and he'd taken the one closest to home. He and Kyp were planning to keep their pack in the area for the foreseeable future. Raven got her graphic design internship and would be doing the internship full time next year to finish her high school requirements and work toward earning her degree at the same time.

The only things left were graduation and Rachel and Kyp's wedding. Then Cade and I would have to go back to New York, too. I was sad to be leaving our friends, but part of me was excited to bring Cade back with me to my pack of origin and start our lives together there. Besides, Rock Falls was only a few hours away. There would be lots of weekend visits and some summer get-togethers before things started back up in the fall.

****

Rachel and Kyp were getting married the weekend after graduation.

Friday night was the rehearsal dinner. The venue for the wedding was stunning. It was an old historic building that had been converted for special occasions and functions. It held a rustic elegance that fit Rachel and her werewolf side perfectly.

I ran my fingers along the aged wood grain as a smile pulled my lips up. Rachel was at the front of the spacious room on a raised platform. She was pointing, dramatizing, ordering, and organizing like a true theater director. She was loving it. Kyp stood off to one side, arms crossed as he leaned against the wall, watching Rachel with amusement and with utter adoration.

"No, no. I think we need this here," Rachel said with a dramatic point of her finger. The flower people moved a column and rearranged the flowers on top. "Much better!" Rachel praised.

"Do you wish we would have had a big affair like this?" Cade asked softly as he came up behind me, his hands slipping around my waist and pulling my back against his chest. I sighed as his lips grazed my neck.

"No. Not really. I might have preferred our Claiming to have been a bit more formal, but I don't regret any of it." I smiled at the memory of clobbering Cade in the middle of the *Lacessere* ring.

"Jump me anytime, Alpha Girl."

I snickered.

"Sarah, sorry to pull you away, but can you help me with some table arrangements?" Megan asked as she walked over with several buckets and bunches of ivy.

"Absolutely. Put me to work," I said.

"Thanks. Cade, Sam and the guys are working on some lighting something or other out at the gazebo," Megan told him.

"I'm there."

Cade gave my hip a quick squeeze that sent butterflies flapping in my middle before heading back out the double doors.

"I'm kind of surprised he didn't grab your butt on the way out," Megan quipped as she handed me a bunch of ivy.

My lips twitched. "He definitely would have, but it makes me feel conspicuous in public."

Megan chuckled. "I get that. I mean, not enough for me to stop Sam when he does it, but he at least tries to be discreet."

I laughed as we put our stuff on the table. "Yeah. Discretion isn't always Cade's strong suit," I replied, thinking of Cade's snarky comments.

"Megan, are these the right flowers and pearl pins?" Raven asked as she rushed up in a flurry of petals and sparkles.

"Yes. Okay, so here's the model one. I have no idea how we managed to miscount off by fifteen, but we did. This does not bode well for our business tracking. We're going to have to find a better model," Megan mussed, getting down to business as she started arranging ivy, pearls, sparkles, and a collection of reddish-, pink-, and wine-colored roses.

"How is the business planning going?" Raven asked.

"Well, it kind of went on standstill with all the wedding stuff," Megan said with another smile. "But we did just get another catering order for thirty-five servings of desserts last night, actually. It'll be while Rachel and Kyp are still on their honeymoon. Any chance you might be up for some icing piping?"

"So long as it's after five o'clock, I'm good."

"Is the internship going well?" I asked. Frowning at a sparkly pin, I nudged it behind a blush pink rose. I nodded. That was much better.

"It's definitely been an adjustment. It's keeping me plenty busy, and it's going to be a learning curve, but I think I'm going to love it." Raven's eyes twinkled. "And, of course, the best part is that I can do the internship and get both high school and college credit for it at the same time. I'm relieved that I won't have to juggle both. Plus, I get vacation time. So Bowen and I can come visit you guys in New York," she said with a smile.

"That's fabulous. You know you're welcome anytime. The guest room is always available," I told Raven, meeting her shining eyes for a second before we returned to our arrangements.

"Are you sure you guys need to leave tomorrow?" Megan asked me. My middle twinged.

"Yeah," I said slowly. "I need to be with my pack. I've been gone a long time. When can you all come up to New York?"

Megan's eyes lit. "I think we should all make a road trip up as soon as Kyp and Rachel are back from their honeymoon."

"I second that," Raven chimed.

"You all have an open invitation. You don't even need to call. Just show up." I meant it. The friends I'd made in Rock Falls would be lifelong.

"You *know* I'll take you up on that," Rachel chimed as she waltzed down the aisle to us and draped an arm around me and Megan.

"I hope you do," I told her sincerely.

The guys came in from outside as Kyp trailed his fiancée down the aisle. We all conglomerated around the table.

"So we were thinking," Rachel said, glancing at Kyp before addressing the rest of us. "Since Cade and Sarah are leaving for New York tomorrow, and we're leaving for the Caribbean, we thought we should all get together. One last time," Rachel said.

"Our flight doesn't leave until tomorrow evening. We don't have to be at the airport until four o'clock," Kyp added.

Cade's hand grazed my low back as a lump rose in my throat. Things would change once we left. It would be good to be just the group of us once more before then.

"Come over to our place," Bowen said. "The pool and hot tub are open. We can grill."

Raven nodded enthusiastically.

"That sounds great. What time do you want us to come over? Eight?" Rachel asked as she twirled a jeweled pin between her fingers, crease between her eyebrows.

Sam's lips twitched, and Cade outright smirked. "Let's make it midmorning. Kyp won't want to be going anywhere early," Cade quipped.

Bowen snorted while giggles broke out around the circle. Rachel's cheeks flushed as mischief lit Kyp's eyes.

"Well, if you put it that way," Rachel amended good-naturedly. I winked at her. She might not want to go anywhere early either, but I kept that to myself as I laced my fingers through Cade's.

****

Rachel was the most stunning bride I'd ever seen. She and Kyp were so well matched and so obviously in love. The whole wedding had a feel of magic about it. When they were pronounced man and wife and kissed, the entire crowd literally sighed. Mrs. Crumb dabbed her eyes while Joanie, Rachel's sister, smiled shakily as she sat between her parents. Mr. Crumb and Rachel's other sister, Clary, both beamed.

Kyp's mom, Jennifer, and her fiancé, Jonathan Stone, sat opposite, peace and contentment on their faces. I fully expected Jennifer to be married and a newly bitten werewolf the next time I saw her.

The entire day went off without a hitch. We danced into the early twilight, then waved Kyp and Rachel off with bubbles and birdseed.

"She's going to have fun digging that out of her dress later," I commented dryly as we tossed the last of the seeds.

Megan laughed. "I bet she will."

"If Kyp's half the man I think he is, he'll help," Sam quipped. Cade snorted beside me.

We helped clean up and then went back to our house. It was the last night we'd spend together in the house like this.

"Are you worried? About leaving your pack?" I

asked Cade later that night as we were snuggled in bed.

"No. Not worried," he said. He toyed with the ends of my hair, wrapping them gently around his finger. "I'll miss it here. I'll miss my parents, Raven, and Sam the most. But I'd miss you more if I had to choose one over the other."

I craned my head to look up at him. "Really?"

"Really." He dropped a kiss on the end of my nose. "You're more than worth it."

I smiled as heat wrapped around my heart and squeezed.

I love you, I sent over our link.

I love you back.

Chapter 50

Cade

It was mildly bittersweet as I locked the door of the house where Sarah and I had first lived together as mates. I'd give the keys back to Sam today when we saw him at Bowen's. Tonight, we'd be in New York at Sarah's house where she grew up. I tried not to cringe at the idea of living with her dad in the same house. I liked Austin. But I liked his daughter more. And I really hoped it wouldn't be weird for Sarah and me to be sharing a room with him living in the same house. Sarah and I would be house shopping in the near future.

"Any last goodbyes to the house?" I asked her as I put our bags in my truck.

She stared wistfully at the brick exterior. "No. But so many memories here. Here in Rock Falls."

I nodded. We'd stop by and see my parents once more before we hit the road, but it was true. Rock Falls held many good memories. It always would.

****

Sam and Megan were already at Bowen's when we pulled up.

"Looks like Kyp and Rachel are late." I smirked as I cut the engine.

"Gee, wonder what held them up?"

"Come on, Alpha Girl. I want to see you in that swimsuit. Raven said they heated the pool last night, so it should be plenty warm to swim in."

"Well, even if not, there's always the hot tub."

Raven hugged me hard when we walked through the door. Sarah, too.

"You guys want burgers or sausages?" she asked as we followed her back to the spacious kitchen.

"Both," I answered.

Raven grinned at me. "Sarah?"

"Hamburger for me today, I think."

"Sounds good. Sam and Meg just stepped out to get the patio furniture from under the tarps."

Just then another car pulled into the drive. The back sliding door opened, and Sam and Megan popped back in the house.

"They just now getting here?" Sam asked as he glanced at the clock.

The door cracked open, and Rachel's wild halo of red hair bounced through first, followed by the rest of her glowing face. I'd never seen Kyp look so at peace. I understood why. That total trust and acceptance by another person was something extraordinary.

"Aren't you glad you didn't come over at eight?" Megan teased as they came into the kitchen with the rest of us.

"Definitely," Kyp answered. Rachel just smiled and blushed prettily.

****

After playing around in the pool and getting the meat grilled, we all moved to the hot tub to soak and eat lunch and talk. I was struck by how similar this was to that night that felt so long ago. The night Sam and I talked about his ancestors' *Lacessere*. That was practically a lifetime ago.

"I guess we all knew this year would be an exciting one—most of us being seniors. But I don't think any of us planned on as much excitement as we've had," Rachel said as she put her sausage on her plate. "All is fair in werewolves, war, and love, I guess."

"Who knew we'd *all* end up finding our mates—for that matter, finding out werewolves exist." Megan grinned.

"And becoming werewolves yourselves," Raven added.

"Finding your enemy is actually your true mate," Bowen chimed.

"That your genes don't matter, because true love doesn't care," Kyp said.

"Love is a choice," Sam said softly.

"That some friendships run deeper than blood," Sarah said. She squeezed my knee under the water.

"And that love and friendships are worth fighting for," I said.

I glanced around at my friends—my family, my pack.

Life was changing. Our packs were changing. But the love we held for each other, the bonds of friendship that we'd forged in time and blood—those would never be taken from us. Those ties forged in Rock Falls would remain.

Forever.

A word about the author...

AJ Skelly is an author, reader, and lover of all things fantasy, medieval, and fairy-tale-romance. As a former high school English teacher with a master's in Creative Writing, she's always been fascinated with the written word and has spent many years working with teenagers. She lives with her husband, children, and many imaginary friends who often find their way into her stories.

http://www.ajskelly.com